A LIGHT
IN THE
JUNGLE

JOHN F. SCHORK

ACKNOWLEDGEMENTS

The author gratefully acknowledges the invaluable advice from Dr. Roger Hanson on all of the medical aspects of the book. As a retired U.S. Navy flight surgeon, his extensive military background provided authenticity to the manuscript and helped to portray the real challenges experienced by men and women in the cauldron of World War Two.

Please email comments/omissions directly to
john@johnschork.com

PROLOGUE

I have come to the conclusion that memory is a dual-edged sword. For every warm and happy thread of what happened in our past, there are those gut-wrenching, repellant shadows we all carry like Marley's load of chains. Some people seem to have the ability to bury the ugly shadows while focusing on the bright memories of their times. I envy them. The ability to suppress those haunting reflections of my past has escaped me for the last forty years.

Perhaps it is just who I am, how the neurons run around my brain. Or, as I am beginning to suspect, my problems originate with the particular path I followed through life. I ask myself if the dark years of the war changed me from a normal man to one who was branded by the events and sights of those terrible times. I surely know many of my fellow Marines who are different from the average men I come across as the years fade from the Second World War. But I also see the same from the men I knew who fought at the Chosin Reservoir in Korea or the rice paddies of Viet Nam. While I don't know many who have returned from the modern horrors of Afghanistan, I suspect the same will happen to them as well. And I am sure it will happen quietly to them also. Over time, as the horrific events unfold around you, a change will take place. That change may not reveal itself until long after the last shot is fired. Hell, it took two years after the end of the war before I began to realize that I was never going to be the same man I was in 1941. But in those days, so many were doing the same thing that I was doing: trying to get their lives back in order. Focusing on school, work, families--everything that was supposed to be important--not four years of death and destruction. But it was still there and rightfully, it will always be.

So, I will tell my story. I think it will help me to tell it, perhaps you will understand what happened to the young man who put on the Marine uniform in 1941. Maybe it will help me do the same thing.

CHAPTER ONE

May 1942

In the distance I could hear sounds of men moving toward my position. Should I try to move further into the underbrush, risking the noise I knew would come from my efforts? Or stay still and silent, hiding under the low-growing vegetation at the base of the small hill? I had always been comfortable in the jungle, but now the jumble of foliage seemed hostile as I tried to blend into the tangles of brush.

As I slowly rolled over to lie on my back, sweat ran stinging into my eyes. My fatigues, now filthy from two days of evading enemy patrols, were soaking wet. The heat and humidity had come early this spring, and with a considerable vengeance. The cover of darkness would be here in an hour; too late to help me hide. My pulse increased. I could now hear men's voices. All I could do was remain motionless and hope my cover was good enough.

Listening, it seemed that the men were heading directly for me. I found my holster and slowly opened the leather flap. Putting my hand around the pistol grip, I moved the .45 Colt just a hair, ready for whatever was to come.

"Goddamn it, Parker! Where the hell are you? The exercise is canceled."

My body relaxed. I knew that voice.

Sitting up, I called, "Edwards! Over here."

In a minute, three Marines walked into the small opening in the underbrush.

"Shit, Rob. We've been looking for you for two hours," Dean Edwards said, a tired, sweaty grin on his face.

"What's up?" I asked. My class was on the final field exercise of our Basic School training program at the Marine Corps Base at Quantico, Virginia.

Edwards laughed.

"You're asking a second lieutenant?"

He was right. Student officers at The Basic School were so far down the chain of command, the cooks in the mess hall knew the scoop before we did.

Twenty minutes later, we all were sitting on the wooden benches in the back of a Dodge one-and-a-half-ton utility truck on the road back to mainside. As we jostled over the gravel road, I wondered what could have caused our training officer to stop the field exercise. It was the first time since arriving at the school that a training event had not been completed as scheduled. To do otherwise was simply not the Marine way.

I'd learned an awful lot about the Marine way in the last six months.

My father had served in the Corps during the war. A sergeant in the Second Marine Division, he'd seen action at Belleau Wood. Because of that, I always considered myself part-Marine growing up. Now I was a Marine, legally anyway, about to take my first steps into the Fleet Marine Force. The ardor of only a year ago was now being tempered by the reality of what I'd signed up for. I wouldn't have changed my mind, but any glamour I had about fighting the forces of evil had long since passed. The inspections, obstacle course runs, rifle range drills, and an unending series of field exercises had taught me how hard being a Marine actually was. But there was a war on, and like my father, I felt I had to be a part of it. And, at least at that point, I was pretty good at doing what the Marines told me to.

I never really liked my father. I loved him as most sons do their fathers, but we weren't friends. He had his job and I had my schooling. But he did pass on his stubbornness and temper, so I guess that's something akin to a bond. Sometimes he could be a real son of a bitch, and I always wondered if I would become one as I grew up. Not so far, I enjoyed going with the group and I was the last guy to ever confront anyone. Just not my way.

The trucks stopped in the parking lot of the Bachelor Officer's Quarters and we unloaded, our equipment clanking in that unique manner only infantry equipment does. Dust rose from the graveled lot, adding a level of grime to the sweat-streaked faces making their way towards our BOQ wing.

"Hey, Parker, Major Hersch wants to see you in his office."

I turned to see the Assistant Officer of the Day, another student officer wearing the duty armband. Major Fred Hersch was our training officer. An old school Marine, he had stayed in after the war, seeing action in Honduras and the Dominican. Everything about him was hard, his language, body and attitude. But he was fair and if you didn't fuck up, he'd treat you square. That's all anyone can ask, I suppose.

I knocked on the frame of his office door.

"Lieutenant Parker, reporting as ordered, sir."

"Come in, lieutenant."

Hersch was sitting at his desk, the two windows open and an oscillating fan rustling the papers held by a paperweight. A Navy commander sat in the single wooden chair across from the desk. We called it "the hot seat" after a number of my compatriots had enjoyed a "major to shit head" discussion with Hersch.

"Get a chair from the outer office and sit down," Hersch ordered, his voice remarkably civil.

The commander was no spring chicken. He was maybe forty, but he looked squared away in his blues, the three gold stripes looking pretty impressive to a boot like me. Unlike most Navy commanders, this one didn't have a gut on him. In fact, he looked like a tough son of a bitch, if I were any judge of looks.

I realized it was his eyes that struck me. They looked hard, almost mean.

"This is Commander Herrick, Naval Intelligence. He's down from D.C. and wants to ask you a few questions."

I found that I was a little uncomfortable as the senior officer looked me over, almost like he was buying a piece of meat. He didn't offer to shake hands, so I knew this was likely not going to end happily for me. I'd been worrying about an altercation in a Georgetown bar two weeks ago. I tried to get out of the place without letting them know I was a Marine, but someone must have connected the short hair. But how had they tracked me down? It must've been the girl. I'd given her my name and told her I was at Quantico. Shit! But it was still the other guy who started it. A smarmy little prick who tried to hit on the girl I was working on. He was three sheets to the wind and when I told him to shove off, he made the mistake of taking a swing at me. After I decked the guy, he yells that he's a lawyer and will have my ass. A Washington lawyer. What a waste of flesh. Looks like the little shit is getting even.

"Lieutenant Robin M. Parker, you graduated from Georgia Tech last June, correct?"

The commander held a clipboard in front of him.

"Ah, yes sir."

Where the hell was this going?

"And your family sent you to the states for college?" he continued.

4

"Yes, sir, in 1937. My father went to Tech. There weren't any schools on Borneo, and I wanted to study electrical engineering."

"And you were living in Borneo, right?"

"Yes, sir, Balikpapan. My father was a petroleum engineer for Shell."

"How long did you live there?"

My thoughts flashed back to our big white house with the wide veranda and the huge lawn.

"As long as I can remember, sir. My parents moved there when I was two."

"Your service record says that you speak Malay."

"Yes, sir."

"Are you fluent?"

"I'm pretty comfortable, sir." My thoughts went to Nadira, who had really raised me and taught me the local language. She was my governess, teacher, and friend. I called her Maksi and she called me Ajib and I loved her like a mother. Hell, I probably loved her more than Mrs. Felicia Parker, the queen of the Dutch East Indies cocktail circuit, who always seemed to be going to a party and leaving me with Nadira. From Maksi, I learned the traditions and a respect for the people who called Kalimantan their home. But now, that seemed like a lifetime ago.

Herrick had been taking notes. He reviewed what he had written, then asked, "Where are your parents now?" But I sensed he knew the answer. What was this all about?

"In California, sir. My father is working for Occidental Petroleum in the Santa Barbara oil fields."

Seeing events unfolding in the Pacific, my family had left Borneo in November of 1940, going to Australia, then back to the mainland. As I tracked the Japanese invasion of the East Indies in January of '41, I thanked the good Lord every day that my father had seen the writing on the wall. Like I said, he was a son of a bitch, but a pretty savvy one. What would you expect from an old Marine? So he, my mom and my younger brother and sister were safe in California. But I would never forgive him for leaving Maksi behind. I could only hope that she was alright.

"I assume you've been following what's been happening in and around Borneo?"

"Yes, sir, although there's not much in the papers." The headlines covered the fall of the Philippines and the raid on Tokyo by army bombers. I did know the Japs had swept through that part of the world like a hot knife through butter. We lost several ships, as did the Aussies and the Dutch. Bottom line, we'd gotten our asses kicked. Now the Japs had all the oil they needed—which was not a good thing in my book—but it seemed like the world had forgotten Borneo.

"You understand the strategic importance of the oil fields in the area?"

Why was this guy asking me this stuff?

"Yes, sir." I was about to qualify my answer by saying that I thought so, but I was starting to get pissed.

He sat back and closed his pad.

"Lieutenant Parker, it goes without saying that we're in a pretty tight spot in the Pacific."

I didn't respond, it seemed he was about to let me know what this was all about.

"Much like in Europe, our first efforts must be to stop the enemy's forward progress. It will take time to mobilize our nation and industry to go on the offensive."

I didn't need a lecture, but the commander seemed unaware that all second lieutenants weren't inherently stupid.

"Part of our effort will be the support of any indigenous resistance activity behind the enemy's lines. The parallel would be what we are seeing with the resistance in Europe."

Now he had my attention.

"You possess a unique knowledge of that area, not just the geography, but the customs and people."

"Yes, sir." I replied like a good Marine, but a chill was making its way down into my gut.

"The Australians have asked for our help in facilitating and supporting fifth column operations on Borneo and surrounding islands. A review of officer records came up with your background and, as you are just finishing a course of instruction that would prepare you for conducting small unit field operations, you seem to fit the bill."

He stopped, apparently looking for some reaction on my part. Marine training took over and I simply said, "Yes, sir." What the hell was I supposed to say? Borneo? Behind enemy lines? I was a twenty-two-year-old second lieutenant who knew a little bit about electrical engineering, played pretty good golf and had a desire to learn more about the fairer sex. But I could tell that wasn't of any great concern to either Naval Intelligence or Commander Herrick.

"Are you looking for me to volunteer for some kind of mission, sir?"

The commander smiled.

"You must have watched too many movies, Mr. Parker. Marines are given orders, which they execute to the best of their ability. What I'm doing is giving you the background on what could be your next assignment. You will, as we all do, go where ordered."

"Yes, sir," I replied, feeling like a true horse's ass. It wouldn't be the last time I stuck my foot in my mouth. But the world had changed. It seemed my days of breezing through classes at Tech, enjoying the social life and not worrying about too much were painfully over.

That night, I lay in my bunk with the window wide open, trying to capture whatever breeze might be available to cool down the stuffy room. Not even three beers had taken the edge off after I left Hersch's office. I'd gone down to the small bar off the main lobby, found Dean Edwards and tried to get my hands around what had just happened.

"There you are."

I'd been given strict instructions by Commander Herrick that I could only say I was going to graduate early and be sent on a temporary additional duty assignment. After ordering a beer I had relayed what little I could to Dean, who was all ears.

"No kidding?"

"No kidding."

"When do you leave?"

I laughed.

"The day after tomorrow. I'm gonna need some help getting my stuff squared away."

"Where're you going?" he asked, his voice excited.

"Can't tell you," I replied, not trying to sound too dramatic.

All I knew was that I would be flying across the country, which certainly told me how important this mission was to somebody. Air transport was strictly for the highest priorities. Camp Elliott, outside San Diego, was my destination. All Major Hersch had said was that I would be getting a brief training course on weapons and tactics. Hell, that's what I'd been doing for the last six months. That part at least had me interested. But I did wonder. Since arriving at Quantico I had been drinking out of the Marine Corp's firehose. The history of conflicts, small unit tactics, weapon employment, physical training, communication, battle medicine and teamwork were just a sample of that information stream. While they had turned us into warriors, they at least had laid the groundwork.

Now I lay on my bunk, sleep still eluding me despite two days in the field and little rest. Until now I'd taken solace from the idea that I would be going to a Marine infantry unit, where I'd be a platoon commander, watched over by a senior NCO who had seen everything. It was going to be my graduate work while I learned how to be a real infantry officer. Now it looked like I was going be out in the middle of nowhere, by myself and surrounded by the enemy. The last six months had taught me how to improvise and adapt, but this wasn't anything like what I'd imagined.

Hell, if truth be known, I had no idea what I was getting into when I joined the Marine Corps. While my father had talked about the Marines, he never really talked about what it was like. Only now did I realize that.

All I knew was that the war was going strong in Europe and most betting men thought the Pacific was going to go the same way. Joining up seemed the right thing to do and I knew with the draft starting up, I'd at least have some control how I would spend the war. Now it appeared like that hadn't worked out too well.

Having only flown twice before in my life, the trip from Washington D.C. to Los Angeles, via Kansas City and Denver, was an adventure. It seemed like I was the junior military man aboard the aircraft with a lot of senior officers and older men in suits. The aircraft was a Douglas DC-3, painted in Navy colors.

But once I climbed aboard, I saw the logo of American Airlines. It seemed everything was being converted to help fight the war.

My previous trips across the country had been by train. I remembered my first trip on the way to Georgia Tech in 1937. It seemed the terrain stretched on forever. But now as the hours droned on, watching the panorama of America pass under the wing, it struck me how really big the country is.

Good weather made the flights comfortable and allowed me to see the expanse of the west. I had barely seen the Rocky Mountains from the train and seeing them from above, I was stunned by the hundreds of miles of mountain peaks. How did the early pioneers cross such a formidable barrier? Then I thought about the mountains of Borneo. Certainly not as large, but they were just as forbidding. I had gone with my father on a surveying trip just before I left for school and we had penetrated northwest into the jungle. Even with spending my life growing up in that part of the world, I had never travelled into the thick primeval forests that cover the highlands in the center of the island. Was I going back into there? The thought was exciting and unsettling at the same time, but lieutenants are supposed to be conflicted. I guess a rite of passage. But despite the Marine uniform, I really thought of myself as a graduate of Georgia Tech, still just acting like a Marine. I wonder when that would change?

A bus from the Los Alamitos Naval Air Station in LA, took me to Camp Elliott, just north of San Diego, where I reported to the Transient Personnel Office. Most reporting Marines would already know their unit and go directly to the unit spaces, but I was an odd duck. My orders directed me to report to the Operations Officer of the 2nd Marine Division, for approximately two weeks of temporary additional duty for training.

A skinny corporal by the name of O'Brien escorted me to division headquarters. He picked up my Valpak and I grabbed my sea bag, happy for the help after humping them both from Quantico. The lack of humidity was wonderful, and it only took us ten minutes to reach a two-story wooden building with a gravel walkway up to a wide veranda.

"I'll take you up to Operations, lieutenant. I can wait around if it won't take too long and get you to the BOQ."

"Thanks, corporal, I have no idea what they'll want from me today."

As it turned out, after a quick endorsement on my orders, I was ordered to report to building 644 the next morning. I was told that a Major Turley would be waiting for me. It was clear that no more information was going to be offered by a very bored looking captain, standing the operations duty officer watch.

So much for my great expectations.

CHAPTER TWO

Camp Elliot
San Diego, CA
18 May 1942

Building 644 was remarkable in its lack of any identifying signs or markings. Most buildings I'd seen at Quantico and so far at Camp Elliott were clearly marked in a telltale correct, military manner. But other than a simple black "644" on a light brown board, there was nothing else in evidence as I approached the single-story building that might give a clue about what might be in store for me.

"Can you tell me where I might find Major Turley?"

A Marine sergeant in summer service khakis sat at a single desk just inside the door. He looked bored, hung over, or a combination of the two, but still looked like he could kick my ass if needed.

"I need to see your orders and ID card, lieutenant."

There was no desk plate or nametag identifying the sergeant and he didn't volunteer the information. What a friendly little group. I'd expected to show my orders, it was just what one did. But what was having to show my ID card all about?

He handed me my ID back, kept my orders and said, "Follow me, sir."

Nothing of note was visible down the passageway that led to the back of the building, just the black tile floor shiny with a new coat of wax. Major Turley was in the last office down the passageway on the left. The door had no markings, unlike most doors in the Marine Corps, that clearly delineated who or what you would find behind the door. In fact, none of the doors had anything showing what function they performed. This was like a Charlie Chan movie for Pete's sake.

"Sit down, Lieutenant Parker."

Turley was unremarkable in any way. Obviously fit, squared away with a uniform that the commandant would be proud of, he seemed like a cardboard cutout.

"When did you leave Quantico?"

"Two days ago, sir."

"You completed the entire course?"

I suspect he already knew the answer to the question, but I played along with him. He was a major, and to second lieutenants, majors sat at the right hand of God.

"Everything except the final field exercise, sir."

He got up and walked to the window. I noticed the creases in his trousers were knife-edge sharp. How did majors always have those? My uniform already looked a little tired and it was only 0730.

"You're going to receive some specialized training over the next two weeks. It should prepare you for operations in the southwest Pacific."

He paused and I decided to jump in with both feet.

"Can you tell me what I'll be doing, major?"

Allowing for no response to my question he returned to his desk and sat down.

"There's not a lot of time for the training we want to accomplish, so report back in one hour, in fatigues. The first several days will be for weapons training."

Obviously, that was all the major was going to tell this lowly fucking lieutenant, so I stood up, said, "Aye aye, sir," did an about face, and marched out the door.

14

Weapons training? In the last six months, I had trained on every piece of infantry weaponry in the Marine inventory. What the hell else was there?

One hour later I found myself in the fenced compound that covered the area behind building 644. The sergeant with no name had escorted me directly back and left me standing under a large field tent with two of the sides raised for ventilation.

I turned when the crunch of gravel told me I was no longer alone.

"Lieutenant Parker, my name is Forsythe."

A man wearing a uniform I didn't recognize was offering his hand.

"Captain Jeff Forsythe, Royal Australian Army. A pleasure to meet you."

A large smile threw me a bit off guard, but there was no doubt this man was professional soldier. He was average height, but looked like an athlete and carried himself like a man not lacking in confidence.

"Ah yes, sir. Nice to meet you."

He laughed.

"Tell me that next week."

But maybe this was my chance.

"Captain, can you tell me exactly what I'll be doing here."

He led me over to a table and sat down, putting his boots on the attached bench.

"Surely. Have a seat and I'll give you the general run down."

Finally, I thought, the lieutenant would understand.

"Your training will be in an area we're starting to call unconventional warfare. What that really means is operating quietly with little notice in the Japs' backyard. The idea is to be able to conduct intelligence gathering, sabotage, or working with local resistance. Whatever helps defeat the little yellow bastards."

I wanted to nod knowingly, but I realized my nuts were in my mouth.

"Yes, sir." I sounded like a third grader.

"Since you'll be operating in our backyard, we've offered to help you yanks with some of the lessons we've learned recently. The Japs may have booted us out of Singapore, but we learned a lot fighting them—information that you might find useful. Over the next two weeks we'll go over some weapons you haven't seen before, but might encounter. We'll also give you a quick course in jungle medicine and radio procedures. That's a lot to accomplish in a short time, but no fear, we will."

No fear here... None at all.

Forsythe turned out to be the opposite of every trainer I'd encountered so far in my formal Marine Corps training. He'd fought in Malaysia and been one of the lucky men to make it out as Singapore fell to the Japs. Alongside Forsythe, Sergeant Major Derek Ramsay spent many hours introducing me to the wonders of the British Sten gun, the Fairbairn-Sykes fighting knife, and several Japanese weapons, including the Arisaka rifle. As they said, you use what you have at hand, and that may well be enemy equipment.

The Sten was remarkable. I'd learned to use the Thompson .45 caliber submachine gun at Quantico. It was a great weapon, but as I was to learn quickly, it was too bulky for the jungle. The Sten was completely different. Light, easy to maneuver, and simple to maintain. I hoped the Marine Corps would buy it for the fleet. The Arisaka rifle reminded me of the trusty old Springfield '03 that we trained with, which had been the mainstream rifle of the Corps since the war. The Aussies had the new type 98, which had a heavier bullet than the original type 38. It was good weapon, which bothered me a bit. I knew there was talk of adopting the M-1 Garand as the main rifle for the Corps, but for now it looked like we were on par with the enemy.

The sergeant major was a veteran of twenty-five years' service, having joined up in 1917. He'd seen action during the first war and decided to stay in the army. He reminded me of the top sergeants I had run across in the Corps, no nonsense, no bullshit, get-the-job-done types. He was also very familiar with many of the islands north of the continent, including Borneo. But his real expertise was in hand-to-hand combat and using a knife to kill. I thought I'd learned a lot at Quantico, but it turned out that my course of instruction had only scratched the surface. Many bruises and sore muscles eventually got me to the point of confidence with a fighting knife.

The weapon he introduced me to was different from any of the knives we had seen at Quantico, including a trench knife designed in the first war. The Fairbairn had a stiletto point with a razor sharp, equally proportioned blade. The ribbed handle fit comfortably in your hand and the balance was remarkable. It was almost an extension of your hand. I hoped I could get my hands on one when I got wherever I was going.

Two full days were dedicated to a cram course on how to stay healthy in the fetid tropical climate of Borneo—when not living in a large, comfortable house with servants to cook and clean for you—which was my actual experience. Commander Louis Killgallen, Royal Australian Navy Medical Corps taught me as much as he could on the potential pitfalls, diseases and remedies one might need to walk out of the jungle in one piece. He covered the most prevalent problems I would see in the jungle including Typhoid, Malaria, Cholera, Dengue Fever and Encephalitis. There were some common-sense precautions to take, like water purification, but my best chance was to simply not get sick. I assured the doctor that was my fervent hope.

"The jungle plays no favorites, I assure you," he said on the first day. "It hit our troops hard in Malaysia. The heat and humidity saps the strength of everyone and any wound, no matter how small is likely to get infected. All anyone can do is their best, but the jungle will take casualties."

He also went over the deadly creatures I might encounter, such as the Cobra and Krait, in addition to the multitude of crawly creatures such as centipedes and the ever-present leeches. While I had always felt a little uncomfortable crawling around the boonies of Quantico, it appeared my anxiety level was going to increase by a large factor. Maybe the Japanese were going to be the least of my problems. And did I mention the headhunters?

The Dyaks were and are the indigenous people of the central highlands in Borneo. A primitive culture, they had gained some amount of notoriety for taking the heads of their enemies. I did recall that the taking of heads was officially made against the law in 1930 by the colonial government, but had heard nothing since. Of course the Dyaks of Borneo was not high on the list of things that Georgia Tech undergraduates discussed regularly.

My memories of the locals growing up were of the Chinese and Malays who had immigrated to Borneo. The Americans and Europeans who worked the oil fields and refineries had little contact with the Dyaks. But I had actually met some of the tribesmen that lived in the interior because of Nadira's relationship with local churchmen. There were white missionaries who had been active in the mountains for years, and I knew some of them. That connection was the reason I had met the Dyaks on several occasions. They had struck me as quiet and proud people. But their reputation as fierce fighters and killers told me I didn't want to be on the wrong side of them. Where would they fit into this mission?

When I finished my two weeks of training it struck me that all I really knew now was how little I really knew. I had damned well better get smarter and do it quick. Unfortunately, there were no training manuals for boot lieutenants going behind the lines in Borneo.

A USMC staff car took me on the short trip from Camp Elliott to the North Island Naval Air Station. Located on San Diego's protected harbor, North Island was one of the bases from which the clippers flew to Hawaii. Pan American Airways had pioneered trans-Pacific flight in the mid-30's with a remarkable Boeing aircraft they had nicknamed "the clipper." Now those venerable aircraft were providing priority air transport for the war effort. Never did I think I would ever see one, let alone fly in one. But now I stood on a pier about to get into a shuttle boat to take me out to where the massive flying boat was tied up to a mooring buoy.

The harbor looked forbidding in the June overcast, and only my thrill at getting on the clipper allowed me to forget my ultimate destination. In my mind, it struck me that all of my boyhood haunts were now overrun by enemy soldiers. But it was still where I had grown up, the only place I had ever really known as home. Now the idea of returning there made me as uneasy as I had ever been. But I was a Marine officer and it was expected that I press on, regardless of my trepidation. Easier said than done.

If the transportation office at Camp Elliott was correct, I'd be travelling by ship from Pearl Harbor to Australia. At that point, I'd be directed by my new command, which would be delineated in my final travel orders. At that point in my limited experience, I still believed that military travel plans actually worked as laid out.

I turned as a Navy staff car pulled up at the head of the pier and watched a Navy captain get out. He picked up a single small bag, and after saluting the driver, strode down the pier.

"Good afternoon, sir," I said, raising my hand to salute, only to freeze momentarily.

"Lieutenant Parker, good afternoon."

"Captain Herrick, you'll be on the next boat with the lieutenant," I heard the chief petty officer running the dock say.

"Sir, I--this is a surprise."

Herrick smiled.

"As I told you in Quantico, lieutenant, we go where we're ordered. All of us."

I decided to keep my mouth shut for once. Maybe he wouldn't think I was a complete idiot. He had been a commander when I saw him at Quantico, now he was wearing four stripes. But I felt a strange camaraderie with the man I had only met once. Perhaps that was part of what people meant when they talked about the profession of arms. It struck me that most men in this war would be doing the same thing I was, leaving life in America and going into the unknown. Then I realized my situation was actually different. While I was surely going into the unknown, I was going by myself. During the last two weeks at Elliott, I began to wonder if I could hack it. It was just a little thought that kept slipping into my mind as learned more about the jungle of Borneo and how to kill Japs. But that must be natural, right?

We watched in silence as a forty-foot utility boat approached the pier, the coxswain throwing the engine into reverse and sliding the stern smartly up to the wooden bumpers. Engine exhaust fumes drifted over us, the turbulent water at the stern quickly subsiding as the coxswain put the engine in neutral. Two crewmen secured the fore and aft lines to small bits on the pier with the practiced nonchalance of old hands.

Luckily I had been awake during the customs and traditions class at Quantico and knew that senior officers boarded boats last and debarked first. I climbed down into the forward compartment, followed by Captain Herrick. I was surprised when he moved to my side, steadying himself on the port railing.

"Reports are coming in of a major sea battle near Midway Island, lieutenant. It sounds like we came out on top," he said quietly.

"The carriers, sir?"

Everyone knew that our carriers had avoided the disaster at Pearl Harbor and likely were going to be our main weapon to strike back at the Japanese. The Battle of the Coral Sea in May was the first round. We lost one carrier, as did the enemy. Sounds like the flyboys may have taken the second round. Thank God it it's true, this country needed some good news.

Herrick nodded.

"Maybe the tide is turning, sir."

He shook his head.

"Even with a tactical victory, it will be a long time before we'll be ready to take the fight to the Japs. Ships to build, men to train and we still have that little problem in Europe."

As we approached the clipper, I saw the boarding hatch was open and a crewman stood ready to assist passengers aboard. My stomach felt a little uneasy, I just wasn't sure why. But I began to feel like a bit of a fraud. I was wearing the uniform of a Marine officer, leaving for overseas duty in a combat zone and I wasn't sure what the hell I was doing here. I told myself just act like you've done this before.

"Sir?"

The offered hand of a sailor broke me out of my thoughts and I scrambled onto the flat sponson that served as a boarding platform. Ducking inside I expected to see a full cabin, but there were less than twenty passengers sitting in the large interior. Hell, we were probably going to have to wait hours for the rest of them to show up. I removed my uniform blouse and slid over to a window seat.

21

Captain Herrick removed his coat and sat in my row with an empty seat between us.

"Would you like to sit by the window, sir?" I asked, pissed that I might have to give up the chance of a lifetime to see the Pacific from the air.

"Thank you, no. I've made this trip several times and I find the aisle is actually more comfortable."

Several times? The good captain's stock shot up in my book. He must have a hell of a job to be zipping back and forth across the Pacific.

I heard the main hatch close and the sailor latch it. Now I was confused. Were we going to take off with all these empty seats or were we just battening down to wait for more passengers?

"I guess we have a wait for more passengers, captain?"

"Actually, we should be ready to go. With the length of the flight, they can only take about two dozen passengers, weight you know."

Yes, the lieutenant is a rookie, I thought, feeling my face flush.

"Ah, yes sir, of course, I hadn't thought about that."

Herrick smiled as the sailor began a takeoff safety brief.

The few times that I had flown, I'd always been awed by the power when the pilot rammed the throttles forward for takeoff. This time was no different, but I wasn't ready for what happened next. Twenty seconds into the takeoff, the hull slammed into a wave, the big clipper staggering from the blow, then in succession it happened again, bam, bam, bam and suddenly we were in the air. As my heart rate slowed, I was more convinced than ever that pilots are crazy. But then, I was a grunt and I'm sure they felt the same way about me.

My wonder over a flight across the Pacific waned at about hour seven of what eventually became a fifteen-hour flight. The deep blue of the ocean had slowly turned dark as the clipper pressed on into the setting sun. Now all that kept me company was the constant drone of the engines and vibration of the aircraft, which began to push me to the point of screaming.

Most of my fellow passenger read or slept in cycles. The sailor who had provided the pre-takeoff briefing brought out sack lunches which were a brief relief from the monotony, but provided a weak excuse for a real meal. I normally don't mind bologna, but this was a poor substitute, on stale bread with a slice of cheese that only a sick cow would have been proud of. But what the hell, it was something to do. My God, why didn't I think to bring a book?

Captain Herrick closed a notebook he'd been reading and raised his arms in a long lazy stretch.

"So, tell me about Borneo, lieutenant."

The question caught me by surprise. We hadn't spoken for hours, even during the bologna assault, and now he wants me to talk about Borneo. Are all captains this strange, or it is just that second lieutenants don't understand the world around them?

"What exactly would you like to know, sir?"

"Tell me about the people. What are they like? How will they deal with the Jap occupation?"

"Sir, they're normal people, just like us. I can't imagine what it must be like for them. What would it be like if the Japs invaded California? What would the people do? I don't know for sure, sir, but I'm pretty sure a lot of the people I knew would fight the Japs."

I saw the look in Herrick's eyes and realized that his questions were not just to pass the time.

As much as I wanted to push him, I knew this wasn't the time or place. But it began to dawn on me that this was not just a random encounter. I was playing in the big leagues even if I didn't think I was ready, but what the hell, who was ever ready to get called up to the big leagues? The thought was sobering,

"Tell me more about them."

The next hour went quickly as I told him about the people I had grown to know as a youth. He was particularly interested in my stories about Nadira and her connection with the local Malay population. I told him everything I could remember. I knew she was the second generation of her family to live on Borneo.

Originally from a small town north of British Singapore, her grandfather had followed a Christian missionary to Borneo. The family, already Christian, had been recruited to help setting up a school system for the Dyaks. Her grandfather had seen an opportunity for his family to become part of the white man's system.

Spending much of her time as a young girl around the native schools, she became familiar with the people and their ways. But there has always remained a gulf between the Malays and the Dyaks. Many of their customs were an anathema to the Christian Malays, everything from their sexual laxness to the brutality of taking heads.

Nadira's future was to become an assistant to the missionaries until a fateful encounter with a senior missionary resulted in her being sent away to secondary school in the south. Four years of schooling brought her back as a teacher and nanny to the local Dutch community.

Our family was the second one she had worked for over the years since her return from school. We were fortunate to arrive just as another engineer was returning home and she was a perfect match for the Parkers from America. While I did attend the local European school, I think my real education came from her. She was always there for me, teaching the young boy about the lessons of life that my parents didn't seem to have the time to share with me.

We talked as the miles clicked off and I came to like the older man. He seemed like someone who was dedicated to getting a job done and did not carry the big ego I would have expected of a senior officer.

"Where do you report when you get to Hawaii?"

"My orders say to CINCPACFLT Headquarters, sir."

"That's convenient for you, Mr. Parker. There's a BOQ at Makalapa Heights. I have a driver meeting me and I can run you up there."

Maybe this wasn't going to be so hard after all.

CHAPTER THREE

Naval Station Pearl Harbor
Oahu, Territory of Hawaii
7 June 1942

After checking in with the Fleet Headquarters personnel office, I was told to report to Building 17, which was directly behind the main building. Not surprisingly, there was a buzz of activity as I walked through the polished tile corridors toward the back exit. This was the real war; these people were actually running our battle with the Japs. From here, Quantico seemed like the other side of the world.

A helpful yeoman had told me I should find room 126 and report to the chief in charge. As confident as I tried to appear, second lieutenants love to get a helping hand.

"Chief, my name is Parker. I was told to see you."

The nametag on his desk said "YNC Charles Little."

He smiled, "I was told you were going to be here, sir."

Standing up, he walked over to a table with a coffee pot and set of cups on it.

"The captain had a meeting in the main building. Care for a cup of coffee while you wait?"

"Thanks, chief." My God, I thought. The chief was the equivalent of a staff sergeant in the Marine Corps and I was certainly never offered a cup of coffee by a staff sergeant. I think I might like working with the Navy. I sat down in one of the chairs and picked up the morning edition of the Honolulu Star Bulletin.

The story of the final surrender of Corregidor was on the front page. It seemed like the goddamned Japs couldn't be stopped. The action in the western desert wasn't much more encouraging with the recapture of Tobruk by the Germans. The entire world was being ripped apart by this war. How long would it take to play out? It seemed that the scope and horror just kept expanding every day. My memory brought up the names like the 30 Years War and the 100 Years War. Could this war go on that long? How many people were going to die, how many cities would be destroyed and how does a world rebuild itself after something like that?

Hell, the first war was called the war to end all wars, and that was only twenty years ago. Maybe the history books would just say this war was simply a continuation of that one. It sure seemed that the twenties and thirties were a never-ending chain of crises: the Great Depression, revolution in Russia, the Fascists in Italy, Nazis in Germany and the complete foolishness of the League of Nations. This must just be round two.

"Good morning, lieutenant."

I was stirred from my thoughts to see Captain Herrick come through the door, remove his cover and walk into the inner office. The look on my face must have amused Chief Little, who grinned at me and followed the captain. Hell, he knew all along where I was reporting. Once more I felt like a boot.

"This way, lieutenant."

Captain Herrick was hanging his blouse on a coat rack in the corner. He gestured to a seat.

"Now we can get down to the basics, Lieutenant Parker. As you might be figuring out, your being here is part of a larger plan. I'm going to brief you on all of the key points and then you'll spend about a week here going over all of the intelligence data we have on the situation in Borneo. Then you'll be on your way to Australia."

My stomach tightened, but it wasn't from fear yet. I realized I was about to have the first job in my life that really mattered.

"Yes, sir."

Everything of any note in the war seemed to have a code name. I suppose a good code name would not denote anything about the underlying mission, but I wondered who came up with these crazy names. I was told that my particular mission was going to take place under an overarching code name of "Bluebell." It was joint operation, which would be under the operational control of the Australians with support provided by the Americans; meaning I would be working for the Australian military. So far, it appeared that much of what I learned at Quantico was so much wasted information. What did I know about how the Australians did things?

Captain Herrick described how the Australians had been working on setting up an infrastructure of observers throughout the islands north of the continent. Operation "Ferdinand" was the code name for that activity, taken from Ferdinand the Bull, the cartoon character who would rather smell the flowers that fight in the arena. He made the point that the coast watchers were specifically directed to avoid combat, their value came in surviving to pass intelligence to the allied command. "Bluebell" was an Australian flower, but unlike Ferdinand and his flowers, our operation was to create problems for the Japs in Borneo, not just watch them.

"Initial reports out of Borneo are reporting some resistance activity in the mountainous areas. One area we're interested in is the highlands east of the Balikpapan oil fields. There's a mixture of Dyak tribes, displaced immigrants and a few criminal bands. The question is, how have these groups reacted to the Japanese?"

I'd assumed that everyone would hate the Japs. The idea that some of the people might actually support the invaders caught me by surprise, but the Dutch and British were colonial powers and resentment had been part of their empires for years. Perhaps some people thought this was their ticket to freedom.

My mind was swimming when I finally left the headquarters. Chief Little escorted me to a gray Navy jeep parked on a side street. It was early afternoon and I was getting damned hungry. The captain had another meeting and asked the Chief to run me down to get something to eat.

Ten minutes later we passed into one of the gates to the main Pearl Harbor Naval Base. I'm not sure what I expected to see, but nothing could have prepared me for the panorama that unfolded. Six months after the attack, the devastation was starkly evident. Certainly, I expected broken and twisted ships, but there was damage everywhere from bullets and shell fragments. The destroyed hangars on Ford Island looked like I had seen in the newsreels, but at least now there were real airplanes parked on the ramp, not just destroyed pieces of metal.

This was the real war. Men had died here, killed without a declaration of war. It was hard not to be filled with a simmering rage seeing the fallout up close. As the chief drove down to the big canteen, I tried to take in the magnitude of what had happened. The more I saw, the more my stomach wound into knots.

Approaching the jetty, I could see activity across the entire harbor. Boats moving across the harbor, a destroyer moving slowly toward the harbor entrance, water flowing from pumps set up along battleship row. Then I saw the *Arizona*, or what was left of her. As I looked across at the charred, jagged metal that was all that remained above water, it seemed like the great ship was quietly resting, oblivious to the ministrations of mere men. Captain Forsythe's words returned to me, "the little yellow bastards."

That night I walked to the Makalapa Officer's Club, my mind still reeling from the intelligence briefing. The bar was jammed, but mostly with Navy types, and no one paid much attention to the lone Marine, which was fine with me. It had been a long day, which finished with a late afternoon briefing by a Navy lieutenant on the Japanese invasion of the island and subsequent naval engagements. I had already known the public story, but the classified information highlighted how poorly our side had done. They had been overwhelmed by a larger, better-equipped invasion force. The Dutch, British, Australian and American navies clashed with the Japanese in a series of battles that resulted in sunken ships, dead men and an occupied Borneo.

It seemed that the world had thought the British Empire could provide security for the entire area, but it turned out they simply couldn't deliver. I was shown what we knew about the sinking of the two British capital ships, *Prince of Wales* and *Repulse*. At sea, without any air cover, the two ships were sunk by Japanese aircraft in only a little over an hour. They'd kicked our ass and now the entire southwest Pacific was under their boot.

I kept remembering the reports of atrocities committed by the Japanese invasion forces against civilians. Men, women and children, had been executed in brutal reprisals by the imperial troops. Either in response to the destruction of facilities, or to gut the colonial administrative system, the troops had been merciless against the helpless captives. Echoes of the brutality in China told a story of a culture that viewed their enemy as something to destroy regardless of the laws of warfare. As I downed my third

31

bourbon and water, I accepted this was going to be a war with no rules in the Pacific. The world had gone crazy and it was taking me with it.

The next few days passed quickly as I began to feel that I was getting a handle on the situation on the island. Borneo is a huge place as islands go. The primitive nature of most of the interior made it a very difficult place to control. There were very few roads inland and transport via the rivers the only real way to travel inland. As expected, the Japanese, so far, had concentrated their troops and personnel around the larger towns and valuable sites like oil facilities. The best estimate I could get from the intelligence officers was that there were less than 3000 Japanese military personnel on the entire island, mostly army with some naval forces.

"We have travel orders for you, lieutenant."

Chief Little had a clipboard in his hand and began reading as I looked up from a briefing folder.

"You'll be going aboard a destroyer, the *Bagley,* for the trip to Australia. She's in the South Loch and due to get underway tomorrow morning."

"Any idea how long it takes to get there?" I asked.

"About two weeks. If nothing comes up."

"What do you mean?"

"Destroyers are in pretty high demand right now. She could be diverted to some other task with a higher priority, but you'll get there eventually."

"Exactly where is *there?*"

"Brisbane."

I had no idea where in Australia Brisbane was, but at least I'd heard of it.

"Do the orders say who I report to?"

The chief smiled.

"The captain will explain."

"This war is being organized much like we saw the allies do at the end of the first war," the captain began. "But I suspect with operations around the entire world, it will be much more complicated. That being said, we're in the process of putting together a combined operational force to battle the Japanese empire. The force will be comprised of the Brits, Aussies, Kiwis, Dutch, Chinese, and everyone else who has a dog in the fight. The U.S. and Australia will carry the ball for the most part, so integrating our militaries will be key to winning this sooner rather than later. You're going to be part of that initial vanguard. You'll be attached to a unit within the Australian command structure that works behind enemy lines. This is something they have more experience with, and we want to learn from them. That's where you come in. They'll put together a team that will be inserted into Borneo to link up with the locals and create problems for the Japs. You will be part of that team."

What the hell was I doing here? At least I would be a team member, not alone. I'm sure they will be experienced soldiers, or sailors and show me the ropes. This was getting very real.

"Captain, except for growing up there, I don't see why I'm doing this. I don't have any combat experience. I mean I'm ready to go, but I'm just trying to figure out why I was selected."

Herrick didn't appear to take any offense at my remark, but instead he said quietly, "This may come as a surprise to you, but there aren't many Americans who do have combat experience right now, most of them are prisoners of war in the Philippines."

There was a slight edge to his voice, too somber to be anger.

"Forget what I said, sir. Just tell me what you want me to do."

33

"I thought all engineers were hard-headed, but it looks like you're figuring this out, Parker. The Navy and Marines need to get smart about guerrilla jungle warfare and quick. You're the first of many officers we intend to send to both the Brits and the Aussies to learn what they've been finding out over the last two years. You'll be attached to the Allied Intelligence Bureau. They have an operation near Brisbane. That's your first stop. From there, you go wherever they send you."

For the first time since I left Quantico, I understood the plan. And a second lieutenant who understands the plan is a dangerous man.

"Get down there and pick their brains. Learn everything you can. And stay alive. We want you to come back and be part of our clandestine operating forces. Think you can do that, Rob?"

He actually called me by my first name.

"Yes, sir".

CHAPTER FOUR

Brisbane, Queensland
Australia
30 June 1942

I had plenty of time to find Brisbane on a map. By the time the *U.S.S. Bagley* (DD-386) arrived in Australia, I was ready to get off the ship and I suspect they were happy to get rid of "the grunt." The officers of the wardroom were friendly, but they were working a ship in a combat zone, on port and starboard watches and didn't have much time for me. Port and starboard means four hours on duty, then four hours off duty then back on for four more hours and that cycle continues until they pull into port or get sunk. During the four hours they are "off duty", they have to take care of the ancillary activities of life like eating, sleeping, and paperwork.

By the time I saw the coast of Australia, I realized that the Navy didn't have a life of luxury, even though they did get to sleep in a bunk each night. Powdered milk is a heinous thing, but that was all anyone in the Pacific Fleet was going to enjoy unless they knew someone who owned a cow. The lack of fresh vegetables was not something I enjoyed. Whoever decided canned peas were edible was certifiably crazy, and Australian mutton ruined any taste I ever had for lamb. My God, it was terrible; but apparently the Australians had millions of the nasty old sheep and that was going to be one of their major contributions to the war effort. I may never eat another piece of anything related to the sheep family again.

Probably the only other thing that just didn't make sense to me was the prohibition on alcohol aboard U.S. Navy ships. Instead they serve something called "bug juice," which was water in different flavors and colors that I could never identify. I finally decided that "red" was the most palatable, if only just.

The Marines are sometimes called "sea soldiers" and there were even Marines aboard John Paul Jones' ship when he battled the British. I guess it was good for me to see what real shipboard life was like. If for no other reason than it convinced me duty on a ship as part of the Marine detachment wasn't going to be on the top of my future duty requests.

The ship was fortunate there was a spot available at the pier when we arrived. Having to use boats back and forth from anchor was something the sailors said was a pain the ass.

I had been on the signal bridge as the ship entered port. It was interesting watching the ship prepare to dock, while the harbor went about normal business around them. The pier was crowded with equipment, vehicles and people who all seemed to be watching the *Bagley* as she came alongside with the assistance of a small boat that looked something like a tug.

Lines were thrown from the ship to waiting line handlers on the pier. Slowly the ship moved toward the pier, the small tug pushing hard from the outboard side. A shrill whistle blew over the general announcing system, which blared:

"The ship is moored, shift colors."

I made my way to the main deck, where I leaned on a lifeline, watching supplies and people make their way on and off the ship. The humidity struck me as if the land had swallowed us from the sea. I'd forgotten what this hemisphere was capable of, but resolved to get used to it and fast.

"Lieutenant, you're wanted on the quarterdeck."

I turned to see a petty officer standing next to me holding a salute and returned the gesture. I had been standing on the starboard side, trying to figure out what made Australia any different than where I had been. Piers looked the same all over the world.

"Follow me, sir."

Dodging a line of sailors moving supplies down the main deck, we arrived at the quarterdeck where I saw a navy lieutenant talking to the officer of the deck. The man noticed me as I stopped and saluted.

"You must be Lieutenant Parker," he said, returning my salute and extending his hand.

"Yes, sir."

"I'm from the Navy Support Detachment, name's Bennett, Fred Bennett. I'm here to pick you up and get you on your way."

I held out a faint hope that this would be easier than I'd thought.

Two hours later I had been processed by the Navy Support Detachment and was on my way out of Brisbane in a 1938 Ford. Bennett sat in the backseat with me, having escorted me personally through the process.

"We're on our way to an Australian forces base called Redbank. It's about fifteen miles west of the city and it's where you'll find Unit 331."

I had first heard of Unit 331 about an hour earlier when we met with a Navy captain named Phillip Creider, who was the officer in charge. Oddly, nothing in my orders specified who I was assigned to on the Australian side. Captain Herrick mentioned the Allied Intelligence Bureau, but my actual orders directed me to report to the Navy Support Detachment. Creider

37

confirmed I would be attached to the AIB, more specifically a Unit 331, whatever that was.

"We don't know much about what goes on out there, mostly army as I understand," Captain Creider told me. "In any case, Lieutenant Bennett will get you out there and then you're on your own. Good luck, Lieutenant Parker."

My first impression of Redbank was barbed wire and lots of it. There were two rows of wire fences running along the frontage road as we approached what looked like a main gate. Concertina wire was much in evidence around the buildings near the entrance, which were painted a nondescript brown, most looking almost new.

Following an inspection of my orders by a very large corporal, we were directed to a single-story building about a quarter mile inside the base. A simple sign denoted that this was the location of Unit 331, but the exterior offered no clues as to the purpose of the outfit.

Once more I went through the ritual of reporting. It was funny how there was little difference between the Marines, Navy or Aussies when I was escorted into the commanding officer's office and offered a chair. I had done a little homework and was able to recognize uniforms and rank insignia, which held me in good stead. The young man who was manning the outer office of the commander was wearing the uniform of a petty officer in the Australian Navy. That only raised more questions; I thought this was an army operation.

The door to the inner office opened and a stocky lieutenant commander in a khaki uniform walked over to me.

"Lieutenant Parker, my name is Coyne. Please come into my office."

Once I was seated, he sat back in his chair.

"Welcome to 331, Mr. Parker."

"Thank you, sir."

"Looks like you've been on the road for some time now."

It had been a long time and a longer distance since Quantico. Coyne's ruddy complexion showed a man even more tired than I was, still maintaining a pleasant and positive air about him.

"Yes, sir."

"You were able to spend some time with Forsythe and his lot, correct?"

I nodded.

"At Camp Elliot."

"Good. Jeff was attached to 331 for a period of time and did some very good work for us."

For some reason that gave me a strong feeling of camaraderie. We were all in this together or something like that.

"I'm sure you're wondering what we have in store for you."

"Sir, that would be an understatement."

Coyne smiled.

"Well, you'll be here working up with your team for several weeks. Once you're ready to go, we'll get you into your operating area."

My mind blossomed with questions. What team? My team? Was I going to be in charge? Christ! And where were we going? Operating area?

"I know you have lots of questions and I'll be happy to answer them all in time. However, it's been a long day and the sun is well over the yardarm. I'll give you the basic plan but first I'm going to have a drink. Will you join me?"

Was this some kind of test? I would love a drink, but this is certainly not the way it works in the Marine Corps.

"Well, yes, sir. If you are going to have one."

"Or would you prefer a beer?"

After the corporal brought in a chilled beer bottle, the commander took a long drink and raised his glass to me.

"To your health."

I raised my bottle and settled back in anticipation.

"You'll be leading a team of three Australians. Two of these men are combat veterans, the other, the radio operator knows his radios, but has never been in the field."

"Where will we be going, sir?"

He got up and walked over to a map of the southwest Pacific. He placed his finger about two thirds of the way up Borneo, near the eastern side of the island.

"About here. As you know, much of this war is about resources, specifically oil. The Japs don't have it and so they've damned well taken it. The Balikpapan complex," he said, pointing to a smaller spot on the map, "supplies a significant amount of oil for the Japanese war machine. It's too far for us to try and bomb, so we've been using submarines to cut off the supply leaving Borneo. The subs are stretched thin, however, and it's a bloody big ocean. Now if we had someone watching the tanker traffic leaving the port, our subs could be waiting for them. That's where your team comes in. Setting up an observation post that can radio back to us what's happening in Balikpapan."

The reality of this mission was settling between my eyes like an ice pick.

"Operating behind the enemy's lines is becoming more and more the way it's got to be done this time. There was a bit of this business done in the last war, but not on this level. The resistance in occupied Europe surely is one reason for the escalation in guerrilla tactics, but the new technology we're seeing also lends itself exceptionally well to these types of operations. The Brits and Italians seem to have taken the lead with their harbor penetrations. Using swimmers with self-propelled devices, they can sneak up to a ship, put one of the new limpet mines below the water line and boom, sunk at the pier. Makes a hell of a mess, but there'll only be more of that as the war continues."

Two more drinks for the commander and a couple more beers for myself accompanied a remarkable deluge of information from the Australian. Coyne possessed a frightening level of knowledge. He covered logistics, weather, enemy forces, and the indigenous people, all in depth and without any notes. I couldn't believe this was just the overview.

After an hour and a half of briefing and answering my questions, he paused, then continued.

"Now I need to tell you about Sergeant Mullen. Then we'll go get some dinner and put you to bed."

I wonder why he waited so long to tell me about this sergeant.

"Your second-in-command is Sergeant James Mullen, nicknamed 'Moon'." He's something of a legend around here, and we're lucky to have him. Tough as nails and a no-nonsense NCO. He was wounded during the retreat to Singapore and evacuated south. Actually, you have two veterans of the Malaysia fighting. Corporal Abernathy was with him, wounded also. Moon is a bit of a character."

"A character?" I asked, more than a little curious.

"He sees the world as he wants to see it. He has very little use for most of the rules and regulations of the service, but he's a hell of an effective soldier, have no worries about that. He's seen the Japs in action." Coyne paused, then said, "The truth is he comes from rough stock and grew up the hard way, perhaps that's why he's such a fighter."

"How's he going to like working with an American boot lieutenant Marine?"

41

"I'll not kid you, Parker. Moon Mullen will test your patience, but above all else, he'll keep you alive."

That sounded like a reasonable trade off to me, but also was a shock. Coyne wasn't kidding.

"Abernathy is the complete opposite: quiet and unassuming. You'll probably wonder how he could be a soldier, but don't let that fool you; he's experienced and capable. Even Mullen gives him his due. When they were in Malaya, they were separated from their unit in thick jungle for almost an entire day. Both came back wounded. No one ever has heard exactly what happened, and they aren't talking."

"And the radio operator?"

"Private Jon Bever. Bit of an odd duck, but knows radios like the back of his hand.

We sat silently for what seemed like a long time. I wondered if it was time to make my withdrawal.

"There's one more aspect of this mission that I want you to consider. Not that it would make any difference on whether you go or not, but it's more along the lines of knowing what you might be facing out there."

"Sir?"

"What do you know about the Japs' war in China?"

Commander Coyne gave me a quick history lesson, culminating with the vicious attack on the civilians of Nanking. What he described was almost hard to believe, that troops could be so brutal and undisciplined. I had heard some of the stories, but Coyne had many of the specifics.

"They don't play by any semblance of the rules of war. Whether it's their attitude toward non-Japanese or simply a lack of humanity, I don't know, but you need to be ready. We saw some of what they are capable of in Malaysia and at Singapore.

Your boys saw it on Bataan. What I'm saying is that if you're captured, expect death and hope it's quick."

Those words kept me awake almost the entire first night. Hope it's quick - son of a bitch.

"Sergeant Mullen."

The next morning, I watched an average size man detach himself from a group of soldiers and walk over to where Coyne and I stood at the edge of the small parade ground.

"Sir," was the sergeant's less than enthusiastic greeting as he saluted.

"This is Lieutenant Parker."

I returned the salute along with the commander.

"Sergeant," I said and extended my hand.

A strong handshake was accompanied by a very direct look from Sergeant Mullen.

"Sergeant, introduce Mr. Parker to the team and get him kitted out."

"Yes, sir."

"Mr. Parker, I'll see you back in my office in an hour."

Mullen turned and walked toward the two soldiers he had left earlier and I followed him. Not a man of many words, apparently. Sandy-haired, the side of his head was scarred with a livid pink strip that looked like a scar from a grazing bullet. Stocky, he was right on that fine edge between rock-hard and beer gut-strong. Not someone I wanted to get in a street fight with.

"This is Lieutenant Parker," he said with a notable dearth of approval.

The two soldiers saluted.

Mullen nodded toward the older one of the two, who I guessed was in his mid-twenties.

"Corporal Abernathy."

The corporal was a strapper, well over six feet and athletic. If he'd been wounded, there was no evidence of it. He looked fit and ready to fight.

"Nice to meet you, sir." His grip was firm and he looked me straight in the eye. My impression was that he was a man who could and would get the job done, period.

We shook hands and I looked at the other man, or should I say boy.

"This is Private Bever, our radio operator."

Wiry and lean, Bever barely looked the minimum age for enlistment.

"Hello, sir," the young man said, grinning.

He seemed genuinely happy to meet me.

"I'll see you two back in the hut in thirty minutes," Mullen told them.

"Nice to meet you both," I said as they saluted and turned on their heels.

"Armory's this way," the sergeant said as he started across the parade ground.

As I followed Mullen, I was able to check out his uniform. The material looked very rough, almost like a brownish-green felt. I didn't much care for that, but he was wearing the iconic hat that I had seen before in the newsreels, an Australian cowboy hat. That, I did like.

Entering through a break in a secondary fence surrounding another single-story building, we entered what was immediately and clearly the armory. The smell of gun oil permeated the air and I saw two men at tables poring over disassembled rifles.

"Sergeant Lally, get the lieutenant here all kitted out, yeah?"

The skinnier of the two men put down a greasy rag and walked over to the counter. Lally's lean face sported the heaviest shadow of a beard I had ever seen. He must shave with a blowtorch.

"The commander said you'd be by," Lally replied, or at least that's what it sounded like, his accent was so thick I wasn't totally sure.

He knelt under the counter and got back up with a small wooden crate, which he put on the counter.

In the box, I saw a weapon I didn't recognize laying on top of an oily towel. It looked like a Sten, but clearly wasn't. A leather holster was next to it, the butt of a pistol visible.

"Owen sub-machine gun, Webley Mark Six and a Fairbairn. I'll need you to sign the logbook," Lally said.

I paid close attention to his lips as the accent flowed over me.

Not what I expected in the way of weapons, but I'd heard of the Webley. Brits had used a version of it forever. The knife was a plus, but I was curious about this Owen gun.

I signed where the sergeant indicated.

"Thank you, sergeant."

Mullen picked up the box.

"Will you need uniforms for the boonies?" he asked me.

I was still wearing my winter service uniform, which wasn't meant for the field.

"I have Marine-issue dungarees with me. They'll do fine."

"Back to the hut, then," he said, heading out the door.

Mullen was starting to piss me off. I was ten years his junior, but I was a commissioned officer in the United States Marine Corps. It was clear that my relationship with the sergeant would be a leadership challenge for me. I didn't give a shit if he didn't like me, but he was going to show me military courtesy. God damn it, I'm a Marine Officer.

As I followed the sergeant back across the open area toward the group of small buildings, I decided I would not follow my first inclination, which was to chew his ass. Actually I wasn't sure how well I could actually do it. Plus, a little voice told me it wouldn't work. No, Sergeant James Mullen was going to be treated as a consummate professional non-commissioned officer of the Australian Army. Even if it killed me.

Abernathy and Bever came to attention when we walked into the hut. I looked around and saw four single bunks in the back of the room. To one side a temporary screen was open, showing another bunk with a footlocker serving as a nightstand. Two tables were centered in the front of the hut. The mess gear on one table told me this was their dining area and barracks. On the wall were shelves that held various items of equipment; the main commonality was the khaki color.

During my earlier discussion with Commander Coyne, he'd told me that the team didn't know any specifics of the mission. It seemed like a good time to see how they would react to where we were going.

"Stand easy," I said. "Grab a chair."

They scraped the floor, pushing the folding chairs into a semi-circle.

"We don't have a lot of time for niceties, so I'll cut to the chase."

The two younger men looked at me like I was speaking Japanese.

"Sorry, American phrase." The looks remained neutral, not a hint of friendliness. "I'll get right to the point. We'll be going into Borneo in about a month, to see what kind of trouble we can stir up for the Japs. Specifically, we will set up an observation post

46

to watch for Jap ships sailing from Balikpapan. If our subs can get a report that allows them to sink those ships, the japs will run out of oil. This is very important to the war effort."

The continued lack of expression on any of their faces told me that they expected something like this. Good start.

"We have a month or so to learn to work as a team, get smart about where we're going and be ready to move out."

Folding my arms across my chest, I paused, getting my thoughts together.

"I'm certain you're asking yourselves, what in the hell is an American doing here taking us into Borneo? Good question. Well, I grew up on the east coast of the island. I lived there for fifteen years there before going back to the states for school. I've also spent the last six months learning small unit tactics at the Marine Corps training school in Quantico, Virginia. I know how to beat the enemy, but I've never heard a shot fired in anger."

I looked at the corporal.

"That's where I'll be looking for your experience, Corporal Abernathy."

Turning back to the team, I said, "But let there be no doubt about this, Sergeant Mullen will be running the show."

I looked at Mullen and his face was expressionless. Yup, a card-carrying asshole, more the challenge.

"At Quantico, they taught us that sergeants run the Marine Corps. My assumption is that it's no different in your army. It will take all of us working together to stay alive and accomplish our mission, but we will get the mission done, one way or the other. That includes getting back here. So pay attention to everything having to do with our target area and what we're going to be doing. This mission is classified, so no one outside the team has any need to know other than the intelligence folks who'll be briefing us."

I turned to Mullen, trying to act like I did this all the time.

"Sergeant, I have to meet with Commander Coyne. Please arrange for weapons training this afternoon. Is there anything you want me to bring up with the commander?"

The sergeant looked surprised for the first time since I had met him.

"Ah, no, no, sir. Weapons training it will be. Anything particular?"

"Whatever you feel is appropriate, Sergeant Mullen."

I turned to leave, but paused. Time to tighten things up a bit.

"In the States, Marines are part of our Navy. As such, we do not salute indoors, ever. Although I respect all your Australian rules and customs, I can't comply with that one. But as a Marine, I am very particular about all other military courtesies. It is part of who we are."

"Yes, sir," came the response in unison by Abernathy and Bever.

I turned and walked out the door, trying to keep my face impassive. Sergeant Mullen and I were going to become fast friends; he just didn't know it yet.

"I'm a big fan of the Colt .45 ACP," I said, picking up the Webley pistol and feeling the balance.

"Damned reliable. That's the Webley. Stopping power, too," Mullen offered, his tone actually a bit friendly.

The British-designed pistol had been around for something like 50 years, coming into its own during the first war. A .45 round certainly gave it the weight of my Colt, and the six-inch barrel would provide the accuracy we needed.

We were standing at a firing line about 20 yards from a row of circular paper targets mounted on wooden frames. What surprised me was the lack of any organization at the range. The

Marine ranges I was used to were very structured and controlled environments with stringent rules that everyone obeyed on pain of having a gunnery sergeant kick their ass into the next week.

"Right," Mullen said and handed me a cardboard box of cartridges. Bever and Abernathy stood to our rear.

I hadn't been exposed to firearms until I joined the Corps. It conflicted with my Georgian roots, but my father never had much use for guns. When I first started firing at Quantico, no one was more surprised than myself when I turned out to be a natural shot. Under the withering instruction of Sergeant Hiram Hunsucker, I learned the Marine mantra of sight alignment and trigger control. It might have been my vision, which was recorded as 20/15 on my induction physical, I never figured it out. But it didn't matter whether I was shooting a Colt .45, a Springfield '03 or a Thompson sub machine gun, I could hit the target. Timed fire, slow fire, standing, prone, it didn't matter. The bullets hit where I aimed.

Raising the Webley to the target, I found the sights were superb and the balance allowed me to keep them aligned on the black center. As always, the shot surprised me, my concentration totally on the sights while I squeezed the trigger almost without thought. Quickly refocusing down range I saw the bullet mark just at the top of the black circle. An easy adjustment, I lowered my sight target three inches and smoothly fired the remaining five cartridges.

Breaking the pistol open, the rounds were automatically extracted. I put the weapon on the small stand.

"Superb weapon, sergeant. I think I've found a match for the Colt."

Mullen was squinting downrange.

He cleared his throat, quietly saying, "Right."

From behind us I heard Abernathy echo, "Too right."

49

For the next thirty minutes, each member of the team fired the Webley, and it was clear that whoever had trained them had done a good job. The opportunity to fire the Lee Enfield was good from a professional standpoint, but we would not be carrying them on the mission. Then it was time for the Owen. It reminded me of the Sten, minimal parts with a clear purpose, to pump out rounds like a fire hose. I quickly became totally infatuated with the weapon.

Developed by an Australian Army officer, it seemed the Aussies realized the available stock of Stens would be taken up by European requirements. The result was a quirky-looking gun that was a cross between a Sten and a Thompson. It fired a 9mm round, which I hadn't seen before and held a vertical magazine of 32 rounds that could be fired semi or full automatic. Using the same technique I'd learned with the Thompson, I fired the first clip in 3 to 4 round bursts, hitting a target forty yards down-range.

"By God, that's a fine piece of weaponry, sergeant. Each member of the team will be carrying one, correct?"

"Yes, sir."

"You and I need to sit down and plan out logistics."

"Not sure what you mean."

"We'll be going into the jungle for an undetermined amount of time. I want to tell the commander how much ammunition we need to take with us. Also, I want to check out your hand grenade."

"The Mills, sir?"

I nodded and said, "Set an hour aside this afternoon to talk about tactics."

"Sir?" For the first time, the sergeant looked truly surprised.

"1600 or so, I'd like to sit down as a team and talk about situations and responses when we're in action. If you can get some cold beer, we can relax after our run."

"Our run?"

"Let's call it combined training, Sergeant Mullen. A whole new way of approaching warfare. We'll set the standard, right?"

The sergeant's face showed a mix of bewilderment and confusion.

"Right."

"Shall we meet here?"

"Uh, yes, sir. You said run, lieutenant?"

"Pick a route that's 6 or 7 miles, nothing real hard. Basic kit, and we'll carry our Owens. Until then, sergeant. "

I stepped back and came to attention and raised my hand in a salute. The three of them immediately came to full attention and saluted, whereupon I returned the salute, smiled and turned on my heel. Round one to the Yank.

By the end of the run, it was clear to me that my team was in fair shape, but nothing spectacular. There wasn't any time to remedy the situation, but at least I knew what I had to deal with. Mullen surprised me. He was the old man of the group, but held his own with the two young ones. I could tell there was some steel inside of him and that made me feel good. Abernathy was the hotshot of the three, more likely to make a smart remark if he said anything at all. Bever seemed to be the most serious of the group; he would listen intently to what anyone else was saying. I'm sure that if I'd ordered him to jump off a cliff, he would've done just that. But I got the impression that he'd be someone I could depend on when the going got tough.

I was pleased with the basics I was seeing. Now I wanted to get a feel for what they thought about fighting the Japs.

Mullen came through holding two metal buckets with bottles of beer in ice. We made ourselves comfortable in the main area of the hut, sitting at the tables, open beers in front of us. Our uniforms were soaked through with sweat and I thought that was a good way to kick things off. It actually reminded me of Quantico, which hit me in an odd way. I kind of missed the place, something I never would have expected during my six months there.

Taking a drink, I looked at the label. "Carlton Draught."

"Not bad," I said "They'd like this in the states. Now, we don't have time for much field training, but we still need to understand how we're gonna approach situations that we're sure to find on this mission. I just spent six months training in small unit tactics, and I want you to know how I think, what I feel is important and how you should expect me to communicate with you. Then I want the same thing from you."

The military is not a democracy. But it is a fool, in my opinion, that tries to run a small unit like a larger unit. I wanted these three men to know that I knew what I was doing, but at the same time, valued their experience and was open to better ways of doing things. As a Marine officer, I had learned clearly that my job was to do whatever was needed to get the job done.

We talked for over two hours. I hadn't planned to go that long, but the time seemed to be well spent. Mullen and Abernathy had learned a lot of things during their time battling the Japs in the Malaysian Peninsula. I asked questions about what tactics the Japs used, how their weapons performed and how things could have been done better. The more we talked, the more comfortable they seemed to be sharing their experiences and thoughts. Poor Bever said almost nothing, but looked like he was trying to absorb everything that was being said. After a while, I discussed basic ops we would have to deal with:

traveling through the jungle, crossing rivers, what to do when encountering people or villages. I talked about mutual support, communicating with hand signals and concealment. I was heartened as I sensed that even Mullen was buying into what we I was saying. My guess is that he hadn't ever done anything like this in his former units, certainly not with officers. I knew I was taking a risk. He could look at me as a weak officer who was going to ask everyone's opinion before taking any action. But that was my challenge.

"What's Borneo like, sir?" Bever asked. The conversation stopped while everyone opened another beer.

"Most of the oil industry is on the coast and that's where I grew up. Inland you'll see some of the world's densest jungle. Much like you must've seen on the Peninsula. Our operating area will be closer to Balikpapan, so we can keep an eye on Japanese shipping, but we'll be working in the jungle."

For a moment I thought Mullen was going to ignore me, but he nodded and said, "Fucking hard to believe how thick it can be. Between the mud and bugs, it's a damned nasty place."

"How do the Japs do in the jungle?" I asked, having seen some of the newsreels that made their infantry out to be superhuman.

"Not much different than us, just always seemed to be so damned many of them."

Abernathy joined in.

"They can move pretty fast. It seemed that once we left the roads, they could flank us pretty easily."

"I'll remember that, corporal, we don't want to lose any footraces in Borneo."

Their expressions told me they agreed.

"How are we gonna get there?" Private Bever asked. The others nodded in their desire to get an answer to that question.

"Borneo's a long way behind the lines. The only way we can reach it will be via sub, then small rubber boats to get ashore." It sounded so easy, but I'd been going over the list of probable fuck-ups that await anyone trying to find a place to land on a hostile shore. I'd spent enough time at sea to know that the ocean is seldom smooth or cooperative, and no doubt we'd be trying to go ashore in the dark.

"You all know how to swim, I assume?"

They all nodded, but my confidence wasn't buoyed by their glances at the floor.

Over the next two weeks, we kept busy with weapons training and intelligence briefings. The lack of current knowledge was intimidating, but it was intrinsic to the nature of the mission. We were going to be the first observers that would be in place with any means of communicating back to allied headquarters. All we had now was peripheral information that had come out via third-party intel.

I was introduced to the AWA BZ3 radio we'd be using. I'd always been fascinated by radios and all things electric, which made my decision to study electrical engineering at Tech that much easier. I knew that efforts were being made to make transceivers portable and that AWA was one of the companies that was working on it. The BZ3 was literally the newest and the best, but it was still a big, cumbersome piece of equipment. More than 200 pounds were spread between five components. I couldn't see how it was going to be usable in the middle of a jungle. The difficulty with transportation was bad enough, but the climate of Borneo couldn't be more hostile to anything electric. The moisture, dirt and bugs would render any delicate piece of equipment so much junk in my mind, but that would be where young Bever would earn his pay.

My briefings from Coyne continued and over several sessions he laid out the mission in its entirety. We were also to attempt to contact a group of locals who had apparently become active in opposition to the Japanese. The problem was, we really didn't know exactly who these people were, or where their loyalties might lie. Our ultimate goal was to conduct recon and if possible, an attack on the Balikpapan oil refinery. This was to be a step-by-step plan according to Coyne, and any follow-on plans would be finalized as we discovered what the real situation was in Borneo. In any case, observing the Jap tanker sailings would remain our primary mission.

One of the steepest challenges would be communicating between Coyne and the team.

"We have a simplified code system to make it easier on you in the field. Much of what you will be reporting will likely be very repetitive and dealing with the tanker traffic out of Balikpapan. But your other activities could run the gamut from intelligence reports to after-action reports. Because of that, we've got pre-formatted codes that'll let you lay out generalities and give you the ability to specify what you need with coded Morse. Bever's been studying the system and can assist, but I'll need you to go over the procedures closely before you leave to make sure you don't have any lingering questions."

While I was thinking about codes, Coyne switched subjects again.

"Do you remember any of the Christian missionary groups that were around in the 30's?"

That seemed like an odd question, but of course I did. Nadira had come to Borneo because of her family's connection to Kemah Injil, a Protestant church that had been active for years on the east coast of the island.

"Reports that have come out of Borneo indicate the Japs were particularly vicious with the missionaries and many were executed."

I heard what he had said, and recoiled at the idea. Those people were harmless and many of them were women and children. What kind of animals were we dealing with? And in the back of my mind was my Maksi. She could easily have been with the missionaries. After all, she had a longstanding connection to the local church group through her family. The sense of dread and apprehension I'd been beating down in the back of my mind was quickly replaced with a burning, desperate anger.

"I would expect that'd make the locals more inclined to be friendly toward you, or at least not hostile."

"Except for the ones who want a bounty from the Japs?"

Coyne glared at me, but didn't dispute my point. The world had seen collaborators across the globe as this war had progressed. Despite my affection for the island, no one could say for sure that Borneo would be any different.

Everything to do with this war was a goddamned nightmare, and it seemed like we were a gnat trying to bother an elephant; then Hostetter changed everything.

CHAPTER FIVE

Redbank Operating Base
Queensland, Australia
17 June 1942

"Change of plans, lieutenant."

Commander Coyne stood at the window, his back to me. As he turned, I saw a new expression take hold of his face. It was uncertainty.

"We have a unique opportunity and I think we would be foolish to pass it up."

"This area of the world seems to attract some of society's more interesting characters," he said as if he was searching for the right words. "We've found a man who spent a great deal of time in and around Balikpapan between the wars."

"Sir?"

"He operated on the...underside, as it were. You know, running contraband, perhaps a bit of light fingers, that sort of thing. The Dutch were never able to catch him and when the war started, he came back to Australia."

"He's Australian?"

"Couldn't beat Queensland out of him."

"You think he can help the team?"

My voice was shakier than I'd have liked. Coyne's unease was as infectious as his confidence.

"Knows the lay of the land, local contacts, the like. Should be valuable to the team."

"Yes, sir, I'm sure he would. But I sense you're not telling me the whole story."

Coyne sat down, rubbed his face and said, "He's been given the chance of a pardon for a long list of crimes, if he'll offer his services to us."

"Hostetter's a bit long in the tooth, but he fought at Gallipoli, heroically, I'm told. In any case, he returned home when the war started, knowing he might be in a spot of trouble, and tried to enlist. That's when his questionable activities in the islands came to notice. The police realized he might be valuable, having escaped from there, and they contacted army intelligence."

It sounded like the commander was trying to convince himself that this was a good idea.

"Have you met him, sir?"

"Just yesterday. He's a bit odd, but his knowledge of the area is superb and he wants to get back at the Japs. They killed a number of civilians when they came ashore last December, including his wife and young son."

Coyne looked me square in the eyes.

"It'll be your choice. Give him a fair go. If you want him, we'll enlist him, kit him up and over to you. But it's your call."

I found Hostetter in one of the small side buildings just across the parade ground from the team hut. Coyne had sent me there by myself, saying that it would be better for me to meet the man one-on-one. I expected to meet an Australian version of Jimmy Cagney: tough, nasty and ready to take on all comers. The only problem was that if he fought in the first war, he was probably at least forty-five.

I knocked twice and swung the door open.

"Mr. Hostetter, I'm Lieutenant Parker."

While he might have been short like Cagney, that's where the resemblance ended. Hostetter looked like an elementary school teacher! This was a tough, underworld character of the Far East? He was average height, weight and just looked like a normal guy. So much for that. How tough could he be?

He stood up from a chair on the opposite side of plain table, a single glass of water in front of him. Looking a little unsure of himself, I inserted myself in the best tradition of a take-charge Marine, extending my hand.

"Glad to meet you."

He smiled ever so slightly and God help me, but I immediately liked him. That's the curse of being a young officer, too easily swayed by emotions.

"No one calls me Mr. Hostetter, just Hoss."

"Okay... Hoss."

The son of a bitch was charming my socks off, I better tighten this up.

"Commander Coyne tells me that you spent time around Balikpapan," I said in my best Marine officer voice.

He nodded.

"After the war, a mate of mine told me there was money to be made, trading with the Dutch up and down the coast. He had a boat he inherited from his old man. I didn't have anything to keep me in Oz, so I went along."

What would I do when this war was over, I thought, seeing the almost wistful look on his face? He must be remembering what it was like to have a future ahead of you.

"Did you make any money?'

He grinned.

"My partner was right on the mark. Didn't take long to build a network along the coast. Once that happened, the rest was easy."

"Commander Coyne told me the Dutch authorities weren't very happy with you."

Hostetter cut his eyes at me.

"Lieutenant, sometimes you just do what you have to do. I didn't have a bloody penny to my name and the world wasn't gonna give me one. So, we gave people what they wanted and they paid us well for our trouble."

I wondered if I would have done the same thing were I in his shoes.

"So why are you ready to go back there? Miss getting shot at?"

"Revenge, Lieutenant. Simple, apolitical, biblical revenge. The Japanese burned down my whole world and I'm going to take back what I'm owed, with you or someone else."

Mullen and Hostetter were not the kind of men I thought I would go into combat with when I was at Quantico, but the more I grasped the reality of what was about to happen, the better I liked them.

The team was in the hut the next morning when I arrived with Private Hostetter, freshly minted from signing enlistment papers.

"This is Private Hostetter. He'll be joining the team."

His new uniform must have been a giveaway.

"Private?" Mullen asked, his tone was at best derisive, if not downright hostile.

"Private Hostetter has an extensive knowledge of the area where we'll be operating. It'll be up to us to get him integrated into the team as quickly as possible."

Mullen stepped up to Hostetter.

"Where were you before coming here?"

Hostetter replied, "Jail."

The sergeant came around the table and stepped up nose to nose with Hostetter.

"Private, I don't give a good God damn if you were in jail or the seminary, you'll call me sergeant or I'll wipe up the bloody floor with you. Understand?

This was not going well.

"Stand easy, both of you."

For a moment, I thought there would be blows, but the two men relaxed and moved back from each other.

"Corporal Abernathy, show the private where to stow his gear. I want everyone outside in five minutes and ready to move out."

Another leadership challenge.

When I think about Mullen and Hostetter, the maxim *opposites attract, likes oppose* couldn't be more applicable. It was as true of them as it is of magnets.

Over the next week, I discovered that Hostetter was more than competent on the weapons range, able to keep up on our runs and likely as not to kill Sergeant Mullen before the month was out. But I suspected events were going to overcome all of our problems and I hoped that would make everyone focus on the mission and not each other's varying degrees of friction. Slowly, the team polarized, with Mullen and Abernathy on one side, while the two privates, despite being so far apart in age, seemed to bond with each other. The only constants were that we were all tired and Mullen wouldn't hesitate to act like a complete hard-on.

Just as I began to feel like things were coalescing, I learned Coyne was not done doling out his little surprises.

"You wanted to see me, sir?"

Coyne was wearing a khaki uniform, acting much more relaxed than the last time we'd met.

"Have a seat, lieutenant."

He handed me a folder.

"Here is a summary report on what is now being called the Battle of Midway. Your pilots, in a very brief period of time, literally changed the situation in the Pacific. Take time to read it and leave in with the yeoman before you leave.

"How's it going with the new man?" he asked.

Fair question.

"He'll do fine, sir. Some static between him and Mullen, but I'm sure that will sort itself out."

"Good to hear, but don't let it get out of hand. Mullen can be damned hard-headed and you don't need that with the mission about to push off."

'Sir?"

"We were just notified that an American submarine will be departing Brisbane in six days. The plan is to have you and your team aboard."

Just like that, there it was. I knew it would come, this just seemed too soon. But I was learning that things happen and you just get on with it.

"Right."

"You'll be spending at least two weeks aboard the submarine, depending on their mission requirements. The hope is they'll drop you first, then go on their merry way. We gave them a suggested insertion point, but you and I can discuss what discretion you have on that later."

Discretion. Interesting word choice, I thought. I was going to be a thousand miles from my immediate superior, so it struck me that I was going to have a hell of a lot of discretion. More than the average Marine lieutenant, for damned sure.

"One other thing, not sure it's relevant, but you should be aware. We've been getting sporadic reports of some type of group operating north of Balikpapan. The intel boys have no idea, or at least they are denying that they have anything going on and I believe them. So, keep your ears open, who knows what you might find."

I found the team in their hut, cleaning up after the noon meal.

"Listen up. We need to be ready to move out. There's an American submarine leaving Brisbane and we've been booked for the trip."

"How much time have we got?" Mullen asked.

The rest of the crew said nothing, but everyone had stopped what they were doing and turned to listen.

"The sub, the *S-43*, leaves port in six days. I don't know when they want us aboard, but we need to be ready to move out at any time."

I didn't tell them that I was trying to get some kind of rubber boat practice before we went aboard the submarine. One of our exercises at Quantico involved a river crossing in inflatable boats, and it'd turned into a full-blown mess. Everyone thought paddling the boats would be easy. But we ended up with a lot of Marines in the water. And that was a relatively calm river, something I knew wouldn't be the case when in Borneo.

Coyne had a real gift for getting things done. Two days after our last briefing, the team was riding aboard an old bus from the camp to the Brisbane waterfront. The U.S. Navy offered to give us a briefing on the submarine and help us practice launching the inflatables.

"One more time," I asked the team, "Everyone can swim, right? Don't blow smoke up my ass, because if you can't, I'm not fishing you out."

They all looked back at me, no one admitting any weakness in the water.

"Remember, we'll be going in during darkness. That makes our problem a lot harder. This is not a little row across a lake on a breezy summer day. Few things are harder than landing from the ocean, and at night it's significantly worse."

"He's right," Hostetter said. "I saw what can happen at Gallipoli."

Abernathy turned in his seat and looked at him.

"You were at Gallipoli?"

Hostetter nodded. "A real clap-up, getting ashore."

"My dad was killed at Gallipoli," Abernathy said, "You were really there?"

Hostetter offered only a solemn nod.

As an afterthought, Hostetter said, almost to himself, "I was a sapper in the third brigade of the First. We were the first Aussies ashore that night, and it was a damned mess all around. I ended up in the water. Barely made it to shore."

The other men were watching the exchange with marked curiosity and saw Abernathy start to say something, then stop and sit back in his seat. Mullen said nothing, but he was certainly paying attention.

The bus continued to bounce along the road, which had turned to macadam from gravel. I had never mentioned Hostetter's war record to the team. Apparently, he hadn't, either.

Ten minutes later Abernathy turned around in his seat, facing Hostetter.

"Heard of the Battle of Lone Pine?"

Hostetter paused for a moment, again his thoughts likely returning to those days.

"I was there. Bloodiest damned thing…"

"That's were my dad was killed," he said quietly.

"A lot of good men died on that ridge. But we killed a lot of theirs, too, by God."

Hostetter narrowed his eyes, focusing on the young corporal.

"There was an Abernathy, I knew. Jim. Jimmy, we called him. He got it on the ridge. Damned good man. From Freemantle, if I recall."

Abernathy's eyes widened.

"That was my dad."

"I'll be damned," Hoss said.

The first ship we saw at the naval base wasn't a submarine, but a big tender, the *U.S.S. Griffin.* As we got closer, we could see a sub moored behind the tender and several subs tied up alongside. I knew that submarines needed a "mother ship" that could provide support between their patrols. We soon learned that the *S-43* was the sub moored pier-side, behind the tender.

A short gangway sloped down to the deck of the submarine, where men were busy working all over the deck. Using the best naval protocol knowledge I could scrounge together, I walked down the gangway, saluted the American flag and then returned the salute of a sailor who apparently had the watch. He was wearing a white sailor hat while everyone else was uncovered, and a .45 hung from his waist.

"I'm Lieutenant Parker," I said, hoping that would be enough.

"From the Aussie base, sir?"

"Right."

"Yes, sir. Mr. Taylor is waiting for you, I'll get him."

He walked to the ship's island and leaned inside a hatch. In a moment, he was back.

"He'll be right up, sir."

Lieutenant Bob Taylor came on deck, and offered his hand along with a broad smile. He was a tall, lanky man who walked with a quiet confidence. He looked like he would've made a hell of a Marine.

"Welcome aboard," he said, returning my salute and offering his hand. "Bob Taylor, XO. Let's head aft. I have the boatswain and one of his men standing by."

The deck felt solid underneath my feet, but I was surprised that there were holes everywhere. As if sensing my question, Taylor offered that the deck was part of the external hull, which surrounded the pressure hull. He pointed out the main aft deck hatch, noting that it would be the hatch used during the boat landing.

A pile of gear was arranged between the hatch and the stern of the boat. It looked like two deflated rafts and life preservers.

"What we have here are two LCRS inflatable rafts. I wanted to show you how they're inflated on deck. Then we can give you a chance to practice with them. We also have B-3 life vests for each of you. You may have heard of them, they're nicknamed "Mae Wests" for reasons that'll become glaringly obvious once they're inflated."

The lieutenant picked up a vest and gave us a quick brief, covering how to put the vest on, the CO_2 inflation bottle and the manual inflator tube.

Two crewmen came aft towards our group, with a coiled tube in their hands.

"Our crew will get the rafts on deck and inflate them with compressed air. Chief Pickett, go ahead and inflate the boats."

He turned back to us.

"All right, now. On with the life vests, but don't inflate them."

A tall sailor knelt, attaching the tube somewhere in the aft hatch area. The unrolled tube now reached the rafts and his companion rolled out the black bundles, which began to look like boats, only flat. In a moment the air began to flow and the first raft took shape. Quickly the second raft was inflated, and two more sailors came aft carrying paddles.

"We'll lower the rafts using a bow and stern line. The lines will stay attached until you're aboard and tell us to cast off."

We watched the two rafts as they were lowered into the water, the fat hull of the submarine providing a wide path down.

"All set here. Now Chief Pickett will show you how to use the knotted rope to get down to the raft."

Two knotted ropes were tied to fittings in the deck and tossed down to each raft.

The chief, who I then realized was built like a brick shithouse, went down the hull, hand over hand, his back to the water with both feet spread wide against the sloping side of the sub. Then he reversed and scrambled back up to the deck.

"Be careful as you go down. The hull's pretty slippery," he said, dropping the rope on deck.

The obstacle course training at Quantico held me in good stead and I was able to climb down to the first raft without making a fool of myself. Abernathy followed me down in to the first raft with no trouble. Private Bever demonstrated the slipperiness as his feet slipped and he banged sideways into the hull.

"Damn," he yelled, but managed to hang on with both hands, scrambling back to his knees, then planting his feet against the hull.

"In you go," I said and Bever climbed into the raft.

How much harder would this be at night on the ocean?

"Okay, Sergeant Mullen, down you go," I said, looking up at Mullen, who was holding on to the knotted rope leading down to raft two.

"Right," he said, his voice sounding resigned.

As he started down the rope, his feet slipped sideways and in an instant, Mullen slammed into the hull with his body, his head snapping sideways into the steel plating. Like a rag doll, the sergeant collapsed, tumbling into the water, a mule-sized splash erupted next to the second raft.

"Shit!" I yelled and twisted around in my raft to see a cap floating away from the submarine's hull and Mullen face down, his arms limp at his side. My realization that Mullen needed help was interrupted by Hostetter entering the water feet-first next to Mullen.

I heard Lieutenant Taylor telling his men to throw a line to the men in the water as I watched Hostetter roll the sergeant on his back and pull the toggle on the vest. The line from the deck landed across Mullen's chest and Hostetter grabbed it while hanging onto the still limp, but now buoyant Mullen.

"Standby, soldier!" Taylor called as two of his men scrambled down the ropes and pulled Mullen to the side of the hull. Bever and Abernathy turned around in our raft and leaned out to help the rescue party. The sailors had run the line around Mullen, tying a knot and positioning him with his back against the hull.

"Steady pull," I heard Taylor order and saw that several more sailors had joined him, straining on the lifting rope.

By the time I climbed back on deck, Mullen was laying on a blanket with a corpsman examining him. His vest was off and I saw his hands clenching and unclenching. Looking down I saw his eyes were open and the corpsman was wiping blood from a nasty scrape on the right side of his head.

"How is he?"

"A little banged up, but he should be fine. My experience is that most army types have damned hard heads."

I was joined by Hostetter, dripping salt water on the deck. A sailor unfolded a dark grey blanket and wrapped it around him.

"Quick thinking, Private. Thank you."

"Saw a man drown once, right next to our boat. Can't take any chances."

Funny, I thought, the oldest one of us was the quickest to act when it was needed. Did that say good things about Hostetter or bad things about the rest of us?

"It's called Cellophane. All the radio components came pre-wrapped from the manufacturer that way. We'll add heavily waxed paper and seal the packages with more wax. Should be able to handle anything but a full immersion. The final package will also have carrying straps."

Coyne was standing at a table in the supply building upon which lay the five packages, which comprised the BZ3 radio set. It'd been two days since our adventure on the submarine and events were moving fast.

"We've packed the remainder of your supplies and ammunition in these ruck sacks to make transport easier," he continued. "You'll find ammunition along with medical supplies, some radio parts and what food we could fit. We've kept the weight to no more than 35 pounds. We've been able to get our hands on what your people call Jungle Rations. Made for tropical weather, it has mostly dried, dehydrated foodstuffs. It'll only get you started. For the long haul, you'll have to live off the land."

Coyne and I had discussed the equipment and we agreed that stashing a portion of the material near the landing site and making several trips to our first staging area was the only reasonable plan. What we couldn't know was how many enemy troops might be in the area. The few reports we'd received noted most of the enemy activity had been centered on Balikpapan and we'd be landing about twenty miles north. With luck, we'd be able to move inland unnoticed by the Japs. Then we could contact the locals.

Earlier in the day, we'd completed our introduction to the rubber rafts under the supervision of Lieutenant Taylor and Chief Pickett. The raft entry process went smoothly as did the paddling drill around the submarine. Getting back aboard the sub was a little rough, but that wasn't something we expected to have to do.

"I'm not certain that two rafts will be enough for the equipment and the team," I told Coyne.

"We don't want the rafts overloaded, that's a sure recipe for problems. What do you suggest?" he asked.

Remembering the sailors who had helped us on the S-43, I said, "Can we get the Navy to paddle a third raft in with us, then they return to the sub?"

"Let me check on that."

Heading back to my billet from Coyne's office, I saw Mullen walking toward the team hut. He still had a thin bandage around his head, but wore his cap anyway.

I assumed the motion with his right hand was a salute, so I returned his gesture sharply.

"Mending well, sergeant?"

He nodded.

"Well enough."

"Private Hostetter was certainly on top of things, wouldn't you say?"

"I still think he's going to be trouble once we get in the field."

That surprised me.

"What makes you say that?"

"He's been a civvie too long. Get him back in his old runs and who knows what comes up."

I looked at Mullen, wondering if he was just being an asshole as usual.

"Sergeant, you're the top NCO. I expect that you won't let anything happen."

"Yes, sir."

His enthusiasm was underwhelming, and I couldn't help but wonder who really might fall short when we found ourselves subject to the jungle's challenges.

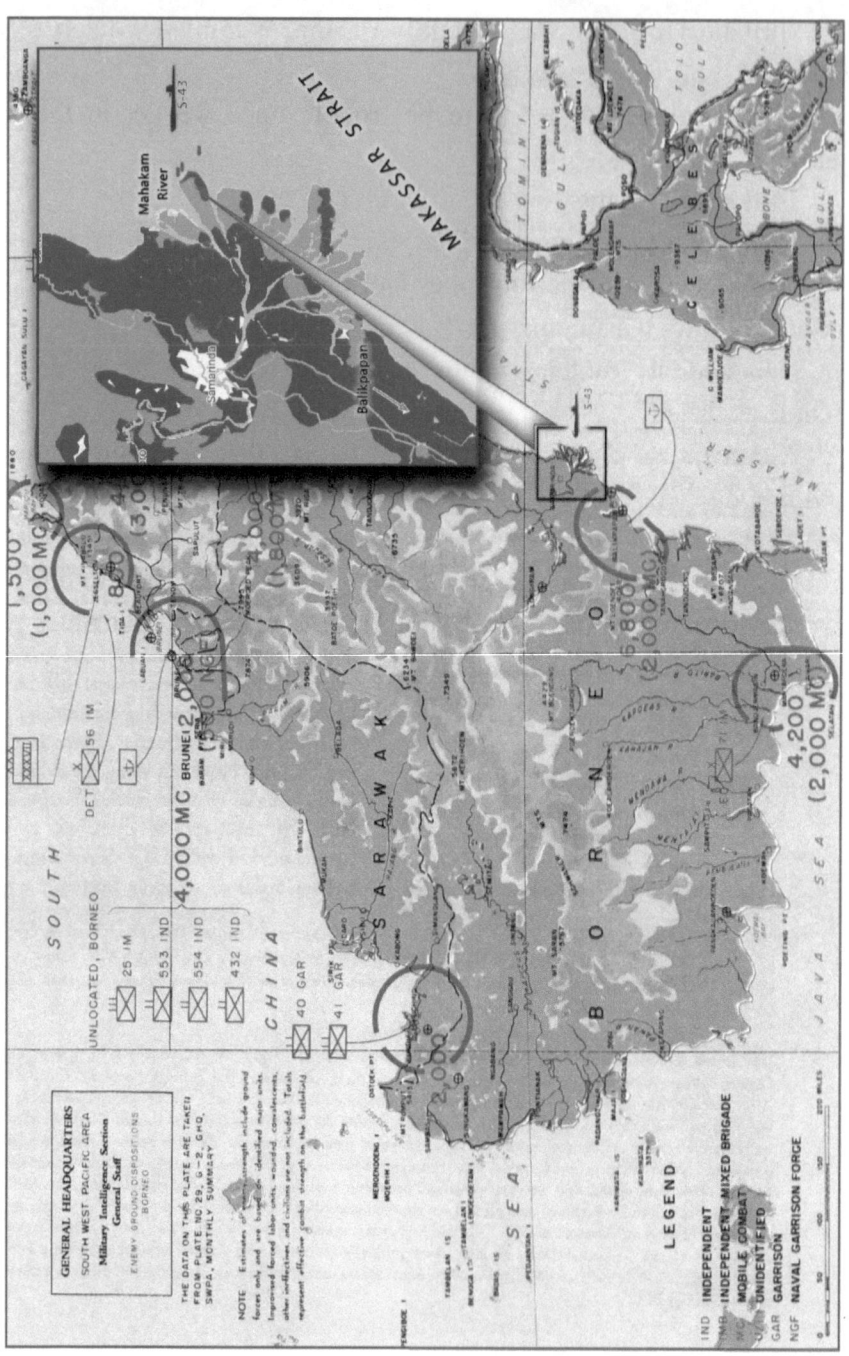

CHAPTER SIX

Aboard the S-43
Outbound from Brisbane
August 1942

On the 4th of August, 1942, the *S-43* departed Brisbane with our little group crammed aboard. The strange world of a ship, to say nothing of a sub, was totally confusing. From the sounds and smells to the bizarre rituals of diving and surfacing, we felt like we were on a different planet. We discovered the Pacific Ocean is somehow even more immense from within than it seems from above, especially so when traveling at 6 knots submerged during daylight hours and at 12 knots on the surface at night. The advantage of traveling by ship, though, is that you're constantly moving toward your destination for 24 hours each day. Under normal circumstances, anyhow.

There are, of course, events that can disrupt a straightforward transit. On the third day, we found ourselves swept up into the ongoing naval battle that had taken hold of the region since the Japanese invaded the islands. The only threat to the Japs were the remaining submarines of the Americans, Dutch and Aussies. Their target was the ongoing need for the Japs to move refined petroleum products from Borneo to the many forward bases that had sprung up across the Pacific. Tankers were fat and slow, which made them perfect targets for the allied submarines that had been dueling with the Japanese navy since December of 1941.

Getting underway seemed to be a well-orchestrated drill. I had briefly met the commanding officer, Lieutenant Commander E.R. Hannon, who welcomed me and said we would talk once at sea. That told me to stay out of the way until summoned. Once our gear was stowed, the team found the crew's dining area and a table to call home.

Submerging at dawn, the *S-43* had been continuing our transit, when, in the late morning, the sound of propellers prompted the captain to raise the periscope. He was rewarded with the sight of a 7,000-ton, tanker flying a rising sun flag, steaming east, accompanied by two destroyers.

Due to the dual layers of operation inherent in seafaring battle, there are times when a submarine commander will be ordered to avoid enemy action in order to prevent hazarding the primary mission. This was not one of those times.

The announcing system told all hands to man their battle stations. I was in the crew's mess with the team, going over procedures and maps for what seemed like the fiftieth time. As passengers, we had nothing to do but stay out of the way, which was easy in the mess, it became a ghost town in less than 10 seconds.

"What do you think that means, lieutenant?"

Bever, the source of all questions on all subjects, had me on that one.

"I suspect we'll find out one way or another," I said as the metallic click of the announcing system sounded through the boat.

"This is the captain speaking. We've sighted an enemy tanker and two destroyers eastbound. Right now, we're in a good position for a torpedo attack. Stay on your toes, we should be in a firing position in about ten minutes. That is all."

Taylor, who was now my roommate, had told me that this might happen, but it seemed far-fetched to me. Now it was happening, with all the urgency and tension inherent in an undersea torpedo strike. The war had finally come to me. I found that I was tense but also excited. Although I didn't understand firing torpedoes from a submarine underwater, I knew something deadly was in the process. I remember some of the newsreel films from the Atlantic of blazing and exploding ships with men in boats or floating amid the debris. This seemed very different. I was sitting at a dining table with a half a cup of coffee. But up there, enemy sailors could be only minutes away from fiery annihilation. It hit me right then that I hoped the skipper did sink the tanker and kill everyone on it. They were responsible for all of this, after all.

Around the table, no one was talking, but eyes were moving as we listened to the sounds of the attack around us.

"Tell us about Georgia, lieutenant," Hostetter asked, with a grin before I could say anything.

Smart guy, I thought. Talk about something other than what was happening. Ignore the fact that we could get killed at any time.

"It's a good place," I said, trying to act nonchalantly. "Friendly people, great food and pretty girls. The best the south has to offer."

"You have a girlfriend back there, sir?" Bever asked, jumping into our effort to remain unaffected by what was going on around us.

I forced a laugh.

"No, Bever, I loved 'em and left 'em, in the finest Tech tradition."

"Tech?"

"That Atlanta institution of higher learning, The Georgia Institute of Technology, which everyone calls Georgia Tech."

Bever asked, "That's a school, then?"

I felt the ship shudder once, then again, then one last time. I knew it must be the torpedoes leaving the tubes up forward.

Around the mess table, a series of querulous looks in my direction pushed me to offer my most uninformed opinion.

"Torpedoes firing, I bet."

"Right," Abernathy offered. The others remained quiet.

A rumble from outside the hull got our attention and the captain confirmed two hits on the tanker. It was nice to have some degree of confirmation that the enemy was not, in fact, invincible.

"This is the captain. Rig for silent running."

From the galley, a cook appeared and he quickly shut off the two wall fans that always ran at either end of the dining area. Walking back to the galley, he held his finger up to his lips and said, "Shhhhhhh."

We felt the deck tilt under us as the captain changed course. I knew submarines do turn and change depths to confuse the enemy. That meant the destroyers must be after us.

"What the hell," Bever whispered as we all heard a rhythmic rumble which began to grow in intensity. A distinct ping echoed from outside the hull and I knew that had to be the Jap version of SONAR.

"Enemy destroyer," I said without thinking. The Jap ship was looking for us and it sounded like he was coming in the right direction.

It hit me that the pulsating was from the rotating propellers of the destroyer as the sounds grew. I felt the course changing and the bow nosing down as the skipper tried to outmaneuver the Jap commander.

"He's right overhead," Hostetter said quietly as the propeller sounds began to recede. The skipper was twisting and turning the boat, but that made it clearer that we were being actively hunted.

The crash of an explosion outside the hull brought every one of us to the immediate terror of death. Grabbing on to the mess table, not a word was said, before a second crash echoed from the hull's port side.

"CHRIST!" Mullen managed to blurt out just as another explosion rocked the sub. The overhead lights blinked several times before going out. Single rays of light pierced the darkness as battle lanterns came on automatically. The dim light was full of clouds of suspended dust and lone paint chips flitting around in chaos before gently, silently falling to the floor.

The next explosion seemed farther away and the hull remained stable.

"That's more than enough of that, for Chrissakes," Hostetter said.

"Too right," Abernathy shakily chimed in.

Saying nothing myself, I sat on that damned bench, trying not to make my mortal terror a dead giveaway.

Taylor told me later the Japs had dropped a total of thirty-seven depth charges. I wasn't counting, but thankfully after the first attack, the remainder exploded much farther away. The *S-43* still maintained silent running for three hours after the last charge went off. All I wanted to do was get to Borneo and feel solid earth under my feet.

That evening, I was summoned to see the commanding officer.

"Come in, lieutenant. Have a seat."

The commanding officer's cabin was spacious compared to the broom closet I was sharing with Taylor, but still cramped. I saw a large chart on the skipper's bunk and he was bent over it making notes on a pad.

He sat down in front of the small fold-down desk and smiled at me. His face was youthful for a man in his mid-thirties, but it showed the unimaginable strain of commanding a warship in combat.

"Your men hold up okay during our little tussle?"

"Yes, sir. I guess none of us expected anything like that."

Hannon chuckled.

"I would have preferred to avoid it, but even the Pacific is only so big. Now, let's talk about getting your team off this sub and back where you can do some good."

We looked at the landing area I'd discussed with Coyne. While the Australian had been focusing on the post-landing mission, Hannon was looking at the landing as a naval exercise.

"According to intelligence, the Japs have patrol boats all over the area. Small, not much of a threat to us, but deadly if they find your group."

"How close can you take us? The closer we are to the beach, the less time we're vulnerable."

"The charts of the area are spotty, but I think we can get you within a mile of the river entrance. Of course off the mouth of that river delta, you could get some choppy water."

Thinking back on our rubber boat travails in a placid harbor, the reality was beginning to become palpable.

"What does that mean to a land lubber?" I asked, not even sure what I wanted to know.

"Maybe a two to three-foot chop, but we won't know until we actually surface."

"What will that do to your sailors helping us ferry our gear into the beach?"

He paused, looking up from the chart.

"Makes it a tougher go, but I've got two good men. They'll be fine."

"One of my men spent years sailing this coast. I'd like to get his opinion."

The skipper nodded.

"Just let me know. And I thought you'd like to know, I received a backchannel message that the Marine 1st Division has landed in the Solomon Islands. Someplace called Guadalcanal."

To hear that gave me a sense of pride, but I also knew I must know men who were on that island, and I wasn't. Orders, however, were orders.

After transiting the Makassar Strait, the *S-43* surfaced off the mouth of the Mahakam River which flows to the east from the mountains and forests of East Kalimantan. My curiosity led me to check the charts before we went on deck. Our little band was going to land on a peninsula that was about ten thousand miles from Quantico. That's a long way from home.

The area that Hannon selected turned out to be a good choice according to Hostetter. There were very few people living in the area and inland, there were few roads, making it less likely the Japs would be conducting land patrols. Besides, their interest had to be in and around the petroleum facilities, and we'd be well north of those during the landing. In any event, I was ready to get off the boat. The only thing stymieing my enthusiasm was the heavy apprehension that had become a constant companion as we drew closer to Borneo. I tried to push it out of my mind as often as I could, chalking it up to nerves, but nothing about this was going to be remotely easy or safe.

As I have often found, the anticipation of a difficult event is sometimes the worst part of it. In my mind, I saw wind-blown spray crashing over the deck of the sub as we struggled to load our gear into ungovernable rubber boats. In fact, the sea we were about to launch into was like a pond, with a moon illuminating the low-lying land in the distance. I'd take it any day over towering squalls, but it didn't keep my apprehension at bay. I had to remind myself that as complex and fraught as this whole thing seemed, it was really pretty simple, get in the boat and go. There weren't any other options.

Taylor supervised the entire evolution on deck with a minimum of chatter. Red flashlights provided extra illumination, but staring down into the inflatable boat, my stomach tightened. Remembering Mullen's fall during training, I held the rope with a death grip as I lowered myself down the side of the sub. The rubber boat felt incredibly flimsy and kneeling down in the bow, I wondered how we would ever get the thing ashore. But despite my misgivings, we followed the plan and in less than ten minutes, everyone was in the boats with our gear aboard.

"Good luck," I heard the XO call as we pulled on the paddles.

My concern about the ability to navigate over a dark ocean proved pointless as the moon clearly showed the way. Once I got my paddling rhythm down, I found the movement of the ocean was a help, lifting the boat for a better view of the beach. My confidence began to grow by leaps and bounds until I remembered I was the unit commander and was responsible for all the boats. Turning backwards as far as I could, I saw the second boat over Hostetter's right shoulder. Mullen was in charge of the boat and kneeling in the bow while Abernathy and Bever paddled on opposite sides behind him. Our boat had a bit more gear and the third boat carried an equal amount. Paddling at the end of the line was Chief Petty Officer Dennis Pickett and Seaman Bob Springer, the two men who had been on deck that first day we came aboard *S-43*. Both had the XO's seal of approval, which was all I needed. They'd offload their boat and immediately paddle back out to the sub.

As we got closer, I realized the entrance to the left fork of the river was not as evident as I expected it would be. Hell, I couldn't make out anything except a low-lying land mass. Despite the calm water, waves would slap into the boat, throwing water into my eyes and soaking the rest of me. Shit. The wind had been moving us north, but I couldn't tell how far.

Behind us, the world erupted in a combination of automatic weapons fire and tracers, which lit up the darkened sea. I ducked involuntarily, the sound unmistakable after hours on the weapons range at Quantico. Twisting around, I couldn't tell for sure what was happening. The only thing I could make out for sure was that *S-43* was being attacked by the Japs.

"Keep paddling!" I hollered behind me, immediately realizing what a damned stupid thing that was to say.

The lack of response told me that everyone was pulling for their lives. I twisted my head around, paddling hard at the same time. I saw lights in the distance and a single searchlight glancing off the water. To hell with trying to find the river entrance, we just needed to get ashore and away from the Japs.

Ten minutes of hard paddling had my shoulders burning and my breath coming in desperate gasps.

"How you doing?" I finally asked Hostetter, who'd been silent the entire time.

"Okay," he wheezed, making me think he was anything but okay.

Glancing back, I could see the two other boats trailing us. The third boat with the two sailors in it was abeam the second boat and they were both about 20 yards behind us.

"Beach," Hostetter called as I was trying to see if the Jap ship was nearby.

As I turned, I saw the breaking waves not more than ten yards in front of us, the beach was a flat black expanse, with no evidence of any river mouth. Behind the sand, I could make out a tree line that looked solid up and down the beach. After two hard pulls, I decided to go over the side of the raft.

The water was only three feet deep and I grabbed the rope that ran down the side of the raft as Hostetter rolled out of the raft on the other side.

Without a word, we pulled the raft clear of the water and looked to see the other two rafts twenty yards to our right, also dragging themselves ashore. I jogged down the beach, watching them pull their rafts clear of the water.

"We've gotta get off the beach. Grab your rafts and drag 'em to the trees," I ordered, and ran back to our raft.

The tree line was fifty feet away and I knew it would be a bitch to get the raft up there, but there was no way the Japs wouldn't come check the beaches with that searchlight.

Thank God the sand was hard. Not only did we not sink into it, but we didn't leave a trail leading to the trees. At least one thing was going right for us tonight.

"What the hell happened?" Bever asked as we pulled the rafts together under the cover of the first line of trees.

Everyone else was breathing hard, kneeling down on the ground or bending over with hands on knees.

"Damn," Mullen offered, swiveling his head around.

Chief Pickett came over to where I was kneeling, my binoculars out and sweeping the area.

"Did you see what happened to the boat, sir?"

"Sorry, chief. I didn't."

"Right," he said.

The reality of the situation was becoming starkly obvious in the dark night. If the *S-43* had been hit, who knows what might have happened. If they'd been able to submerge and escape, the Japs now knew an enemy sub was in the area and more ships would likely arrive to hunt it down. In either case, Pickett and Springer had just been seconded to the Marine Corps, whether they liked it or not.

CHAPTER SEVEN

The Telukladang Peninsula
East Kalimantan, Borneo
17 August 1942

Dawn brought an empty ocean, the Japanese long gone. Why we hadn't seen the beach combed for survivors, I didn't know. but at least I could pinpoint where we were, and it wasn't as bad as I had feared during the night. The plan had been to enter the mouth of the river and travel inland. I fixed our position left of the river mouth, on a peninsula that jutted into the sea. The good news was that we could reach our intended landing spot by going overland.

For the time being, I decided to hide the rafts and carry our supplies inland, stashing them for later. Having two extra men would make humping the gear a lot easier. No one had suffered any injuries during the landing and after a quick breakfast, we got busy covering the rafts.

I expected the chief wanted to discuss his situation, but for now he and Springer were going about their business as if they were longtime team members. Both men carried .45 pistols, but that was the extent of their gear. They wore their everyday uniforms, the chief in khakis, Springer in dungarees.

Very quickly everyone was drenched in sweat. The heat climbed along with the humidity and soaked us all through, which at least provided some amount of cooling paired with the light breeze coming off the water. In an hour, the rafts were hidden by thick layers of underbrush and we were ready to move out.

I motioned to Chief Pickett to follow me beyond earshot of the rest.

"Chief, you and Springer can stay here and see if the S-43 comes back tonight to pick you up. Otherwise you're with us."

The chief removed his cap and ran his hands through his curly red hair.

"I think we best stick with you, lieutenant. We don't know if the boat'll be back and with no equipment, we'd be up shit creek without a paddle."

"It's your call, chief. We'd be happy to have you, but I'll be honest, we might be here for some time."

"Chance we'll have to take, I guess."

I was glad to have them with us. If the Japs now suspected someone might have come ashore in the night, we'd need all the help we could get.

We spent an hour going over our storage area for the gear. Protecting it from the elements as well as concealing it was critical if we needed to retrieve it later. Encountering unforeseen complications in the jungle was an inevitability, but even so, it was critical to think ahead and try to plan as much as possible in spite of the chaos.

Putting Sergeant Mullen on point, we headed southwest, paralleling the river. I wanted experience leading us into the unknown and now was time for the sergeant to start earning his attitude. According to the map, the area didn't have any big villages, but Hostetter had said that it wasn't unusual to find small camps where several families might live, particularly near the river. As we moved deeper into the jungle, the underbrush grew thicker and the flying insects began to bother everyone. It made even the dead of summer at Quantico seem like a temperate paradise.

As a boy, I hadn't spent that much time in the jungle, but the earthy smell and humidity brought back memories. I was having more trouble with the mosquitoes, gnats and a particularly nasty looking type of fly. We stopped and everyone applied a bug repellent called "612" and we were relieved that it seemed to deter the little bastards. A small, but significant victory we were all too happy to accept.

At Quantico, land navigation had always come easy to me, but the rolling hills of Virginia bear little resemblance to the flat jungle expanses of coastal Borneo. The best I could do was dead reckoning with my compass and map, then estimate our progress. The other problem I was beginning to recognize was that the map I was using lacked any real detail. We had no choice but to improvise and make our own map as we went. Maybe our amateur cartographic endeavors would be useful to the mapmakers of the world if we made it out of this in one piece.

Seaman Springer had been extremely quiet during the two hours since we had left the beach. Everyone else had been carrying on a quiet commentary as we traversed thorn belts, small streams and overhanging branches. It had proven the best way to prevent injury on the many unfriendly bushes that seemed to infest the area. Springer had been at the end of the line and took all of the cautionary comments on where to step or what to dodge without reply. I couldn't tell if he was scared, exhausted or just the quiet type. Physically, he was the polar opposite of Chief Pickett. While the Chief was big and burly, Springer was wiry and skinny as a rail. Which gave me an idea.

"Springer," I called during a break.

He walked over and squatted next to me.

"Where do you call home?"

"New York, sir, Binghamton."

"I bet they have some big trees in Binghamton, right?"

"Uh, yes, sir. I guess so."

"You ever climb those trees when you were growing up?"

Looking at me like I had slipped a gear, he nodded.

"Sure, sir."

"Think you can climb a tree like that?" I asked him, pointing to a tall palm type tree at the edge of the clearing we had stopped in.

He looked at the tree, which was probably forty feet tall, the trunk bare most of the way up, but angling at about thirty degrees.

"I'll give it a try, sir."

Twenty minutes later the young sailor was back on the ground, grinning like a Cheshire cat and describing on the map what he had seen from his elevated perch.

"Right about here, there's a clearing. I saw smoke."

"You ever work in this area?" I asked Hostetter.

"Not here, but I knew some local blokes who worked this part of the river. Might help."

An hour later, with the rest of the team still out of sight, Hostetter and I slowly approached the open area, the smoke now clearly visible. We had cached our gear near a rock formation and now only carried our weapons.

A cry of welcome or alarm broke the silence and the two of us stopped and raised our hands out to our sides, even with our waists.

Two men wearing loincloths and nothing else walked toward us. Both carried long poles, like walking sticks but heavier. I also noticed that both men wore long blades in scabbards hanging from ropes around their waists. They appeared to be in their late twenties, wiry and lean. They each wore their jet-black hair tied into long ponytails.

I called hello in Malay, trying to sound as friendly as I could.

Between Hoss and myself using a combination of Malay and English, we were able to communicate with the two men. They had known several missionaries, which explained their rudimentary knowledge of English, and our Malay worked pretty well with their local dialect. Soon, two older men came down from a long structure that had been constructed at the edge of the clearing, parallel to the river. Using the same mixture of languages, we were able to exchange greetings with the older men.

Amulong and Prehanan were the two headmen of the small village. I estimated that there might be thirty people living there. We found out later that they fished the river and cultivated several crops including rice and a local variety of corn. Probably a dozen kids were soon in evidence, playing or doing chores under the supervision of a half-dozen women who bore the unmistakable aura of motherhood. Most of them were wearing a type of wraparound shirt, some had a strange corset-type affair around their stomachs, and they were all bare breasted. One woman, who looked older than the rest stood back from the others and I saw she was wearing a western smock-style dress. *Where the hell did that come from?*

I focused my attention on our hosts and explained that there were more of us nearby, which was met with some amount of concern on their parts. In short order we had the whole team gathered in the center of the village.

"Be friendly. Be polite, but keep your eyes open and be ready with your weapons," I passed to the team as they gathered in a small circle.

The people seemed relaxed, but were clearly giving us the once over. I knew we had to figure out what was happening with the Japanese. I tried to talk to Amulong, but he stopped me and called to a group of men who had been standing at the edge of the clearing. As they approached, I noticed every one of them carried a long knife and several also carried long poles that seemed menacing absent any explanation.

The men escorted all of us to a long structure that was elevated off the ground and looked like a fancy lean-to. The side facing us was open with what looked like woven mats used to close the side. The back was made of woven strips of wood, with several window-like openings. Sloped ramps with notched steps led up to the platform. We climbed up on their gestured invitation and were invited to sit around a rock fire pit, which had been constructed in the middle of the building. I'd heard of these longhouses before and while this one wasn't that large, it was certainly big enough to house all of the villagers.

After sitting in a circle around the fire, we were served balls of rice that tasted vaguely fishy and a drink that must have been their version of moonshine. The incongruity struck me as we smiled and nodded to our hosts. Realizing we didn't truly know their intentions or where their loyalties lay, I realized how far in over our heads we really were. I wanted to trust them and knew that we had no choice but to continue the charade. Coyne had told me that most natives were to be considered friendly or at least non-threatening, but after last night's fiasco, I wasn't putting too much faith in our blind luck.

I asked them what they knew of the Japanese. At first they didn't seem to understand, then Hostetter used the term "Nippon," and that was all it took. An hour later, we had put the picture together. The Japs hadn't visited their village, but a similar village upriver had been attacked by a patrol several months before. Many of the men had been killed along with some of the women. The village's longhouse had been burned to the ground. Their crime had been hiding a British family that had fled from Balikpapan. I wondered what had happened to all of the English and Dutch civilians that lived in the area. It seemed strange that the world where I had grown up in was gone, not reclaimed by natives, but torn apart by invaders.

"What do you think?" I asked Hoss, "Can we trust 'em?"

He shrugged.

"After what happened to the other village, I'd guess they're more on our side than not. Before the war, these river types were considered pretty honest as a whole."

"Sergeant Mullen, what are you thinking?"

"That things just got sticky."

I turned to where the sergeant had been looking and was stunned to see a western woman, in a loose-fitting sun dress walking slowly toward the longhouse. Her long hair was pulled back in a ponytail, a deep tan evident on her face and bare arms.

Standing up I motioned everyone to stay in place and made my way back down the ladder. The woman had stopped, a look of fear or trepidation on her face.

"My name is Parker, Lieutenant Parker, United States Marines."

She stepped up to me, her blue eyes still showing fear.

"Do you speak English?"

"Yes, I do, of course," she said with a British accent. Then she smiled and shook her head almost as if to clear her mind of the strange vision in front of her.

I extended my hand, which she looked at for a moment then slowly grasped.

"Nice to meet you."

Tears ran down her face.

"My name is Lynda, Lynda Noble. I never thought I would see Americans in Borneo."

"What in God's name are you doing here?"

She put her hand to her face, wiping away the tears. She had a tiredness that made her look wizened and older than her years, but her head was held high, unrepentant. I sensed this was a woman who should not be underestimated, too frequent a fault of mine when it came to women in general.

The story slowly came out of her escape from Balikpapan with her parents. Her father was a doctor and she was a qualified nurse. Two months ago, she had been summoned to this village because one of the women was in labor. Her father was sick with a fever, so he remained behind. While she was here, the Japs had descended on the other village. Her parents had been taken away and the village was ravaged. She'd been here ever since, not knowing what to do or even where to go.

"Why are you here? Are the Americans retaking the island?"

I shook my head.

"Sorry, the war's still a long way from that happening."

She didn't seem to understand what I meant.

"We're here to check on enemy operations and report back to headquarters."

I thought that was enough for her to know.

"You might want to come back up here," Sergeant Mullen called down.

Back on the platform I saw the older women in the smock was kneeling behind Amulong.

Hostetter leaned over as I sat down.

"Apparently, they've decided we're not the enemy and so we now have a villager who is a little better versed in English. I take it her name is Mamsettan."

Mamsettan, the woman I had seen earlier in the smock dress, whispered in Amulong's ear and he replied in the same manner.

"Amulong is very pleased that you are able to be with us," she said, her English tinged with a Dutch accent.

"Thank him for his hospitality. We don't want to remain here for long, our presence is a danger for your village."

"Amulong asked what we can do to help you and if you will take the two English with you when you leave."

"Two English?"

"The woman and her brother."

I heard Mullen chuckling beside me, I think it was the first time I ever heard anything humorous out of him.

Lynda spoke up from the bottom of the slanted ladder, "My brother was at the edge of the village and watched the Japanese attack. He was fortunate that another boy who had befriended him was able to lead him to me. It's taken a terrible toll on him. He hasn't spoken since the attack. I'm responsible and I don't know anything I can do for him."

The look in her eyes conveyed the pain and frustration she must be feeling, but what could I do? We were on a mission, as dangerous as anything could be, and I couldn't take civilians along, to say nothing of sorting out the boy's problem.

I asked, "Can I see the boy?"

She smiled briefly and nodded.

"His name is Richard, but everyone calls him Dicky."

In short order, she returned, leading a skinny young boy, wearing shorts and a pullover shirt.

I went down the ladder and knelt next to the boy.

"You must be Dicky."

He looked back at me. He was thin and wearing shorts and an undershirt. I knew he was registering what I had said, his eyes giving me the once over. But he made no attempt to reply.

I put my hand on his shoulder and said, "I know you've had a tough go of it. But don't worry now." Underneath the shirt it felt like he was all bone.

"Thank you, lieutenant," I heard her say.

What the hell had I gotten us into? Events were overwhelming our mission. Civilian refugees and a native camp that now had seen us and knew our strength. Too many variables. Quantico had beat into our brains, simplify and focus on key objectives. I was losing my focus and that could be fatal.

I returned to the circle and sat down, still wondering what I was going to do with the woman and a young boy in the jungle.

Hoss said, "They say we can use two of their canoes. I've seen the type before, not big, but you could put three men in most of em."

The ability to move on the water would be a great advantage.

"The headman also said that he heard there was a camp north of here that has men who were fighting the Japs."

"What kind of men?" I asked, thinking this was one more variable, damn.

"He's not sure, just jungle rumors. But he thought it was about two days by boat." He paused then continued, "I'm not sure, but from how he described what he knew of those men, it sounded a little like Weller and his crew. He offered to try and find out more about them for us."

Before we left the village, I talked with the two headmen again and told them we would consider any information about this group very useful and would be very thankful.

We would have to find out who those people were, but first we needed to establish a camp and get the radio working.

CHAPTER EIGHT

The Kalimantan Jungle
20 miles north of Balikpapan
18 August 1942

The canoes were dug out of large logs. While not very wide, they were about fifteen feet long with a carved bow and flat stern. Not something I would want to take on the open ocean, but they were stable on the river.

It took us a full day to ferry our gear across the river to a hill about five miles north of the village. I wanted our base of operations staged away from the village for their protection and ours. While they seemed eager to help us, you never knew where their real loyalty might lie. I had turned down the headman's offer of a scout to go with us. While someone familiar with the area might be an asset, that person could also lead the Japanese to our camp if their loyalty was simply a ruse.

I wanted to get the radio up and running as soon as possible to let Coyne know we'd made it safely ashore, with two extra sailors.

Mullen had been quiet as we packed up our gear and made ready for the move. I found him sitting with his back to a palm tree. He looked up at me, but then looked away.

I sat down next to him and took off my bush cap, which I had pulled out as soon as we got ashore.

"The chief seems to have things well under control," I said.

"Seems so."

"That a problem?"

"Not likely."

"Sergeant, you, Abernathy and Hostetter have more combat experience than all of the rest of us combined. I need you to do your job and make sure we're ready. That's why you're the second in command of this team."

He sat there without saying anything.

"Did you forget that, sergeant?"

"I thought the yank had taken over."

"Have you heard of positional authority?"

"Nah, not me."

"It means that you are second in command, regardless of who is the ranker."

He turned to look at me and I met his eyes with a direct look.

"Then I'll do my job."

"I'm counting on it, sergeant," I said, keeping my eyes locked on his as I stood up. "Don't disappoint me."

I walked away, surprised by my tone and language. Then I stopped and considered how things had gone so far. All right was accurate, but it seemed I was just going with events. But that wasn't my job, I had to drive events, consider all factors, make a decision and get the job done. Looking around I reminded myself that this was my responsibility, period. The survival of these people and our mission depended on it.

Chief Pickett had quietly taken the lead on getting the gear and men across the river. His physical presence coupled with a positive attitude seemed to settle the team and even Mullen joined in the effort without comment. He did seem more comfortable with the chief. I guess senior non-coms the world over have the same qualities – and troops recognize that in short order. I suspected that in a fight, Mullen, Abernathy and probably Hoss would carry the load, but for now, I was happy with Pickett's organizing.

"Bever, I want you to get the radio unwrapped and see what we have. The sooner we're able to transmit, the better."

"Yes, sir. I didn't see any damage after we came ashore, so unless something's broken inside, we should be alright."

I watched the young private go about his business and marveled that he seemed so matter of fact about setting up a clandestine radio transmitter in enemy-held territory, a thousand miles from home. As I looked around, though, it was obvious that everyone appeared to be relaxed. It was like a Saturday afternoon at home, even for our stranded sailors.

"Sergeant Mullen has three spots selected for watch posts", the chief offered as I walked up to where he was cutting bamboo for a radio platform. "I'll send Abernathy down for now to the one overlooking the river."

"Good idea, chief. How's Springer doing?"

Pickett laughed.

"He's fine. Good sailor and a sharp kid. He's going to apply for machinist mate's school after this patrol. I think he might make a career of this man's Navy."

"Suppose it's up to us to make sure he gets there."

Pickett was good with the small machete and I moved down to the lean-to that Hoss had constructed for the young woman and her brother.

"All the comforts of home, Miss Noble," I said to her as I knelt at the entrance.

A small cloth bag lay on a woven reed mat that provided a floor for the small shelter.

She turned and smiled slightly.

"It will do just fine."

"Where's Dicky?"

"Mr. Hostetter came by and asked if he could help gather firewood. I didn't see any harm."

"He'll be fine. Hostetter had a son of his own."

She looked quizzical.

"Something happened?"

"The Japanese killed the boy and his mother."

Her eyes flashed, the memory of her own parents likely flooding back. I probably shouldn't have said anything.

"Lieutenant, what's going to happen to us?"

Her eyes conveyed fear and exhaustion, but her tone was very subdued. I guess she had seen so many bad things that she was starting to accept that it was only a matter of time until they were killed or captured.

"Call me Rob. We were delivered here by a submarine. At some point that submarine will return for a resupply run. My plan is to put you and Dicky on that submarine and send you back to Australia."

She put her hands together and turned away from me, which seemed strange, then I realized she was crying as her voice broke.

"Thank you, Mr. Parker, thank you for giving me hope."

I turned away and started to head for the radio.

"Lieutenant—Rob," she called.

Walking back I saw her wipe her eyes.

"Would you call me Lynda?"

I found Private Bever unpacking and setting up the radio. Springer was with him and the two were talking like two magpies. What I overheard told me that Bever was much more educated on the principals of short-wave radio operations and transmitting aerials than I would have expected. And listening to Springer, it was clear that he had some level of knowledge as well.

"I made up sixty feet of two-wire antenna feedline before we left Australia and it's packed in with the 200-foot wire antenna that comes with the set. Should give us much better performance from the antenna. The 3BZ has terminals for it."

Springer looked around and asked, "Where do you want to run the wire?"

Bever saw me and continued, "I thought we could run the main length of wire from that large tree there, across the small gully and connect it to the far tree by that large rock. We run the feeder straight down from the center of that wire down to the radio. We'd be below the ledge and out of sight. If our wavelength calculations are right, we won't need to adjust the lengths."

We were in good hands with Bever technically, but those trees were over fifty feet high.

"How do you propose to string the wire?"

"That's where Tarzan here comes in. Can you get up those?" He asked Springer.

"Sure," the sailor answered, surveying the heavy ringed trunks of the palms.

"Springer, you must like climbing trees," I said, glad that he did.

He grinned.

"Yes, sir. Don't get much of a chance on a sub."

"Have you checked the orientation," I asked Bever.

"Yes, sir. That set up will put the horizontal within ten degrees of our receiving station. Assuming the Japs have receivers in Balikpapan, that'll give us the best signal concealment, less chance they stumble on us."

I wondered if the Japs were even watching for strange transmissions? I knew they had the capability. Coyne had told me that. But here? The lack of roads would make it hard, but not impossible, to triangulate for an intercept. Minimum transmission times would remain a priority.

Understanding that shipping observation would be our primary duty, we came equipped with a quick code table that allowed us to send a contact report in very short order. Any normal message would likely take less than 15 seconds to send and our transmissions would be random. Any signal can be tracked eventually, but we would make it as difficult as possible for the Japs.

By the end of the day, Springer had the wire antenna running across the gully and it was almost impossible to see. Now it was time for Bever to work his magic. Each radio is slightly different and matching the transmitter to the antenna is more an art than science, although it is based on electronic theory. With the varying impedances of different sets, the BX3 had a tuner matcher that should allow Bever to synchronize the set with the antenna. If not, he might have to adjust the length of the wire. This could be a laborious process, but Bever was done in short order, except for one of the critical bandwidths.

"I recall an instructor once told me that if I ever got an antenna that worked well except for a "problem band", it sometimes works to cut an extra wire 1/4-wavelength at the problem band's frequency and lay it out on the ground away from the antenna and connect it to the radio's ground terminal."

Hell, I may have to sponsor this guy to a scholarship at Tech.

"Where'd you get so smart about radios?" I asked.

Bever grinned, sweat dripping off his chin. "My stepdad got me started. He was always tinkering. It just came natural, I guess. When I joined up, I was able to get into radio training."

"Good job on this. Let me know when you're ready to transmit."

Checking my map one more time, I estimated that we were about twenty miles north of Balikpapan proper. From camp, I figured a three mile march would put us in the hills overlooking the northern approach to the harbor. That was my objective, but finding out the lay of the land was just as important. Now it was time for Hoss to earn his keep.

My plan was to take a small patrol, including Abernathy and Hoss. We'd travel light, carrying weapons and not much else. The objective would be to find the best location from which we could keep the harbor under observation. It would be necessary to cross the river and the three of us would take one canoe. I'd leave Mullen in camp to make sure that things would be secure and there would be enough men to put up a fight if anyone came upon the camp. We were on the high ground and with our firepower, we should be able to hold off or distract any attackers and get to our escape route.

Sergeant Mullen had already found a route east toward the deeper jungle and away from the river, that we could escape down if needed. I was betting the Japs would be coming from the river and not the thicker jungle behind us. If it ever happens I'd better be right, I thought. I'd better be right.

"We'll shove off as soon as the sun comes up tomorrow. Weapons, ammo and canteens. For now, get all the lads together."

I looked at the group in a semi-circle around me. We'd all been busy setting up the camp, but it was time to lay down some rules.

"No one ever expected we would have a woman and child with us on this little romp. But because of that, there are some things we need to get straight. The two of them have their own shelter and latrine. Off limits at all times, understand? This is going to be hard enough on everyone and I don't need any complications. And keep the language civil when she or the boy are around. Any questions?"

I looked them directly in the eyes and their reactions confirmed they understood I wasn't going to put up with any shenanigans.

"One last thing. If you don't want to shave, growing a beard is fine." Common sense had to prevail and this was no place for spit and polish. Besides, I'd never tried to grow a beard.

The original plan had been to make a short transmission to let Australia know we were safely ashore. Because of our two sailors, I told Bever to add the code for an additional transmission 90 minutes later, so we could update Australia on their status. Coyne could pass it on to the Navy.

The grin on Bever's face told me all I needed to know. We were in business and ninety minutes later, we sent a longer transmission:

......Pickett, Springer, USN, ashore safely and working with team.....

It would have been easy to ask for instructions, but I wanted to keep the two sailors, I'd gotten used to having them around. The reply came back shortly.

"Acknowledged."

That's all I needed. It was time to get on with the war.

That night we ate what the Aussie's call porridge: something like oatmeal, with dried fruit mixed in for flavor. The instant coffee wasn't half bad and I think the chow did a lot to bolster morale.

The girl and her brother sat with Hoss while we ate. The group minus Abernathy, who was on watch, sat around the cooking fire and the mood was relaxed. After the events of the last few days for us and the last two months for the girl a bit of normalcy was welcome.

"How long have you lived here?" I asked her when the second cups of coffee were poured.

"Almost three years. My father had a practice in Singapore. That's really where I grew up, but the opportunity in Balikpapan was attractive and so down we came."

I laughed.

"And I grew up in Balikpapan. My dad was an engineer for Shell."

"You lived here?"

"Until I went back to the states for school."

As we talked, she relaxed and I found out she'd left England when she was ten, grew up and went to nursing school in Singapore. I couldn't get the idea of a girl who had been thrown to the winds out of my mind. She hadn't asked to be here, just the debris left from a war that swept across the world destroying people and things. At first I felt that the team had been saddled with her and her brother, just something we couldn't avoid in good conscience. Now this would be one more way of fighting back at the Japs. They couldn't have these two. I would get them home.

Securing the canoe to the far side of the river, we were already well on our way by 0800. Working our way into the jungle, it was possible to weave a path that avoided the densest underbrush. Much like the first day ashore, the humidity and insects quickly made our progress uncomfortable but workable. The insect repellent did the trick again, thankfully.

The effort to move forward increased as we cut our way into higher terrain. The jungle cover broke at times, the tallest trees reaching fifty to sixty feet in height. The ground underfoot was soft and we slipped often, going face down into the tangle of vines and bushes. I tried to ignore the snakes, spiders and centipedes I knew were scuttling through those bushes, but I couldn't force them out of my mind completely.

Four hours after leaving the river, our efforts paid off as we broke out onto a ridge that ran east and west and we saw the port of Balikpapan in the far distance. To the east, a panoramic view of the Makassar Strait. There, we would see any tankers heading for the Empire of Japan.

After the heat and humidity of the jungle, the ridge felt wonderful with a good breeze coming off the ocean. A scattered cloud layer broke the blue sky and only the black plumes from the refineries marred the view. The ships in the harbor were just visible. As I moved the binoculars over the city, I could pick out the area of our old neighborhood.

"Great vantage point," Hoss offered, "Only one problem."

I guessed what that was, but let him lay it out.

"Lookout's here, radio's about four hours in that direction."

Moving the radio up here was a possibility, but did we really have to?

"You spent time sailing these waters, how long does it take one of the big ships to get underway and out of harbor?"

"Hard to say. A couple hours, maybe?"

"So we could do it by runners?"

"Don't see why not."

Corporal Abernathy got up.

"I'm going to check out what's down the ridge."

The ridge extended to the west, the vegetation much thicker as the ground rose about one hundred feet higher.

I wondered if there were enough spare parts to construct a spark transmitter that we could use to send a Morse signal back to the main receiver. We had a good selection of spare parts. Worth a thought.

Twenty minutes later, Abernathy was back with an idea he thought might solve our problem. He led us down the ridge, into the brush and after a short while, we broke out into a small clearing that had an unobstructed view of the jungle to the north, the river, and if we were lucky, our camp.

I hadn't even thought of it. A visual signaling system. No transmissions for the Japs to pick up, totally directional and we could make up whatever we needed for signaling. I remembered that land-based semaphore had been used in Europe during the Napoleonic era. My first thought had been using light signals, but what would work better?

"We need to leave a marker here that we can see from back at the camp."

An hour later, we had built a square frame with an "x' in the middle from bamboo. Around the "x" we wrapped vines to hold yellow and red flowery blooms that were abundant in the underbrush. The result was a distinctive marker, which we placed in an open area right below the crest of the ridge. The question now was whether we'd be able to see it from camp.

Our discovery that the square was easily visible with our Bausch and Lomb 7x50 binoculars was the start of what we called Tarzan's jungle telegraph. With several trials, we were able to come up with a system of semaphore-type flags during the day, and a flashlight with a bamboo tube extending two feet from the lens at night. A quick code which took parts of our original code from Coyne and a set check-in time every two hours put us in business. I decided that the lookout would be manned by two men and we would swap out every two days. Bever would remain at the main radio while the rest of us would rotate between camp and the lookout.

Three days later we reported our first Jap tanker sailing from Balikpapan. The ship was in the 10,000-ton category and sailed with one escort. The other key piece of data that we were able to provide was to confirm the tanker had turned north up the Makassar Strait. Coyne could now get that word out to any allied submarine that would be in the right area to intercept. I was interested in how the communication would evolve between Coyne and myself. Was he going to leave us alone or keep a tight rein?

Coyne's answer was ambivalent:

"Acknowledged."

We were finally fighting our war. Now it was time to see if we could cause more trouble for the Japs.

Our war council consisted of the chief, Mullen, Hostetter and myself. Abernathy and Springer had taken over the lookout duties and would be relieved in two days.

"You spent time around Samarinda and the river?" I asked Hostetter.

"Aye, we did, depending on what we were selling."

106

"It's important to find out what we can about this group upriver. You said that it could even be your old partner."

"Weller. Larry Weller," Hoss replied.

"The villagers might have gotten some more on them," the sergeant offered.

"What are you thinking, lieutenant?" Pickett asked.

"Sending Hostetter and Abernathy in a canoe to see what they can find out. Where are these people, what are they up to and whose side they are really on."

Hoss didn't look surprised but did say, "That's a lot to find out. But if it's Weller or any of his gang, they could help us with anything we need."

"Why did he stay here when you went back to Australia?"

"He still has a wife here and three children."

"Right," I answered, feeling like an asshole.

"I could visit the village and find out what they might know," Mullen volunteered.

"Good idea," I replied, "We'll go first thing tomorrow." Not bad, the sergeant was taking some initiative.

That night I sat with Lynda and her brother after the team finished replenishing our water supply. We'd been issued Lyster bags, which were canvas bags with rubber liners. All we had to do was fill them from the river and add our water purification tablets, wait thirty minutes and we were in business. When I was down at the river I decided that tomorrow I would see if we could get some fish from the villagers. The sooner we were able to subsist off the land, the better. Our supplies would last about thirty days. After that, we'd be on our own. Coyne had mentioned possibly trying for a resupply mission by submarine, but the only things I could think of that might truly call for that would be parts for the radio or ammunition and we were in good shape on both counts.

"Dicky, are you getting enough to eat?" I asked, knowing there would not be an answer from the young boy.

"His favorite are the fruit bars," Lynda offered.

"Good. Maybe tomorrow we'll have some fresh fish," I again directed my question to Dicky.

"From the village?" she asked.

"I thought it was worth a try. But what could I barter with them?"

Lynda smiled.

"Do you have any money?"

That surprised me.

"Money? Actually, I brought both paper and coin." Coyne had given me a leather pouch that contained Australian and Dutch currency and coin.

"The village is close enough to the city that they can use it in barter for some of the things they don't make for themselves."

This opened up a whole new line of thinking. If I came to trust Amulong and Prehanan, then using money in exchange for food or information might solve a lot of problems.

Beaching the canoe east of the village, Sergeant Mullen and I moved quietly through the jungle toward the village. Lynda had bolstered my feeling that the villagers could be trusted, but in the light of day, I decided to remain cautious. Working our way through the underbrush, it was already over 80 degrees. I thought about how the weather here never changed that much. Hot and humid all year long. It made it hard to remember those frigid days at Quantico during the winter.

We raised our hands in greeting as we approached the longhouse and I saw several of the younger men talking in a group. In a moment, Amulong appeared from the longhouse, a smile appearing on his face when he saw us.

We were soon sitting around the fireplace, which was thankfully not burning. Mamsettan had joined us and she told us that Prehanan was not in the village.

"Do you have any more information on the people upriver fighting the Japanese?"

I tried to sound matter of fact, but I wanted to see how he reacted to my question. Was he being honest?

Did he want to help us, or just not cause problems?

The old man nodded. His expression was tentative, almost like this would be a step that would make them targets for the Japanese, rather than just bystanders.

"They are led by a white man, but most are Kayan."

I knew that these people were Malay, but the Kayan was a tribe that lived further inland on the rivers. While their lifestyles were probably very similar, were these people friendly to the Kayan or not?

"Do you know the Kayan?"

Again he nodded.

"We used to fight them, long ago. But not now. The whites have changed everything."

"The Japanese are worse," I said, suddenly irritated.

He looked at me, his face totally blank.

"Maybe," he finally said.

The colonial world had been a goldmine for the European powers that had enriched their homelands for the last three hundred years. But I knew that much of that had been possible because of an iron fist that subjugated the local peoples. Perhaps my perception of the world I grew up within was not universally shared by these people. For now, we were still the good guys, and that's how it was going to stay.

"Amulong, you and your village have been friends to us and helpful in many ways. I would like to give you something to thank you."

The old man looked surprised and wary.

I handed him two gold coins and said, "Thank you."

At first he looked puzzled, then he looked at me and nodded with a small smile. The headman understood.

"And, we would like to buy some fish."

On our way back to the river, the two of us discussed sending Hoss upriver. The information from the village seemed to support the possibility there might be a link we could exploit.

That first shot echoed across the river and it's a sound I'll never forget. It was certainly an Arisaka rifle and sent a shot of fear straight into my heart. Both of us dove into the brush.

Flat on my stomach, I listened for the next shot, my heart pounding in my chest. This was it, someone was trying to kill us.

Another shot rang out. And those shots weren't aimed at us.

"The village!" I called to Mullen, who I couldn't see.

"Right," he said, and I heard him standing up to my left.

Brushing strands of long grass out of my face, I joined him. He was looking in the direction of the village and listening.

We stood there for half a minute, the silence steady now.

"What do you think?" I asked him, hoping he had something to say.

"Jap rifle, no doubt about that. The little bastards must have hit the village."

He took a deep breath and turned to look at me.

"Orders?"

Damn it. I had to think before we did anything. How many Japs were there? What was the firing about? Could the two of us do anything to help them? More importantly, if we took on the Japs, there would be no doubt that we were ashore and that was not something I wanted to broadcast. Smart money was to get the hell back across the river and up to the camp, but something was tugging me back toward the village.

"Let's work our way back and see what's going on."

Mullen looked at me for a moment, then shrugged and took the lead.

Never had I been more careful or paid more attention to movement through the brush. Anything could alert the enemy. A flushed bird, a broken branch, anything. We had to be silent and invisible. It was funny that all of the crawly, poisonous things I knew were around me didn't matter anymore. I was trying to be part of the land.

A loud yell came from the village, but there were no more shots as we moved to within twenty yards of the clearing. More yelling followed and I knew this was it. I checked that the safety on my Wilson was *off*.

As I reached the clearing, my fearful apprehension turned to bewilderment. There weren't any Japs in sight, just a group of strange men, wearing shirts and shorts. The men were definitely carrying weapons, and two of the men were white. What the hell?

No pride here, I was just searching for any answer.

"Moon, what do you think?" I said, not thinking that I was using his nickname.

"Hell if I know, but the villagers don't look too put out." He hadn't reacted to his nickname, but his tone seemed friendlier.

111

Amulong stood talking with the group, and apparently not concerned about what was going on.

Seeing the white man talking with Amulong made my mind up. We could just blend back into the bush and be on our way. But something was going on and I wanted to find out the story.

They all turned, several rifles moving our direction as we emerged from the bush.

"Amulong, hello!" I called one hand up in the air as an indication that we meant no threat. I saw the headman talking rapidly and the rifles were lowered.

The white man stepped forward and I saw he was about six feet tall, thin and in his middle forties if my guess was right. He carried a Lee Enfield rifle in his left hand and I saw a pistol holster on his right hip.

"My name's Parker," I called as we closed to ten feet. I stopped to wait for his answer.

"By, God, it's a yank," the man said in an Australian accent. "Weller's my name, Larry Weller."

"Criminy, he's Hoss's mate," Moon said.

Lowering my Wilson, I walked up and offered my hand.

"I was going to send Bob Hostetter to find you, but looks like that won't be necessary." Weller was medium height, wiry with a thin face. He looked like a man who could take care of himself.

"Hostetter, you say, Bob Hostetter? He's here?"

"He is," I said.

"I'll be damned. This is quite a day."

It turned out that two of Weller's men were from the village. Weller was in the village to see what was happening in this area and to possibly expand what his group had been doing.

The rifle shots were simply a demonstration to the village's other young men as a recruiting trick.

"What have you been doing since the invasion?" I asked as we sat around the fire pit in the longhouse, the village having gone back to its daily routine. Amulong sat with us, but said nothing.

Weller looked a little surprised at my question and actually irritated. But he took a deep breath and went on to relate how they had abandoned their village after the Japanese had attacked it. He had been upriver during the attack and returned home to find his family dead along with many of the villagers. Since then they had been building up their supplies and growing the size of their band. His intent was to snipe at the Japs and cause them as much trouble as possible.

"Good men. Some are river rats like myself, a few were working the oil fields and didn't feel like working for the Japs. We have one former colonial administrator and a school teacher. But we plan on causing a little trouble for the bastards," he said.

"It's likely to be a long time before the allies are ready to retake the island," I told him. "How can you stay in action?"

"A long time, I reckon. I have friends up and down the coast and no one likes the little blighters. And I know people who are willing to fight back."

"Doing what?" Moon asked.

"Whatever it takes, mate."

"What kind of things have you done so far?"

"We ambushed a Jap patrol. Killed all six of them and took their weapons and ammo."

The rifles were evidence to support that claim. This would get interesting.

"Where?" I asked.

"Upriver. About a week ago."

That made me wonder if they had been searching for us, after the landing had been discovered.

I turned as two of Weller's men ran up to the steps of the longhouse, out of breath and with a look of panic on their faces.

"Japs, headed this way."

CHAPTER NINE

"How many?" Weller asked as he stood up and headed for the long house steps.

"Six or seven," one said.

"We saw their boat just before they landed," the second man added.

"How far?" I asked, surprised that I was not scared.

He replied that they'd be there in five minutes, and Weller began to direct his men north.

"What are you gonna do?" I asked him, thinking that retiring north was exactly what we ought to be doing.

"Lay low. See what happens," he said, actually grinning.

He had almost a dozen men, all armed. I liked our odds, but the problem was simply that engaging the Japanese could set off a reaction that would endanger the radio transmitter operation.

"We're with you. Come on, sergeant."

In less than a minute, all of us were hiding in the bushes that surrounded the village. Several minutes later, the first Jap appeared on the trail that led down to the river. They looked just like I had seen in newsreels, but suddenly in color. Their uniforms were a fecal brown, both the shirts and shorts. All of them wore cloth hats. No helmets anywhere to be seen. The second soldier in line carried a sword and had extra red tabs on his uniform, in addition to a sidearm on a leather belt. He had to be the sergeant or non-com. All of the other soldiers were carrying Arisaka rifles with bayonets fixed. At the end of the file walked a man in a white civilian shirt and shorts and some kind of fedora hat.

The soldiers spread out around the central clearing while the sergeant barked out an order and waved one arm.

Amulong stepped forward, his head held high, a long pole in his right hand.

The civilian stepped up beside the sergeant and began talking with Amulong. We were too far away to understand what was being said, but both sides were gesturing with their hands. Amulong was shaking his head.

Suddenly the Japanese sergeant stepped forward and pushed the headman to the ground, kicking him hard in the side. Turning to his soldiers, he shouted an order and they dispersed to the huts and long house. The sergeant pulled the pistol from his holster and stood over Amulong, who lay unmoving on the ground.

"What do you think?" I asked Weller, who knelt next to me in the brush.

"Not sure what to think, but it doesn't look good."

"Moon?"

"If we're going to take the blighters on, better have a plan," he said quietly.

I leaned to Weller.

"Can your men use those rifles?"

"Good enough."

While the Japs continued to search the village, Weller moved quietly, telling his men the plan. Maybe it wouldn't come to that, but these people could be an asset to my team and joining forces with Weller would expand our ability to do the mission. At least

116

that was my twisted logic as we waited in the sweltering heat, insects flitting around our sweaty faces.

I felt the Lee Enfield in my hands, heavier than the Wilson, but just what we needed right now. If we were going to take this patrol, the leader was going to be the first target. I'd told Weller that I would take him out if the Lee Enfield shot true. He assured me it did and took my Wilson.

"Not sure how this works, so I'll take mine back when you're done," he said.

Fifty yards with a good rifle. On any rifle range, I wouldn't miss at that distance. I better hit him on the first shot. There were shouts from the Japanese and the sergeant waved his pistol back and forth at the huts.

"I know a little Japanese. They're gonna burn the village," Weller said. "If we're going to do anything, it'd better be now."

It had all come down to this: a split second in a stinking jungle.

I fired and hit the Jap sergeant directly in the chest, knocking him off his feet and backwards. Several more shots came from the brush as at least three of the enemy soldiers were hit by Weller's men.

"Let's go," I said, grabbing the Wilson from Weller and running forward in a crouch. There had to be two more Japs and the civilian in the huts. Moon was five paces on my left, both of us looking for targets. One of the Weller's men fired again into a prone soldier and then ran off to the right of the farthest hut. Two more of his men followed and several shots rang out. I ran low and covered the distance to Amulong, who had crawled several feet away from the Jap sergeant's body. I motioned to him to stay down as Moon and I circled around left of one of the huts, but saw nothing of the enemy.

"They might be heading back down to that boat," Moon called, all the while he was sweeping the area around us. A person bolted from the undergrowth and I knew it was villager, holding my fire. This was crazy. Where were the other two?

"Alright. Let's go."

Running towards the river, we hit the trail and moved down it with some caution, despite the fact we were breaking all the rules. I didn't want anyone to make it to a boat and escape.

One of the Japs had already been killed by Weller's men, but we caught up to the last soldier, who was pushing the bow of their boat into deeper water as we emerged on the river bank. Moon hit the man with a short burst from his Wilson and he fell sideways into the river. As the boat slipped further into the current, its bow turned and I saw the white shirt of what had to be the civilian, disappear below the port gunwale.

"Shit, the other one's getting away!"

Moon laid his Wilson on the sand and waded into the river. He jumped forward and threw both hands over the side, hauling himself aboard. The boat was starting to drift and I walked along the bank watching Moon pull his pistol and move aft. The boat was about 25 feet long, with a small pilot house and an open after deck. The current had taken hold, pulling it further into midstream. My shadowing was stopped abruptly by a large set of roots and underbrush that suddenly blocked my way.

I ran back up the bank, picked up the Wilson and ran back toward the village.

There was another path that ran north toward the river and I sprinted toward it, breaking into sight of the river about ten minutes after losing visual of the boat. In the distance, I could see the boat now, near the center of the river.

Guessing the boat was now two miles away, I decided against giving chase and turned to head toward Weller to let him know what's happened.

Turning for one last look at the boat, I saw that smoke was now coming from the small stack I had seen just aft of the pilot house.

Ten minutes later, the P-46 patrol boat, former property of the Japs, pushed her bow into the river bank, Moon stepped out of the pilot house and threw a manila rope across to me.

"Always wanted a boat," he said with a quick grin.

I pulled hard on the line and stretched it to a large root, securing it with a half hitch.

Looking back, I saw that Moon had blood spattered over his trousers.

"Are you hurt?"

Sweat covered his face and soaked through his shirt.

He shook his head.

Climbing over the gunwale, he waded ashore.

"Bonus prize. There's a Type 96 machine gun aboard."

By the time we got back to the village, Weller had things well in hand. The enemy bodies lay in a row, stripped of weapons and ammunition. Flies were already clustered around the wounds, the blood turning black in the hot sun. The effects of high-powered rifle rounds up close was something that I hadn't imagined, but I steeled myself to what I saw. The sergeant lay first in the line, on his back with his mouth and eyes open. My shot had hit him dead center chest. There was no blood to speak of on the front of his uniform, but blood was evident under his back. He looked to be about thirty. I found myself reaching down for the pouch on his belt. Inside I found a pack of cigarettes and some kind of official card – maybe a ration card. Ther was a seemed to be a name on the top of the card, "Soichi Tatsunama."

I surprised myself. I didn't really feel anything. I killed an enemy soldier. That's what we're supposed to do. Get on with business.

"There's one more floating in the river, but that body is probably long gone," I told Weller.

He sent two men to search, just in case.

In short order, a water bucket appeared and Amulong indicated we should sit while wooden cups were passed around. He was still suffering from the assault by the enemy sergeant, but more than that, he looked frightened. I couldn't blame him, we all knew that when the Jap soldiers didn't return, more would come looking for them. If it was known they were going to visit this village, it would only play out badly. Now what?

"We take the villagers up river," Weller said as we discussed what to do.

"What do you mean?"

"To our camp. The area's huge, it could hide hundreds of people. There aren't many ways in or out and we know where those are. And I don't think the Japs are in any big hurry to push that deep into the jungle. Their business is on the coast."

It made sense. But how do you move an entire village lock, stock and barrel?

"That boat would help," I said, "You could carry twenty or thirty people and probably tow canoes, to boot."

And so the great river trek began. Amulong didn't even wait for Prehanan to return, but ordered everyone to start packing.

Mullen remained pretty quiet as plans were being made, other than lightly protesting against relinquishing his newly acquired vessel. He did tell me that he dispatched the civilian by shooting through the pilot house bulkhead.

"Was he Jap or Malay?"

"Jap. Must have been an interpreter or a cop."

I knew they had pulled the body from the boat, but never took time to check it out.

"Was he armed?"

"Not that I saw."

I asked him when he thought we should head back to camp.

"They'll be wondering soon, I expect."

"Well it seems Mr. Weller has things well in hand, let's get going."

"You leaving the Jap machine gun with him?"

I'd given that some thought. While more firepower was something most Marines would never turn down, there wasn't much ammunition for the weapon, only two 30 round magazines, and the weight was the real drawback. Humping it up and down these slippery trails would be a nightmare. Better to leave it with Weller, who thought he would be able to get more ammunition for it.

After Weller and I agreed on a location to meet in a week's time, Moon and I pushed off. I still wanted to get Hoss and Abernathy up to Weller's camp to check things out and see what help they could be to us. But that could wait.

"What's Australia going to make of all this?" Moon asked as we worked our way back to the river.

Good question, I thought. Better question, how much do we tell the boys back at base? I never told Weller where our camp was located and he never asked. Just like he didn't show me where exactly they were. I never mentioned the radio, no need for him to know about that, at least not for now. So do we say we made contact with a local band and see what Coyne has to say? No need to let them know we were in a shootout with the Japs. I managed to convince myself of that only after suppressing every instinct drummed into me at Quantico to keep the chain of command informed. This was just different and it was my call.

"I think they'll be fine with whatever we tell them."

"Righto," Moon laughed

We settled into silence as we moved back to where we'd hidden the canoe.

"By the way, when we get back to Australia, I'm going to put you in for a medal for going after that boat."

"Not necessary," he said.

"Maybe not, but you deserve it."

We walked on for a few minutes.

"So, what do I call you?" he asked, clearly referring to my very frowned upon use of an enlisted man's nickname. But this was a commander's discretion, at least that's what I told myself.

"Parker," I said.

"Right," he replied and chuckled.

He was still an asshole, but I wouldn't want to be here without him.

Bever reported they sighted and reported one tanker sailing while we'd been gone.

"Anything exciting happen on your trip?" Chief Pickett asked.

I laughed and shook my head. Time to bring everyone up to speed. Hoss was surprised and pleased when he heard about Larry Weller. I told him about the loss of Weller's family and you could tell he hurt for his friend. I mentioned the other man with Weller, Paul Ellis, but there was no recognition.

Lynda joined us and I related what had taken place in the village. She was concerned, but I assured her that none of the villagers had been hurt. I'd been thinking that maybe she would be safer upriver, once the village was settled in.

"Damn," I said looking at Lynda.

She looked more than a little surprised.

"Pardon, me?"

"I'm sorry, I just remembered I left the fish in the jungle."

Her laugh made me smile and she smiled in return.

I decided I had to report what had happened to Coyne. How the hell do you explain something like that in a concise, coded message?

......Engaged enemy patrol. All enemy KIA. No casualties. Location not, repeat not compromised. Contact made with local resistance......

"Acknowledged, well done. Amplify on local group when able."

God love the Aussie, he was certainly a hands off leader.

The next morning, I told Hoss I wanted him to lead a two-man party to meet up with Weller. He nodded, but something wasn't right.

"Are you feeling alright?"

"Bit crook, actually. Might be the malaria coming back."

We'd been lucky so far. And if he was right, we could handle malaria, even though he would be damned uncomfortable for a time. And with Lynda being a nurse, he would be in good hands. So much for sending her upriver.

CHAPTER TEN

Camp One
Telukladang Peninsula
27 August 1942

Twenty-four hours later, Hoss was off his feet and medically down hard. Lynda had given him quinine and told us that she would monitor his fever, expecting it to break relatively quickly.

I found Hoss in the lean-to he shared with Bever.

"Another bout of malaria," I said, watching Hoss's eyes open. He lay on his back, his face covered with sweat. His sleeveless skivvy shirt was soaked through, dirt stains accentuated by the moisture. My only thought was that he looked like death warmed over.

"Quinine should take care of it," I said with forced optimism.

"It's never been like this," he croaked, his voice sounding more like a bullfrog than a man.

"How so?"

"My arms and legs. Sweet Jesus, they feel like they're broken. The pain's never been like this bad."

"I'll see what I can do," I said, wondering immediately what, if anything, I could do.

Lynda wiped the sweat from her face and shook her hair.

"I've seen a lot of malaria, but this looks worse."

"What else could it be?"

She took a deep breath and said, "Jungle fevers are like stars in the sky. Could be a variation of several known diseases or it could be something brand new. But he's strong and at this point still relatively healthy, so it may be that all we can do is let it run its course."

"He's in a lot of pain. Is there anything we can do for that?"

"I've been giving him aspirin. I guess if it gets too bad we could always use morphine."

I racked my brain, trying to remember the briefs from Commander Killgallen back in San Diego. He went over the menu of problems I might run into, what the hell did he say about some of the diseases?

It came to me that afternoon. Dengue Fever, son of a bitch. The pain was what made my memory click. I remember he told me that in the past, some of the people would call it "bone breaker" fever because of the severe joint and limb pain. When I asked Lynda, she thought about it and then agreed Hoss could very well have Dengue. But, if so, what the hell could we do about it?

"Amulong is not just the headman, he is the closest thing they have to a healer in the village."

"How so?"

"He uses traditional cures the natives have used for generations. He might have something to help Mr. Hostetter. I've seen good things done with their natural remedies. In the meantime, I'll increase the aspirin dosage."

I felt helpless, but I knew that Maksi had used "local" medicines on me without my parents' knowledge and I'd survived.

I found Moon cleaning his Wilson.

"It's three days before our scheduled rendezvous with Weller's people," I said. "If you and Abernathy shove off tomorrow, you should be waiting for them at the rendezvous spot."

"I bring Amulong back here?" Moon asked.

"If he's willing. I'll give you some gold coins to sweeten the pot. But if he absolutely won't come back, you need to find out what we have to do, including getting any herbs or potions they use."

"Fair enough."

Lynda and I had decided to inject Hoss with half a dose of morphine. This was pull-it-out-of-your-ass medicine at best, but if we could ease the pain, that had to be good. They didn't call it "bone breaker" fever for nothing. Hoss was in terrible pain and I couldn't help but wonder how long he could hold up.

"I hope this helps with the pain," she said. "I'm afraid the Dengue may have progressed."

"What do you mean?"

"Dengue is bad enough, but it can turn hemorrhagic. Internal bleeding."

Moon and I went by the lean to, just before the two of them headed off. Hoss still lay on his back, his breathing labored and his whole body still covered with sweat.

"Hey, mate," Moon said as he put his hand on Hoss's shoulder.

Opening his eyes, Hoss looked surprised and a bit confused.

"You look like shit," Moon said, his voice trying for a laugh.

Hoss's expression changed after hearing Moon's voice. He turned his head slightly and looked at his countryman.

"Too right, asshole," Hoss said, his voice raspy and soft.

"Stick to it. I'm off to the chemist and you'll be right as rain."

Hoss just looked at him, his eyes watery. Slowly Hoss's right hand raised up, the palm open.

Moon took his hand and pulled it to his chest.

"Take care, you old bastard."

Lynda and I sat outside her shelter the day after Moon and Corporal Abernathy left. I was getting ready to head out to join Springer and the chief at the observation site, but I didn't want to leave her without checking on Hoss one more time. Dicky was playing with a wooden horse Hoss had carved for him right after we set up camp.

I sensed the exhaustion she was feeling, on top of everything that had happened to her. Now the man who had showed her friendship lay gravely ill and possibly wouldn't survive.

"None of this makes sense," she said.

I waited for her to continue, but she just stared into the distance.

Hell, she's got that right, I thought. I should be working for Westinghouse, chasing some cute young lady from Tech and playing golf every weekend. Instead I'm in the jungle in Borneo, trying to help kill Japanese sailors on their ships and keep Japanese soldiers from killing me and my men. But I realized I was okay with that.

"So, tell me about Singapore," I said, trying to be the consummate leader.

Lynda looked up at me like I had two heads.

"What?"

"I've never been there, but I'd love to see it."

She laughed and again that struck me like a bolt of lightning. There are two different women here, the worn out, exhausted nurse, who was agonizing about her brother and a young girl who grew up in one of the most exotic places in the Pacific. She sat there in the dirt, her clothes literally in rags, without a bath and shampoo in who knows how long.

"It doesn't matter anymore, those days are gone."

The tone in her voice was almost painful to hear, but how would I feel if my parents had been dragged off by the Japs, and probably killed?

I also realized there are few people slower on the uptake than junior officers. Come on, Parker, use your head.

"Lynda, I've come to a decision."

She turned, her eyes apprehensive.

"We have soap in our supplies and you need a relaxing bath and shampoo."

"I what?"

Oh, shit.

"Hear me out. I'm not kidding. I can take you down to that spring by the river, set up a lookout, then you can bath and wash your clothes."

The anger in her eyes dimmed a bit and she looked back at me like I had lost my marbles.

"Bever can watch Dicky and I'll stand guard."

They never taught us this at Quantico.

She looked at me again, her eyes searching.

"Are you really serious?"

"Tomorrow morning."

When Errol Flynn did this in the movies, it always seemed so easy. Not so in real life, I found. The spring was surrounded by thick underbrush, which required twenty minutes of hacking to open an access for Lynda. Then it struck me, how dangerous was the spring itself? Rocks, snakes, insects, what was down there anyway. So I found myself taking off my boots and checking out the pool, which was forty feet across. In the end, it was as safe as I guessed I could expect, so I waded ashore, put on my boots and picked up my Wilson.

I think that was the moment I fell in love with her. She was standing next to a palm tree with vines hanging behind her. That threadbare dress hung loosely on her slender body. In one hand was a bar of soap, in the other her small bag containing the few other clothes she had with her.

"Your bath awaits, madam," I said with the panache of Flynn himself and a wide sweep of my arm.

She smiled and said, "Thank you, Rob Parker, and I'm glad to see you have abandoned your attempt at growing a beard."

Then she stepped up to me and kissed me lightly on the cheek. It wasn't a big kiss, but it stunned me like I'd been hit with a baseball bat. She immediately lowered her head and looked away as she walked to the edge of the pool. Shaving may have been one of my best decisions since arriving on the island.

"Now, Lieutenant Parker, be the gallant officer and please turn your back."

I stammered, "Yes, ma'am," and stepped away, making sure I was directly facing away from the pond.

"Tell me when you're in the water, so I can actually stand watch," I said, planning on moving to where I could watch more of the area approaching the pond.

She cried out and without thinking I turned around.

"What's wrong?"

I stopped in mid-sentence as I saw her kneeling down, her dress already off.

"It's nothing, I stepped on a thorn," she said, standing up and making no effort to cover herself. "Now, I will continue with my bath," she said, stepping into the water.

"Sure, I mean, excuse me. But you're okay?"

She laughed.

I worked my way down an open area that adjoined the southern side of the pond. I'm not sure what drew me in that direction, but as I found out over time, I could sense when Japs were near. At the time, I just thought I was on edge from having seen Lynda in the altogether, but within two minutes, I noticed birds acting disturbed south of my position. It was dawning on me how stupid I'd been to try doing this by myself. Lynda was alone at the pool, unaware that danger might be approaching. Shit.

Moving forward in a crouch, I listened for anything, now wishing the damn birds would shut up. Through the underbrush and trees, I saw a single Jap soldier making his way toward me, his rifle slung on his shoulder. Was he point man for a patrol? If not, what the hell was he doing out here by himself? I raised the Wilson and knew immediately it was the wrong thing to do. A single Jap soldier would not be in this area by himself. Shit. I carefully laid the Wilson down on the ground and pulled the Fairbairn from its sheath.

Everything would depend on where the Jap moved next. I desperately hoped he would veer right around a small clump of bushes, allowing me to get behind him. If not, it was going to be face to face. Time seemed to slow as the soldier stopped for a moment and knelt down. What was he doing? Had he seen me? Damn, the Wilson was five paces behind me. The Webley would be my only choice if he had seen me, but I'd still try to use the relative silence of the knife. Suddenly the man stood up, readjusted his rifle and moved forward, apparently unaware of what was happening. With a sinking feeling I realized he was going to move right at me, having turned left at the bush. Now I had no choice. It was going to be face to face.

131

I remembered later that the sergeant major had taught me what to do. At the time, I simply reacted as the enemy soldier walked forward. The ribs and sternum provide a natural protection for the heart. But a knife thrust up hard just above the belt line will miss, both man-made equipment and God-made bones.

There was no time and no choice, I drove forward into the man, the Fairburn ready. As I hit him, I drove the knife hard up into the Jap's chest and I pushed him down, throwing my left arm across his throat to stop any cry. As we fell to the ground, I felt his body fight me, his eyes wide with terror and pain. Suddenly he went limp. The struggle I expected simply didn't happen, but I held the body down, not really sure what to do next. Slowly I raised myself up, the man's face only inches from mine. I knew he was dead, blood already coming from his mouth, his green eyes wide open in surprise. Getting to my knees, I pulled the knife from his chest with some effort. Then I looked at his face again and for a moment, I thought he was staring at me. I was breathing hard, trying to get my wind, but it was taking time, my heart pounding in my chest. Then I heard her scream.

Stumbling slightly, I shoved the knife back into its sheath and lunged toward where I had left the submachine gun. There was no plan in my mind, how do you make a plan when you have no idea what's out there? A single Jap, like the one I had just killed, or the rest of his patrol? As I approached the spring, I stopped to listen, still hidden by the thick underbrush south of the water. Nothing.

Checking the safety off one more time, I crept forward, trying to get as close as I could to the water without making any noise. A branch cracked under my foot and I froze, waiting for some response. Nothing. I started forward, slowly, listening and watching for any motion. It was as if I was the only person in the world right then. Where were they?

I pushed slowly out of the bush, the Wilson leveled at the water, quickly scanning the area for brown uniforms. My immediate relief at not seeing any Japanese was short lived, Lynda was gone.

Quickly I circled back to where she had entered the water. Her clothes were missing, but her small bag still lay on the ground. I looked for any indication of where she might have gone, but the jungle was quiet. There wasn't an obvious trail in the area, but I had to assume the Japs would return to the river. I grabbed the cloth bag and moved out in that direction, with no idea what to do.

Within ten minutes, I heard a barked order in Japanese off to my left. It had to be her, I thought, pushing forward in a crouch. My first glimpse was of Lynda, ducking her head under a low hanging limb. Then I saw a brown uniform, right behind her. I froze, watching as they moved toward the river. There was only one Jap soldier, but his rifle was at the carry and his bayonet was only a foot from Lynda's back.

Slipping the Wilson over my shoulder, I laid it carefully on the ground and pulled my pistol from its holster. I was well inside range for the Webley and I wanted to make sure that I put this Jap down with one shot. Raising the pistol to the horizontal, I moved fast at the back of the enemy guard. The angle put Lynda left of my line of fire, and I had closed to ten yards when the man turned, swing his rifle in my direction.

"Lynda, get down," I cried and waited for the Jap to stop and begin to raise his rifle. My bullet hit him in the chest as the rifle spun off to one side. The shot must have glanced off the Arisaka. Driving forward, I was next to the man who lay on his side, his

133

hands clutching at his chest, moaning. Lynda had scrambled to her feet, pushing backwards, away from the dying man.

"No, no...," she said quietly, holding her hands like they were a barrier to what had just happened.

The man continued to moan, his breath coming in short rasps. There had to be more enemy troops in the area, these two couldn't have been alone. Bever was by himself in the camp watching Hoss and Dicky. We had to get back there.

"We're going," I said grabbing her right wrist and pulling her north toward the camp.

Lynda looked at me, her eyes still full of shock.

"Yes, alright," she said.

I looked down at the Jap. He wasn't going to survive, not out here in the jungle with a wound like that. But if the Japanese found him alive, he could tell them about the white lady and the soldier. All I could hope now was that the Japs would think the men had been killed by a band like Weller's.

"Now walk," I said and pointed her north. She nodded and started through the brush.

I watched her for a moment, then pulled out the Fairbairn. A year ago what I was doing would've been unthinkable, but the rules had changed.

"Lynda," I called as I caught up to her, reaching out to grab her arm.

She stopped and turned to face me.

"Are you all right?" I asked, not sure what exactly I was asking her.

"We need to get back to Dicky," she said, tears in her eyes.

My heart went out to her.

Slowly I put my hands on her shoulders and said, "Everything will be okay."

"Oh, Rob," she said and we took each other in our arms.

CHAPTER ELEVEN

Camp One
Telukladang Peninsula
30 August 1942

We never discovered whether or not those two soldiers were part of a larger group or not. Bever and I set up a perimeter watch, but we saw no sign of any enemy troops. That was just as well, Hoss had taken a turn for the worse and we wouldn't have been able to move him if the Japs had showed up. Thank God they didn't, it saved me from having to make a terrible decision. I think I could have done it at the time, even being the rookie I was. No one was more brutal to prisoners than the Japs and sick as Hoss was, there would have been no hope. They probably would have bayoneted him where he lay. A year later I wouldn't have thought twice about putting a bullet in his head and I hope he would have done the same for me. But then I still had an awful lot to learn.

At that moment, I was pretty sure that Bob Hostetter wasn't long for this world. Between the vomiting, diarrhea and sweating, it was if he was wasting away right in front of our eyes. He'd begun bleeding from his nose and his skin was covered in a reddish rash. All we could do was try to get water into him, keep him as clean as possible and use morphine. We were losing the battle. Lynda knew it and so did I.

When I had first met Amulong, I had taken him at face value. An old weather-beaten native, steeped in tradition and superstition, likely incapable of dealing with the modern world.

Only as I got to know the old bastard better, did I realize how wrong I had been. But then, like I said, I had a lot to learn.

"They're back," I heard Lynda call.

Moon had come through. He had the headman behind him, carrying a long spear and a bag over his shoulder. Another native I didn't recognize walked behind the old man, carrying a long spear with a nasty looking knife hanging from his side.

"See any Japs?" I asked Moon as he began to unload his gear. "We had a couple around here yesterday."

"We saw a motor launch on the river about ten miles north of here, but they were going north."

I greeted Amulong and nodded at his companion. Despite the heat and humidity, the two of them looked like they had just gone for a walk in the park.

"Thank you for coming to see our man," I said in Malay.

He nodded.

"I will look," he said.

While Amulong looked at Hoss, I got the debrief from Moon. Weller's camp was on a remote hilltop, about four miles from the river. Thick jungle and ravines made access difficult but easy to guard. The villagers were settling in and Moon estimated Weller had twenty men in his group. The sergeant felt they all looked like capable fighters, but you never knew for sure.

"How about supplies?"

"Not the Garden of Eden, if you ask me, but they seemed to have the essentials. I don't know about ammunition, but each of the men was armed."

I looked around, then asked Moon, "Where's Abernathy?"

"Should be here shortly. He's with two of Weller's people that he sent along with us."

"What the hell?"

138

I didn't need more mouths to feed or more people to know about our operation.

"Weller thought they could help," he said, "I was trying to be cooperative. You know, the friendly Aussie."

This operation was turning into a damn dime store novel and it was starting to piss me off.

"There he is now," Moon said as Abernathy came up the trail. Behind him I saw two people that had to be women based on their size. Christ. I might as well face this, I thought and walked over to meet them.

Abernathy had a shit-eating grin on his face, despite the sweat. He was actually enjoying himself. Then the first woman looked up from the trail and directly at me. It couldn't be.

"Maksi?"

She walked up to me and put her hand on my cheek.

"Ajib, my boy."

Her eyes filled with tears as I put my arms around her and hugged her, consumed by complete happiness and wonder.

"My, God, what are you doing here? How did…?" I finally asked after releasing my bear hug.

Smiling, Maksi said, "All in good time, but first you must meet Aliea, my niece and her son Balle."

A young boy, probably eight years old was standing behind the other woman, a small round face peering at me. I remembered that Maksi's sister had lived up north and worked for one of the other church missionary groups.

"Weller figured out who she was and thought that you might want to see her," Abernathy said while he helped Aliea remove a large carrying bag from over her shoulder.

"Right, right," I said, trying to think what to do next. I walked over to Aliea, who looked like a younger Maksi. She looked a little apprehensive, but smiled when I offered my hand.

139

"Welcome, Aliea," I said in Malay. "I'm Rob Parker."

She smiled and slowly answered in English, "I have heard about you for many years."

The young boy moved to her side.

"This is my son, Balle."

I squatted down and said in Malay, "Hello, Balle, my name is Rob."

His round face and bright eyes conveyed a calmness I wouldn't have expected in one so young. But I suspect what he had been through in his short life was not the norm for young boys.

To my surprise, he offered his hand.

In English he said, "My name is Balle, pleased to meet you."

Taking it, I shook it and grinned at him, then Aliea.

Every day a new surprise.

"He attended the Christian school," Aliea said.

"Hello, I'm Lynda Noble," I heard from right behind me as Lynda stepped forward to meet the new arrivals.

The three woman exchanged greetings.

"Let's go down to my hut and I'll help you get settled," she said, taking charge in the best British tradition.

Like Grand Central Station in the middle of the jungle.

There were many things I knew needed to be done, building shelters and preparing food, but I had to find out what had happened to her since the Japs had taken Borneo.

I followed the group and watched as they settled their gear and introduced Dicky to Balle. The two looked at each other and I wondered if Balle was going to offer to shake hands, but he just stood there, being shy. Why was he so forthcoming with me, but shy with another youngster? Clearly, I was way out of my league trying to understand women or children.

When Lynda returned to assist Amulong, Moon started gathering material for building shelters. He took Balle and Dicky with him, and I thought they might get a chance to know each other away from the women.

I sat down with Maksi and her sister to find out what had happened to them since the war started. My last contact had been a letter I had received at Tech, but that was well before the war started. She told me when my parents left Balikpapan, she first worked at the church office, then took another job with a local family as governess and teacher to their young children. That lasted until the actual invasion, when the Japanese occupied the city. While there weren't a large number of Japanese troops, the Imperial Army established their headquarters for the northern coast and refineries.

"I didn't know what to do," she said, her tone very uncharacteristic. Maksi had always had an air of authority and purpose about her. At least that was what it had always seemed to me.

"What did the Japs do when they took over the town?"

She looked down, as if she wanted to forget what had happened.

"There were many new rules. Violations punishable by death. At first it seemed like a nightmare," her voice trailed off. "Then," she continued slowly, "We saw what they were capable of."

It struck me I was seeing my Maksi as never before. Now she was acting like everyone else, afraid of what might happen, not sure what to do. In my memory, she had always been the one person who took charge and knew what had to be done.

She went on to tell me how she found herself working for a senior Japanese officer who had commandeered the family's house. Major Kurita was the second in command of the military port authority. As long as she did what was needed to keep the house running smoothly, he paid little attention to her. But as the brutality of the Japanese occupation became a reality, she knew she had to get away from the city. Deciding two months ago that it was finally time, she told the major her daughter was ill and she must travel to see her. A friend of hers had already agreed to take over the major's house and he seemed to care little for the details, only that his clothes were washed and his food prepared. She traveled north and met her sister in Samarinda, where she had been living since her son's birth. Maksi thought she would be able to spend the war in peace, until the Japanese arrived and arrested all foreigners, which were primarily the missionaries. Unfortunately, Maksi had once again established her connection to the church and by association, she had come under suspicion by the Kempietai, the Japanese military's secret police. She and her sister had been able to steal away and found their way to Weller's band. Since then they had served the Australian as both cooks and provisioners. I began to see my Maksi in a different light. Living in the jungle, surrounded by men with weapons, intent on doing harm to the invaders. Not the quiet, gentle companion of my youth.

A short time later I found Abernathy sitting with Moon and Bob Springer.

"Thanks for bringing them to camp," I said. They were all looking at me with curiosity.

"You really knew her before the war?" Springer asked.

I laughed.

"She pretty much raised me. Her given name is Nadira, but I called her Maksi. She was my teacher, governess and nurse all rolled into one."

"Crazy war," Moon said.

He had that right.

.......Additional contact local group. Twenty men, equipped with small arms only. Believe would be asset for use against enemy and appear cooperative........

That afternoon, I was sitting with her when Abernathy ran up the trail from the river, his face telling me that we had a problem.

"Jap boat down on the river," he reported, "You need to see this."

Grabbing my Wilson, we ran down to the big bluff that overlooked the main channel of the river closest to our camp. What I saw made my stomach turn.

The patrol boat was like the one we had captured, but there was an antenna mounted on the pilot house. Our radio transmissions, despite our best efforts to minimize air time, must have been detected by the Japs. The lack of roads in the area may have been our saving grace, because it made the Japs use a boat instead of trucks to mount their radio detection gear. The problem for them would be more difficult, but unfortunately, our location was vulnerable to detection from the river. Take two bearings from different points, triangulate and the transmitter location is pretty well pinned down. We had a problem.

"Get back as fast as you can and make sure that Bever's off the air. Tell everyone to get ready to move.

Abernathy paused for a moment, then nodded.

"Right," he said and headed for the camp.

I watched the patrol boat, which was barely making way. The antenna was being controlled by someone in the pilot house who was making slow adjustments around the compass apparently trying to catch our transmission. Now that we knew what the Japs were doing, our time at the camp was limited. If we stayed at the camp, we had to transmit. If we transmitted, the Japs would eventually find us. Perhaps the boat being so close was just a coincidence, or perhaps had they already gotten some cuts on previous transmissions.

Moving the transmitter was difficult, but it wasn't the issue. Without a connection to our lookout point, the transmitter was worthless. Somehow, we had to find another way to track ships leaving the harbor and get that information to a relocated transmission site. How the hell we were going to do that, I didn't have a clue.

"We have to move?" Lynda asked.

"The Japs are trying to locate us with radio direction gear."

She looked confused.

"You locate a radio transmitter by taking bearings off the transmissions. That's what they're doing now."

"How long does that take?" she asked.

"I don't know," I told her. I'd never been involved in anything like that, but I knew the technology. Luck and geography seemed to be big variables. "But better to overestimate the little bastards, and get the radio out of here."

"But we can't move Mr. Hostetter, he's too sick."

The two of us walked down to Hoss's shelter. Amulong sat at a small fire near the entrance where a pot sat on rocks arranged next to the flames.

Maksi stood next to the headman, and looked up as we approached.

Her smile brought back so many memories, but those were pleasant. What was happening now was anything but pleasant. How were we going to get Hoss out of here? And how was I going to take care of two more women and another child?

"When will he be able to travel?" I asked.

Maksi and Lynda looked at me like I was crazy. The headman continued to stir the pot, which looked like it contained chopped up leaves.

"We'll know more in the morning," Lynda said. "Amulong is mixing a tea of papaya leaves and another plant called Melissa, if I understand what he said correctly. The tea will fight his dehydration and the fever.

CHAPTER TWELVE

Camp One
Telukladang, Peninsula
2 September 1942

My time in Borneo taught me many things, some good, some not so good. But it did teach me to take seriously the knowledge of the locals when it comes to living and surviving. By the third day of Amulong's treatments, Hoss was sitting up and actually looked human again. But in my mind, we had no time to lose getting away from this camp. If the Japs had any lines of bearing, it would make our discovery easier. I had made the decision to stop any transmissions until we were able to change our location. My reasoning was simple: sending the information on one ship, which might be sighted by a sub anyway, might mean the end of any future intelligence from us. I didn't know if Coyne would agree, but he wasn't here to ask.

The radio had been packed up, the antenna taken down and we moved most of our equipment to a staging area near the river. We were ready to move.

"I want you to take one of the canoes tonight and go north to Weller's camp. We need him down here either tomorrow night or the next with the power launch. Take Bever with you, but watch out for him, he's the only radioman we have."

Mullen nodded.

"Good for the lad to get away from that damned thing for a time. Will Hoss be ready to move?"

I nodded, not knowing if he would be or not. It didn't matter, though. We had to move. I guess that's what they call "operational necessity". If Hoss didn't survive the move, it was a price I was willing to pay. Easy to say, but it was the truth.

"Yeah, he'll be okay," I was learning that things were not black and white out here.

"We'll be leaving here tomorrow night or the next," I told Lynda. She and Maksi were sitting outside Hoss's shelter, watching Amulong feeding him some soup. It smelled awful, sort of like fresh cut grass. I could only guess how it tasted. Aroma aside, it seemed to be making a difference. Hoss's face no longer looked like a cadaver's. He looked like crap, but in this jungle we all did.

"Rob, he's still very ill," Lynda said. "He may not be up to any kind of travel."

Maksi looked at me with concern and I knew she could tell by the tone in my voice.

"I understand that," I said quietly, wanting Lynda to know I understood what I was saying. "But we're going to move. I can't risk the lives of everyone else."

She was a nurse and I know they can be very protective of their patients. But Lynda had also seen what the Japanese had done to her family.

"Alright," she said, the understanding complete.

"I need you all to take care of the boys. We'll be traveling at night. It has to be quiet and we can't lose anyone in the dark. That'll be your priority. I'll have the Chief and Springer work with Amulong to move Hoss as carefully as we can. That's the best we can do."

She nodded.

"How are the boys getting along?" I asked.

"Always together. Balle is very nice and seems unconcerned that Dicky doesn't talk."

"Maybe having a friend will help him get past whatever it is." I had no clue what I was saying, for all I knew Dicky was so fouled up that he would never be normal, but I was responsible for both of them and I hoped something good would come out of having Balle around.

The next night we moved down to our staging area by the river. It took several trips by the men, while the women waited for the last trip with Dicky and Balle. Bringing up the rear, Chief Pickett and Springer carried Hoss on a stretcher they'd constructed from bamboo poles and vines. We were going to be taking a chance if the boat didn't come the first night and we had to spend the day that close to the river. While there generally wasn't much traffic on the waterway, the occasional canoe or small boat might spot us. If they were sympathetic to the Japs, we were done for.

My biggest concern was that the boat might not show up at all. Our only option would be to cache the radio and much of the equipment and head north into the jungle. I suspect that would certainly kill Hoss and any hope of continuing our mission. That was a bridge I hoped we wouldn't have to cross.

Three of us took up positions at night fall near the big bend in the river. We each carried flashlights so we'd be able to signal Weller if he showed up.

I think the hardest part of war is the waiting. Particularly when the wait was out of your control. Those were the times when a man's mind would attack him. The doubts and fears ganged up on you. That night was no different. By midnight, I'd began to think they wouldn't come. The time to make the trip back north, if it was to be made during darkness, was running out. As I sat in my partially concealed position, the insects buzzing around me, sweat dripping off my nose, I began to lose confidence that this was a good idea. The Japs would certainly be patrolling the river. Would moving our group north bring betrayal by one of Weller's people who might be looking for a reward payment? What was the probability this would succeed? I tried to kill time by creating a mathematical formula from my probability and statistics course at Tech to determine our success potential. After an hour I decided it all came down to indefinable factors. That is a scientific way of saying there's no fucking way to figure it out for certain. It will either work or it won't. Simple as that. This was no time to get overly analytical, though. All we could do was take things as they came.

The noise behind me was Bever.

"The chief heard something on the river," he said.

"Let's go."

By the time we knelt down next to Chief Pickett, the sound of a motor was clear, coming out of the darkness, and from the north.

"How do we know if it's Weller or the Japs?" Pickett asked.

Why the hell hadn't I given Moon some kind of signal?

"Just watch," I said, trying to act like I had the situation under control.

Moon knew where our staging area was, but could he find it from the darkened river? A small amount of illumination from the waning moon helped, but it wasn't much.

I could just make out the outline of the boat, when its motor went to idle.

"That's got to be them," I said. No one else would have gone to idle, why would they?

I raised my flashlight and turned it on for two seconds, off for two and repeated the signal.

The engine kicked into gear and began heading directly for us.

The journey north proved to be anticlimactic. We saw no other boats on the river and were back on land, headed for the camp, just as the sun began to provide the light of false dawn. A group of twenty men were waiting for us and we were able to move all of our equipment, including the radio, in one trip.

"How's Hoss doing? I asked Lynda as we prepared to move out.

Standing up from the litter, which was about to be picked up by four of Weller's men, she brushed her hair out of her eyes.

"I think he'll be okay. How much farther?"

"Five or six miles," I answered, trying to remember what Moon had told me.

"He was able to get some sleep on the boat."

He might have, but I know she hadn't. The strain showed on her face.

Stepping over to the litter, I knelt down. Hoss's eyes were closed. I wouldn't wake him, what the hell was there to say? His face was gaunt and he must have lost thirty pounds over the last two weeks. He was damned lucky he was still alive.

"She's quite a lass," Hoss said, his eyes now open.

I grinned at him.

"Leave it to an old codger like you to figure that out," I said. "Are you doing all right?"

"I know who I am and where I am," he said, "That's a lot better than I was, that's for damned sure."

"We'll be at Weller's camp in a couple of hours."

"Then what?"

I laughed. "Get better and help me figure that out."

Turning I saw Maksi watching the exchange.

"How are you?" I asked putting a hand on each shoulder.

She smiled that smile she seemed to save for me.

"I am well, Ajib," she said quietly.

I was sure she didn't want anyone to hear my boyhood name.

"Have you a young lady at home?"

"Not I. Unattached as they say. I belong to the Marine Corps."

"Then I am right," she said her voice still quiet.

"About what?"

"You are in love."

I started to protest, but why?

"I think, yes. She is a very special lady, just like you."

She took my hand and squeezed it, turning to walk up the trail.

The trip took over three hours. But the closer we got to the camp, the better I felt about our chances. The jungle was damned near impenetrable, some of this nastiest bush I had ever seen. If we hadn't been with Weller's people we never would have made it. An attacking force would be hard pressed to surprise anyone in this jungle. I think "Sherwood Forest" would've been an apt name for it. I guess that made Weller our Robin Hood. Smiling to myself I thought of Errol Flynn, playing Robin Hood in the movie. Handsome smile, clean clothes and a hearty good nature about himself. That was not Larry Weller, who struck me more like a Noah Beery's pirate character in "Treasure Island," a dangerous-looking man you don't want to mess with.

CHAPTER THIRTEEN

Weller's Camp
Telukladang Peninsula
3 September 1942

The camp itself was difficult to see. Shelters had been constructed to blend in with the surrounding jungle and there didn't appear to be any large, open areas like we'd seen at Amulong's village. Smoke from several cooking fires drifted up toward the higher canopy, but if I hadn't been right there, I wouldn't have noticed them.

Weller found me and we took a brief tour of the camp.

"You can set your people up in this area. There's plenty of material for building huts, but make sure they cut it well away from the camp."

"I'll need to get our transmitter up and running in short order. The Japs are trying to locate us using radio direction finders."

The older man smiled.

"I think we have a location that'll take care of that problem. We've scouted well up into the hills to find other locations where we might have to fall back. There's a ridge I want to show you."

Lynda, Maksi and her sister came from the main trail, leading the two boys up a small trail that ran into our new "bivouac."

"Welcome to our new home," I offered, with a theatrical sweep of my hand.

She laughed.

"The boys will have lots of new places to explore, I said. Then leaned down to Dicky and Balle. "But you two stay close for now, got it?"

Balle nodded and put his hand on Dicky's shoulder.

Standing up, I turned to Lynda.

"We need to get Hoss settled, a shelter, something."

"No worry," Weller said from behind us, "I have a soft bed waiting for him just over there. I've already told my lads to take the stretcher there. I think the headman is waiting for him."

We all turned to, shelters being the first line of business. Like our old camp, we made sure Lynda had an area with privacy. At least here there were other women and many of them, she knew from the village; to say nothing of Maksi and her sister. Hell, it was almost civilized.

By sundown I was ready for some food and rest. It had been a long thirty-six hours and I was glad it was behind us.

"Looks like your crew's settling in."

Larry Weller walked up, carrying a bottle and two cups.

"Thought a drink was in order. Join me?"

"I should say so."

"This is Lihing, it's a rice wine. Quite a punch, but it'll grow on you."

I'd heard of it growing up here, but had never tried it. Wow.

"You'll find that we have a decent food supply, much courtesy of the Japs. Canned food and rice mostly, but you can do wonders with some fresh fish and the occasional wild pig."

Things were definitely looking up.

Two days later, the team was settled at the new camp. Six shelters took care of our needs and we were ready to get on with the fight. Maksi and her sister took over the cooking duties and, made a massive improvement to our cuisine and morale.

Weller had described a ridge about five miles north of the main camp, where he thought we could rig up an antenna. The area was almost inaccessible—so far removed from the river and any roads that the Japs would play hell locating it. Then, if the Japs tried to get any force near the ridge, it would be almost impossible for them to do so without detection by Weller's lookouts. I knew that Australia would be getting concerned with no transmissions for five days, though. Coyne never struck me as a patient man.

"We've never seen or heard of the Nips having any unit larger than a patrol operate outside the city. I know there aren't any large army units in the Balikpapan area. So far it has appeared they don't want anything to do with coming this far into the bush."

"That may cover the transmitter, but the problem is getting real time information on the tankers," I said. "Without a direct view of the harbor, we're screwed." It looked like our mission was rapidly going down the shitter.

"Some of my blokes have family that work the docks. If they know a ship's sailing, why couldn't they get word up here and you send that to your people?"

I started to tell Weller that couldn't work. There was a time factor. If we were going to hit the Jap tankers, we needed to see them sail. Or did we?

"So, they know when the ships will sail?" I asked.

He shrugged his shoulders.

"You'd think they must have an idea, wouldn't you?"

155

Maybe it would work.

"Can you find out for sure?"

Weller nodded.

"I'll send a man south today. Should have an answer the day after next."

"While we wait, let's go take a look at this ridge."

Weller led four of us west the next morning. The jungle was just as thick, and now uphill. I thought I was used to traveling in the bush, but by mid-day I was out of gas. The effort to push through the heavy foliage was made even more difficult because of the slick mud on the exposed hillsides. How in the hell were we going to hump the heavy radio boxes up this ridge?

"Let's stop here," Weller called back. "It's about one more mile to the ridge."

Everyone simply sat down where they were. The lack of conversation told me that I wasn't the only one who was done for. It wasn't that much hotter today, but I found that I was sweating like nothing I remember. Wiping my eyes, I realized I was actually a little dizzy. Shit. My stomach had been upset earlier, which is why I wrote off the diarrhea I had this morning. Now I wondered if I was coming down with something.

By the time we broke into the open just south of the ridge, I knew something wasn't right. It seemed like my body was just too heavy to go on.

"Moon, I gotta sit down."

I started to kneel down as the world grayed then went dark.

Weller was looking down at me when I opened my eyes. The bright sun stung and I tried to raise my arm to shade my face from it. It wouldn't move.

"How long was I out?" I asked as Moon came into my field of view.

"About half an hour."

Shit. He moved to give me some shade and I was able to open my eyes fully.

"I've seen this before," he said. "You're in for a few very uncomfortable days. We need to get you back to camp,"

"What about the radio?" I asked, my head now throbbing.

Bever appeared next to Moon.

"Great site, skipper. We can run the antenna easily and there's a clearing where we can build a shelter for the set."

That was fine, but all I wanted to do was close my eyes.

"Good," I said with all the enthusiasm I could muster, but it wasn't lost on me that Bever had called me skipper. That felt pretty good.

I found out after the fact that it took almost six hours for them to carry me back to the camp. A litter made all the difference and thank God it was downhill. Not that I remember all that much of the trip. In fact, the next four days were a blur.

If you have to come down with a tropical fever in the middle of the Bornean jungle, it never hurts to have a trained nurse and a local medicine man working on you. I'll never know what variant of fever I had contracted, but my "doctors" decided that they would use the same regimen on me that they had on Hoss. Much of it I don't remember, but by the time I was aware of what was going on around me I was to discover that the green stuff tasted worse than I could have ever imagined. An awful miracle.

It was on the third day that I actually arrived back in the land of the living. As I lay on my back, trying to figure out where I was and what was happening, I was confused to say the least. It was as if I was in a cave with a low ceiling, but it was light around me. Something was cutting into my back and I moved my shoulders in search of a more comfortable position.

"Lynda."

I could hear Maksi's voice, but couldn't see her. Turning my head, I realized a drape of mosquito netting covered me. But focusing past the netting I saw trees. I wasn't in a shelter. Trying to roll on my side proved too hard, so I lay back to wait. Hard bands were cutting into my butt and back. What the hell was going on?

The netting lifted and I saw Lynda leaning over me.

"Hello, Rob Parker," she said quietly, putting her hand on my forehead.

"What happened?" I asked, the words coming out like a croak.

"Fever, it hit you hard."

"How long have I been out?"

"They brought you back from the ridge three days ago."

After drinking water in small sips, I actually felt like I was coming around.

"Where am I?"

Lynda grinned at me.

"We moved you down here."

"What?" This was not making sense.

"It was the best way to take care of you."

Over the next several hours, I would nap, then wake for a few minutes, taking more liquid. As I tried to move around I was more than a little surprised to find that I was naked except for a square of cloth covering my crotch. The bands cutting my butt and back turned out to be vines that had been fashioned into a bed on a bamboo frame. The other sense that begin to work well was my nose. There was no mistaking the sickening smell of sewage.

"It was the best way to deal with your diarrhea," Lynda said.

I closed my eyes tight as the reality hit me. I was shitting through the bed.

"We didn't know how long it would continue. Amulong's potion should have stopped it right away, but it didn't."

What was I supposed to say?

Lynda was a nurse, I knew that, but it didn't help.

"I have to talk to Sergeant Mullen," I finally said, not wanting to talk about my bodily functions to Lynda or anyone else. "And get me some clothes," I croaked, trying to assert some face saving dignity.

She smiled that bewitching smile of hers, taking my hand.

"I do believe the lieutenant is embarrassed. That means you're most certainly getting better."

"We're ready to move the radio up to the ridge tomorrow morning."

I was able to sit up, wearing freshly washed shorts, while Moon briefed me on the plan to use a large working party to carry the radio parts on slings suspended from a four-man carries. Bever and Springer would go up early with Weller and string the antenna. We could be operating by the next afternoon.

"Tell Bever to send a short message, just saying we had to move and are up and running again. No reason to explain the new system just yet."

Hell, it might not even work.

"Right," he answered.

"How's Hoss? I continued, "Lynda told me he's in good shape. What do you say?"

Mullen nodded, "She's right, he seems like the old Hoss. Maybe a little tired, but he's eating and playing with the boys."

More things were flooding into my mind, the dark cloud lifting from my brain.

"Have you looked at the camp defenses?" I asked.

"Weller knows his business," Moon replied. "There's a system of watch posts that are manned constantly, watching the approaches to the camp. He doesn't have any heavy weapons other than the one machine gun you gave them. If the Japs show up with mortars or machine guns, he'll have to pull out."

"Deeper into the jungle?"

"Right. You saw how tough it was to move, Japs would have to do the same thing. Damned hard if you ask me."

I supposed the Japs could attack with aircraft, but it was hard to see the camp when you were standing in the middle of it, from the air it would be been invisible.

"You look better than the last time I saw you."

Larry Weller had joined Moon, squatting down next to him.

"Starting to feel human again," I said.

"My man's back from Balikpapan, when you want to hear about it."

"I'm ready now," I said, even though I felt like all the air was going out of my tires.

He told us there were three men working the docks. Larry said the workers told his man that they knew when the ships were going to be finished loading and setting sail. Two of the men were relatives of his men and another was a friend of theirs. The men also said that they often knew the destination port because there was deck cargo.

Weller said that a messenger could travel from the port to the camp in about twelve hours. If we could get the information up to the radio a couple of hours after that, we would be almost as effective as before. We were back in business.

CHAPTER FOURTEEN

Weller's Camp
Telukladang Peninsula
22 September 1942

I haven't yet reached the age of 80, but I think I know how it will feel. The two weeks after I came back to this world were painful. Moving was a supreme effort once they were able to get me on my feet. Given a choice, I would have just laid down under a tree and slept, but time and tide wait for no man and I could do a little more each day.

My enforced inactivity did give me a chance to pay attention to the two boys. They were within my sight most of the day and it was interesting to watch them. Balle would talk to Dicky as they would play and explore, despite a lack of answers from the young Englishman. Balle's time at the Christian school gave him a fluency in English, although with a bit of a Dutch accent. I knew that would be an asset as he grew up in the colonial world that would return to Borneo after the war. At the time, I could have never imagined how the landscape of the southeast Pacific would change after the war. But that was long in the future.

It was early afternoon and I was sitting with my back against a large palm tree, the camp quiet except for the rustling of the foliage overhead in the breeze.

"The boys seem to be making the very best of it, wouldn't you say?"

"It's been good for Dicky," she said.

"Both of them if you ask me."

"How's the nurse holding up?" I asked her.

"Glad all my patients are on the mend."

I laughed.

"That'd make two of us."

She sighed and sat back against the tree, our shoulders touching.

"You didn't answer my question. How are you?"

Lynda didn't respond right away, almost as if it was painful to relate.

"I'm wondering what's going to happen to those boys… to all of us. We can't stay in the jungle forever."

That struck me like a blow. She had no idea what the future might hold for her and Dicky. This was her life and it had been ripped apart. Hell, I was on a lark compared to that. This was a war and after it was over, I would become an engineer and live happily ever after. A tough load to carry for her after what happened to her parents and the run-in with the Jap by the pond.

Her closeness seemed so natural, although after what we had been through together, I suppose it was only to be expected. But now I sensed there was more to it and I knew I couldn't let that happen.

A commotion below us broke the moment and Maksi's sister emerged from behind a hut, carrying Balle in her arms.

"Nadira, a snake bit him!" she cried.

Maksi came out of the shelter, in time to help her sister lower the boy to the ground.

Lynda and I ran and knelt down as Maksi looked at her sister, the fear clear in her voice.

"Where? What happened?" she cried.

"Look," Aliea said, holding his left arm.

Balle lay on the ground, his body limp.

"Lynda, can you help them?" I asked, my voice quiet but urgent. My memories of Commander Kilgallen's warnings about the deadly snakes on this island coming back as a sickening reality. Depending on what kind of snake had bitten the young boy, there might be nothing anyone could do.

"Here," Lynda said, kneeling next to the boy.

"Get Amulong," Maksi told me. I sensed that she knew there was nothing to be done.

Lynda examined Balle's arm, which was swollen below the elbow where the snake must have struck. Suddenly she asked, "Where's Dicky?"

Standing up, she looked around, but her brother was nowhere to be seen.

"You stay here," I said, grabbing her shoulder. "I'll find him."

Running down the trail, I looked left and right, trying to catch a glimpse of him.

I called out for him. I knew he wouldn't answer, but he would know someone was looking for him.

Fifty feet down the trail, the underbrush opened up, a small ridge rising to the north. Playing a hunch, I climbed the slope, hoping that the higher ground might give me a better vantage.

Behind me I heard someone following and turned to see Hoss pushing up the ridge a machete in his hand.

"I heard," he said.

"Dicky!" I called, Hoss echoing me.

We both heard a reply, not that it was recognizable, but it was a human voice coming from the line of undergrowth at the far side of the ridge. Both of us pushed down the hill, pushing the light vegetation out of the way.

"Dicky! Dicky!"

What sounded like "Yes," came from behind the base of a large palm.

Rushing around the tree, we saw the boy, standing with his back to the tree. A bright orange and black snake lay on the ground, its head raised as if it was getting ready to move. I stopped in my tracks, seeing Hoss come around the other side of the tree.

"Freeze! Snake!" I called to him. I remember the Australian doctor telling me that rapid movements could trigger actions by snakes.

"Dicky, stand very still," I said, trying to sound calm.

The boy seemed riveted to the ground, his eyes on the snake. That gave me my chance.

"Hoss, I'm going to slowly move toward Dicky. Keep an eye on that snake and use the machete if it moves toward us."

As I slowly moved to the boy, the snake raised its head, but didn't move. I grabbed Dicky's left arm and put my right hand under his right arm and lifted him up and away from the snake. Stepping back, with my eyes on the snake I moved out of danger. The snake had followed our movement with its head and never saw the machete.

By the time we made it back to camp, Amulong was tending to Balle. Hoss brought the headless body of the snake. I carried Dicky, who had put both arms around my neck, something I had only seen him do to Lynda. It made me feel strange, maybe this was how a father felt?

He hadn't said anything, but I hoped his calls before might mean that he was coming out of whatever was keeping him from talking.

Lynda ran up to us and I transferred him to her arms.

I put my hand on her arm.

166

"He's okay. He's fine."

Amulong looked up and saw Hoss who had the snake in his left hand, the body hanging almost to the ground. I saw the reaction by the old man and it did not give me much hope.

Only much later did we get the whole story. The two boys had found the snake and had been playing with it for several minutes before it struck Balle, who had panicked and run. His mother had been looking for them already and saw him staggering to the trail and where he collapsed. Amulong had a name for the snake, but it made no sense to me. Later we discovered the snake was a blue coral, one of the deadliest in the area. Perhaps immediate treatment by a doctor in a hospital could have made a difference, but not in a jungle. Once Balle had run back to the trail, the venom had spread through his body making the outcome inevitable. He died in less than two hours, thankfully he was unconscious for much of the time.

That night I sat next to my hut, unwilling to lie down, knowing all I would do is toss and turn. The sadness and finality of a young boy's death was affecting me more than I would have ever expected. Hell, I'm a Marine, I should be able to put anything out of my mind.

"Rob?"

I turned to see Lynda and Dicky coming up the path. He let go of her hand and ran up to me, his arms going around my neck.

"He kept pulling up the trail, toward your hut. Now I know why," she said coming to stand next to me.

I put my arms around Dicky, who was crying softly.

"Don't worry. You'll be okay."

Over the next several weeks, the sailings from Balikpapan were again being sent to Coyne. I was surprised there seemed to be no interest in why we were offline for almost two weeks, but perhaps he didn't want to waste transmission time. In any case, it seemed like things were getting into a comfortable routine as I regained my strength.

Maksi was now aware of what we were doing to help sink the Jap tankers. It made no sense to hide anything from her, I valued her counsel now as much as when I was growing up. She approached me about Aliea returning to Balikpapan.

"She could likely return to the major's household or use that connection to gain employment with another Japanese officer. Whatever she learns could be sent to us by the same messenger from the harbor."

My reaction was instantaneous, "I couldn't ask her to do that. It's just too dangerous."

"Ajib, she has nothing to live for. Balle was her life and he's gone."

Three weeks had passed since the boy's death. I hadn't seen Aliea very much, she spent most of her time in her shelter or walking by herself. I hated the idea of putting her in any peril, but I knew I had to consider every option. The mission had to be the priority.

The decision to send Aliea to Balikpapan was easy once I thought it through. Additional intelligence would only make our reporting more accurate. She seemed happy when she left with one of Weller's messengers. Once she was settled, the messenger would add any reports from her to the information on the ships that was passed back to us. Having her in the city would make everything more complicated, but the situation was far from what I had ever imagined. At least now I was pretty sure it couldn't get any more complicated.

Then Williams arrived.

CHAPTER FIFTEEN

Weller's Camp
Telukladang Peninsula
14 October 1942

I suppose life in general always provides surprises, but war has a way of taking those surprises to another level. The flow of events during conflict can accelerate to breathtaking speed or slow down to an excruciating painfulness. I didn't know it, but I had just moved into the fast lane.

"Skipper, Weller wants you down at his hut."

Looking up from my Webley, which was now immaculately clean, I told Abernathy I'd be right down. As I look back at it, the smartest thing I could have done at that point would have been to run headlong into the jungle.

Moon was standing with Weller, who was talking with a stranger. Three other men I didn't recognize stood back slightly, not taking part in the discussion. One looked American, wearing a type of flying coverall. The other two were wearing plain working clothes, one was a white man, and the other looked like a local.

Weller turned as I walked up.

"This is Lieutenant Parker," he said, nodding toward me.

The stranger extended his hand.

"Williams, Dave Williams, Lieutenant Commander, late off the *U.S.S. Houston*."

The cruiser *Houston,* nicknamed the "Galloping Ghost of the Java Coast," had been in a combined allied task force that had tried to blunt the Japanese move into the East Indies. After several heroic fights, she'd been sunk by overwhelming Japanese forces. What the hell was a crew member off that ship doing here?

"The *Houston?*"

He smiled slightly and said, "Until about nine months ago."

"Parker, sir. Marine Corps," I said, more than a little amazed. While this Williams looked a little rough around the edges with a shaggy haircut and worn khakis, there was no doubt in my mind he was military. It was how he carried himself.

"What are the Marines doing here, lieutenant?"

"It's a long story, sir. But it's Marine. Singular. I'm the only one."

He sighed.

"Parker, I think we need to talk. Can you get my men something to eat and drink?"

We did talk. Williams was a Naval Aviator. A graduate of the Naval Academy class of 1932, he'd been in charge of the aviation detachment aboard the *Houston.* The cruiser carried four floatplanes, which were designed for long-range search in addition to spotting for the ship's 8-inch guns. Dave Williams was one of three pilots who flew the aircraft and he oversaw fourteen aviation technicians who maintained them.

The combined allied task force was under the command of the Dutch admiral De Ruyter. Their task was to take on the Japanese forces expanding into the East Indies. While completely outnumbered, the task force had managed a series of small victories, but the outcome was inevitable with their supply lines cut and more Japanese ships being thrown into the battle.

Williams had been on a mission trying to locate spare parts for the ship when the Houston had their final encounter in the Sunda Strait. A vicious night battle resulted in the loss of the ship and over eight-hundred of her crew. Suddenly he found himself with an aircraft but no ship. Rather than surrendering to the victorious Japanese, he decided he'd go to ground and continue the fight. He and his radioman/observer, Petty Officer John Smith, flew their Seagull float plane north to where they'd flown search missions earlier in the war. He thought there would be a better chance of finding a sympathetic population south of Balikpapan and he knew they would be there for a long time.

By the time he finished his story, I knew briefing him on our mission was the only thing to do. While I did work for Commander Coyne, Dave Williams was now the senior military officer present. It also struck me that he'd survived on his own for over nine months and his knowledge could only help our cause.

"Now you know what I'm doing here, why is there a single Marine lieutenant on his own in the jungle of Borneo?"

I explained my history with the island, Georgia Tech and Quantico.

"When the intel types found out about my connection with Borneo, I was pulled into this mission. The Aussies are calling the shots, but it's part of a combined command."

Williams laughed.

"I know all about combined commands and I'm not sure they work all that well."

"I see, sir."

"So, what are you actually doing?"

It took me ten minutes to cover the team and our radio contacts with Australia.

"Hopefully it's resulted in Jap tankers going to the bottom," I said.

He nodded.

"How about the rest of these people?"

I went on, "A combination of Aussies, Malays and natives who came together over time. Weller's the head man, he's been running a smuggling business in this area since the last war. The Japs killed his wife and children."

"How many people?"

"Sixty or so. About thirty of them were with Weller originally and there are thirty villagers that relocated after a Jap attack. Probably forty fighters if you include the natives."

"Have they done anything?"

"Weller's set up a network of people from here to Balikpapan. They've had several small skirmishes with the Japs, but nothing big."

"Not yet, anyway," he said.

At the time I didn't understand what he meant.

"You had two other men with you, who are they?" I asked, the info needed to flow both ways in my book.

"Two merchant sailors we found after we hid the aircraft, an Irishman and a Malay. Good men who don't like the Japs much at all. They'll hold their own in any fight, I'll tell you that. McGowan can be a bit pushy, but he's just Irish. Finley's a quiet one, but don't let that fool you. I've seen him take out several Jap soldiers without batting an eyelash. Come on," he said, walking back down to the group.

"This is Marty McGowan, Lester Finley and my crewman, Petty Officer John Smith—goes by "Smitty". Lieutenant Parker, Marine Corps, is in charge here."

Williams was right, they looked like they could take care of themselves.

McGowan was built like a fireplug, short hair and a pug face. I suspect he'd been in more that his fair share of fist fights. Finley was average height and wiry. He may have been from Malaya, but I suspect there was some English blood in his family tree. The name must have some connection. Both men wore dark blue shirts and pants, making me wonder if they were crewman on the same ship.

"Nice to meet you, sir," Petty Officer Smith said. He was younger than the other two, but also looked like he had been around the block a few times. He still wore a set of flying coveralls, which were torn and faded.

I offered my hand to each man, looking them in the eyes as we shook.

"Glad to have you here, Sergeant Mullen will get you settled and I'll let Mr. Weller fill you in on the situation here. We're an odd group, but I think we're all interested in making life hard on the Japs. Let Commander Williams know if there's anything you need."

Weller laid out a few rules and warned them to stay away from the tribe, particularly the women. They didn't seem surprised by the warning and I guessed they had been around Borneo long enough to understand tread carefully around the locals.

The next day, Williams and I talked at length. I introduced him to the team and showed him the radio equipment. I sensed a slow change in how Williams was carrying himself. He was asking questions and making comments like someone getting ready to take command. That was going to make for an interesting confrontation.

"Sir, we can contact Australia and let them know about you and your crewman."

Surprisingly, he didn't readily agree.

"Let's hold off, there'll be plenty of time for that."

Right or wrong, it seemed to me that I was starting to lose control of events.

"A rendezvous with a submarine has always been one of the options on the mission," I said. "We expected to need support for the radio or ammunition in any case. And now we have our two crewmen from the *S-43*, who shouldn't even be here."

Williams replied after a moment, "Do you need radio parts or ammunition?"

"No, sir, we're okay for now."

"Then it makes no sense to risk a submarine just to pick anyone up."

Did he want to stay in this miserable jungle? What's driving this guy?

He went on, "It seems like what you're doing here is pretty damned important. For the time being I'm happy to stay here and help the effort. I know Smitty feels the same way. We've spent nine months staying one step ahead of the Japs. I've got contacts down south and I still have our aircraft hidden in an inlet about forty miles south of Balikpapan. Who knows what trouble we could stir up if we combine forces."

The truth was that we weren't making much progress on our mission to raise a little hell with the Japs. What Williams was saying made sense, at least on the surface. Plus, he had a damned plane.

"Yes, sir," I replied.

"And Smitty's a trained radio operator, he can work with your crew."

Things seemed to be working out.

"One more thing, commander. There's a British nurse and her 9-year-old brother. At some point I was going to use a submarine resupply run to get them out of here."

"A nurse? You don't say. Any medical support is a real plus in my book."

CHAPTER SIXTEEN

Weller's Camp
Telukladang Peninsula
15 October 1942

Standing around a map of the area Weller had produced, Williams, Mullen and I listened as he briefed the location of the nearest Japs that he knew about.

"There's one detachment north of Balikpapan, here in Samarinda. We haven't seen them out in the bush much. If they do come out on patrol, they stick to the water most of the time, small patrol boats. They seemed to have had some intelligence of the area when they first showed up, hitting some of the missionaries but since then they stick near their base."

Williams pointed at the chart.

"Where have you seen any activity in the last month?"

"Patrols on the river. Here and here."

I added, "We also saw them using direction finding equipment on one of those boats." I went on to describe our move from the original camp.

"So, if we want to hurt the bastards, we'll need to go after them," Williams said, his conclusion sounding final.

"Whatever we do, the Japs will take it out on the locals." Weller said.

While I hadn't thought about that, I knew in the back of my mind something like that was always possible. Knowing what the invading troops had done to the civilians, I should have connected the dots. How could we justify taking actions that would result in the deaths of the locals?

Williams shook his head, and said, "We can't even think about that. This is a no holds barred war. The only way these people will ever get their lives back is to kick the Japs off this island. That only happens if they lose. Like it or not, a lot of innocent people are going to die. Look at the bombing in Europe, London, Rotterdam or Warsaw. No one gives a shit anymore. We need to do whatever we can to loosen the Japanese grip on Borneo."

He was right. I remembered pictures from London. It was what war had become. But I also recalled the pictures from China of what the Japs did to the Chinese. They were merciless. We must be no different, but I knew the reality would be brutal if people were killed because of what we did. Maybe there was some option that wouldn't put the locals right on the chopping block.

That's when it hit me. I remembered Commander Coyne telling me about anti-ship mines the Brits had developed. He called them "limpets." What if we could place these mines on a tanker at the pier in Balikpapan? If they worked, not only would they put the tanker out of action, but it would block the pier. Suddenly, I realized we had a real possibility to hit the Japs hard. Very hard. And an attack like that would be seen as external, by a hostile military, and the locals would have played no part in it.

I sketched out the idea for the group.

"I like that idea, Parker." Williams smiled like a kid in a candy store.

Weller hadn't said anything while I laid out my idea, but now joined in, "Small boats at night, huh? Sneak in, hook on the mines and then long gone by the time they go off."

"Exactly."

Mullen and Hostetter sat in the circle, watching but not commenting.

Pickett agreed, "Hit 'em right where it hurts."

Williams asked the question I knew was coming next.

"How do we get our hands these mines?"

I had put some thought into that.

"The obvious answer is a resupply by submarine. The problem is that'll take a long time. Probably a very long time, and I don't know if those mines are even in Australia. Like we saw on our inbound trip, submarine schedules are hard to count on. So, I thought we could make our own?"

"One of my men, Tirra, worked with explosives in the oil fields," Weller said. "And hell, Hoss was a sapper in the first war."

Hoss looked surprised at first, but nodded.

"I know a fair bit."

"What about material to make a mine?" Williams asked.

I looked at Weller, our best procurer.

"Depends on what you'll need, but we'll give it a go."

Now, I wondered, what would the good commander back in Australia think about our idea?

…..Believe limpet mine attack on tanker pier side feasible. Gathering material now. Any guidance appreciated…..

There was no doubt in my mind that would elicit a rapid response from Commander Coyne. The idea of an attack on the Japs had always been part of the plan. While Australia might not have envisioned an attack such as this, didn't it make sense? Or would they decide the primary mission remained paramount? The good commander did not disappoint.

179

"Fully support and approve moving forward. Request specific support needed."

It really boiled down to whether we could build an effective weapon ourselves.

Tirra was a short, sturdy man with a pleasant face and shaggy black hair. More Malay than indigenous, he spoke pretty good English and was enthusiastic to help. According to him, he knew where the explosives were stored for use in the fields, but that was before the invasion. Step one, we needed to see if the explosives were still there and if we could get to them. Tirra told us the Japs still maintained their primary oil field support facility on the waterfront at the western end of the Balikpapan harbor area. The explosives had been stored in a separate fenced off compound at the far end of the property.

"Anali knows men who work in the Shell compound. I'll send him down to find out more," Weller said as we all sat discussing the attack.

"What kind of explosives did they have there?" Hoss asked.

"Dynamite," Tirra said.

"Can you make a mine from that?" I asked, not being very well versed in the mechanics of explosive devices.

Hoss laughed.

"We used to make bombs, satchel charges and the like. But they weren't being used under water and surely not against hard steel like a hull. But it's worth a go, I say."

Were we crazy?

That night I sat in front of my hut contemplating all the problems we were going to encounter. I was no expert, but placing a mine against an enemy hull in a patrolled harbor had to be a tough nut, and that was even if you had a mine that was constructed to do the job. A big if, to my mind. We were going to have to jury rig something, including the timer, and make it waterproof and capable of attaching to a metal hull that might very well be covered with weeds and barnacles.

"You certainly seem wrapped up in your thoughts."

I hadn't heard Lynda walk up and turned to see her looking down at me.

"Could you use some company?"

"Please, sit down. I'm a bit preoccupied."

I moved over on the log to make room for her.

"What are you wearing?" I asked. She wore a sari type dress that I hadn't seen before.

"Nadira helped me. The material came from one of her saris and we altered it. I think my old dress was about done for."

I also noticed that she had let her hair out of the standard pony tail and it hung down, just touching her shoulders. For a long moment, I completely forgot about limpet mines and harbor attacks, remembering her standing in the pond, her dress back on the bank. That thought had returned to me many times and I still felt uneasy about it. But war is a strange thing. You take it as it comes and so I guess it's normal to be sitting in a jungle with a lovely woman and thinking about killing Japs. But so be it.

"How's Dicky doing?"

She shook her head.

"I didn't think it was possible for him to withdraw any more. But with Balle's death, he seems like a shell of a little boy. I simply don't know what I can do."

"Weren't he and Hoss connecting?"

"That may be my only hope. Mr. Hostetter is always there, talking to him, watching him for me. Who knows, maybe it will just take time."

"How about you?"

Lynda turned to look at me.

"Because of you, I'm doing well."

Her voice was steady, but soft and she reached for my hand. Raising it to her lips, she gently kissed my fingers.

I kissed her hand, then looked into those beautiful eyes, kissing her softly on the lips.

We both slowly got up, embraced once, and without a word, slipped into my shelter.

The next morning, Chief Pickett and Hoss found me shaving by my hut.

They explained that last night while discussing the project, the chief had come up with an idea.

"Submariners fear depth charges more than almost anything," the chief said. "So I was thinking what looks like a depth charge? A fifty-five-gallon drum. Why couldn't we fill it up with dynamite, slip in a simple timer and float it alongside the target ship?"

Son of a bitch.

"Hoss, what do you think?"

"It makes sense to me. We put as many sticks of dynamite into the barrel as we can, then slip a blasting cap into one with a clock timer, put it in and screw the access tight."

"How do we make a timer?" I asked.

"Pretty simple. A clock with a wind-up spring, use the hour hand as a contact for a battery pack that connects to the blasting cap."

"Will a drum like that float if it's full of dynamite?"

Hoss shrugged his shoulders.

"We'll have to check it out," Pickett inserted, "But we could use external float bags to get it neutrally buoyant," the chief said.

That much explosive would surely rupture a ship's hull, wouldn't it? We could send our idea back to Australia and let them go over it. This could work.

I needed to go there and survey the area. What type of defensive posture would we find in the harbor? What kind of patrols? Were there any kind of booms? How about lights and sentries?

Williams and Weller listened as I laid out my plan. First, we would send our plan to Australia. At the same time, we'd figure out how to get our hands on the explosives at the Shell compound. Then we'd check out the area to determine specifics for the final plan.

"How do you intend to scout the area?" Weller asked.

I had been thinking about options. Traveling to the city and then taking a canoe around the harbor was one option. The problem was transiting the city. I didn't look remotely like a Malay—or a Jap, for that matter. But there was a better way.

"Why don't we take the patrol boat? Make a night run and check out the harbor."

"I like that idea," Williams said.

I continued, "Once we see what we're up against, some of your guys can watch how the Japs patrol the place. Could be they aren't doing much at all."

Weller nodded. "Okay. We'll need to work on the boat so the Japs don't recognize it. But a little paint should be all we need."

"We'll need to confirm that your man is still in place at Shell," I said.

"I'll send Tirra down to find out."

I liked Weller. He was a man who was used to getting things done. This whole lash-up was only possible because he'd decided to take on the Japs all by himself. Now we would use that to do some real damage.

The message to Australia laying out our technical questions took two separate transmissions. I was surprised that all we got back from them for the next three days was a single acknowledgement.

Tirra left the next morning with two more of Weller's men. They would get word back to us as soon as they could. The explosives would be the real key. Without dynamite we'd be out of business.

Williams never stopped asking questions as we put our plan together. I was damned glad he did, as I hadn't thought about many things that he focused on right away.

"Aliea returned to the same major's house in Balikpapan." I went on explain to Williams the story of Maksi's sister and the death of Balle. "The major is the number two officer in the Japanese Port Authority. I don't know how we can use that, but she wants revenge on the Japanese for driving her and her boy into the jungle."

"Unless she speaks Japanese, I'm not sure how much she could help us. We need patrol schedules, passwords, loading schedules, things like that. I can't think that a Jap senior officer would keep those at home."

He did make sense. To say nothing of the fact that she wasn't a trained operative. Better to forget the whole thing, I thought.

"But if we wanted to kidnap the son of a bitch, she could be the key," he said, his tone totally serious.

This was rapidly getting out of control. Kidnap a Jap officer in the middle of an occupied city? To what end?

"Kidnap him?" I asked.

He continued, his voice earnest, "You said we need patrol schedules, passwords, all those things that the number two guy must know."

This was crazy.

"Even if we could kidnap this major, how do we interrogate him?"

Williams flashed that grin that was now starting to irritate the hell out of me.

"McGowan speaks pretty good Japanese. He sailed out of Yokohama for a long time back in the early thirties. We turn the crazy Irishman loose on him."

A good commander explores all options, I told myself. Check out the harbor, then build the mine, grab the major, find out what we need to know and then we'd be ready to attack. Just act like you do this every day.

Then the message came in from Coyne.

"Recommend 5-gallon metal petrol can, 20 sticks of dynamite, single blasting cap with local timer. Place mines at least two feet underwater. Explosion should rupture hull and commence flooding. Three mines one hundred feet apart most desirable."

As an electrical engineer, I had no idea what was needed to do the job. I had assumed that a 55-gallon drum full of dynamite would do the job, knowing it was going to be a bitch to handle. But a five-gallon jerry can would be a piece of cake. The plan was starting to look promising. But how in the hell do we attach the mines to the hull?

Could we find something in the support yard to use? The real limpet mines were attached magnetically to the hull. But how do we get our hands on magnets that would do the job? It took me a few minutes, but then it hit me. Audio speakers have magnets, good-sized magnets if the speaker was big enough. We'd just have to find some in Balikpapan.

"Speakers?"

"Yeah, where can we get our hands on big audio speakers? We can use the magnets from inside to stick the mines to the Jap tanker's hull."

Weller looked at me with a quizzical look, then smiled.

"If I remember right, there are outdoor speakers around the Shell yard. Does it matter what kind of speaker?"

"Bigger is better," I said.

The "Radio Gang" now was made up of Bever and Smith full-time with Springer filling in when needed. I laid out our plan and asked them to get the magnets out of whatever came back from Balikpapan. In the meantime our regular transmissions would continue to Australia. The new system, using the native intelligence, freed up the team from harbor watch and kept us together. That was a good thing.

After two days of getting the boat ready, I felt confident that we'd covered up the previous markings to the point that, in the dark of the harbor, no one would suspect us. What we didn't know was if the other Jap patrol boats used any kind of recognition code. There was only one way we were going to find that out.

"How do we get our eyes on the Jap major's house?" Williams asked.

"This major's house is in the northern part of the city, actually near where I went to school."

A map of the town and harbor lay on the table in front of the group. I went over the area where the Japanese major lived from my memories of growing up. The actual house was only two roads over from our old house. Maksi confirmed the location, and added current information on the area.

"Most of the traffic uses the Balikpapan-Samarinda Road. Right here the road becomes Soekarno Hatta," she said. "The house is right here on Klamono in what was one of the most exclusive areas before the war. A large lawn surrounds the house, but there's no fence or gate. My sister said the major is sometime accompanied home by an assistant. There are also two armed soldiers at the house at all times, but she told me they don't have regular patrols."

Moon looked up from the map.

"We could probably grab this Nip major, but as soon as we do, all hell will break out. Could queer the whole harbor thing."

He was right. Do we run south with the boat and just take our chances on not being challenged? And if we are challenged, as soon as the Japs figure out something's not right, they'll tighten up their defenses. We lose either way.

Over the next hour, we hammered out our final plan. The major was safe, nothing wasted there. Instead, we would run the patrol boat south at night and launch a native outrigger canoe that Finley would take into the harbor, disguised as a fisherman. As much as I knew I should go, it made sense to send a Malay who looked the part and could speak the language better than I could.

The boat that Weller showed us was a lot like the wooden canoes that we'd used from the tribe. About fourteen feet long, it had a small mast and a slatted wood shelter in the bow. An outrigger extended six feet to one side, providing the slim hull with stability. Weller said it was the type used by the local fishermen. The Japs allowed fishermen to go out each day, much like they had always done, but the Japs also ran patrols regularly. I hoped one more fishing boat would draw little notice. Once Finley had a chance to reconnoiter the pier where the tankers loaded, he'd put back out to sea for the pickup.

Chief Pickett was concerned that it would be difficult if not impossible for Finley to find the boat in the darkness.

"That low on the water, no point of reference to steer by, damned hard to make a rendezvous."

Mullen rubbed his jaw and said, "We show a light, and he just steers for the boat."

"Along with any Jap boats that happen to see the signal," Williams said.

They were all right. I knew how hard small boat navigation was, particularly at night. But we'd have to do the same thing when we attacked the tanker."

"We reverse the lights," I said. "Let him flash the signal and we go to him."

The looks from around the table told me we had a plan.

Two hours prior to sunset, Weller pushed the throttles forward and the former Japanese patrol boat P-46, now called "the 46 boat" by everyone, headed out into the river delta enroute to the open ocean at about ten knots. Attached with a length of manila line, the canoe trailed in the wake. Williams had remained behind with the radio team and Mullen, but sent McGowan in case we needed someone who could speak Japanese. I wanted Pickett and Springer along, knowing there's no substitute for real experience on the water. Hoss stood on the port side, his Wilson cradled in his arms.

Standing at the stern, I watched two of the native crewmen organizing the lines and flaking them down as the boat accelerated. Despite the heat, the wind off the water provided a welcome relief.

McGowan walked back, his natural balance as a seaman evident. The older man leaned back against the transom, and we both watched as Weller turned slightly starboard.

"When was the last time you saw Ireland?" I asked McGowan and we felt the swell of the ocean begin to move the patrol boat.

He laughed.

"Winter of '21, it was. Had a bit of a disagreement with the authorities. Seems the Black and Tans finally got tired of some of us."

I could hear the irony in his voice.

"That was the end of the Irish revolt, right?"

"That was when the goddamned British finally went back where they came from and left Ireland to the Irish."

There was a hardness to his voice that I'd not heard before. It seemed that our vagabond mariner had some secrets from a former life.

"You haven't been back since?"

He didn't look at me, his gaze taking in the sunset.

"Nothing to go back to."

I was glad Weller knew these waters and seemed comfortable as the day faded into darkness. His focus was on the compass just forward of the wheel. Hoss related to me that he and Weller had run three different boats up and down this coast.

"Remind you of the old days?

Hoss was sitting inside the small cabin door, eating a rice ball.

"It does," he said. "But we'd have had better food, that's for sure."

Weller had added to our food supply with the augmentation of tinned corned beef and tuna. His people stole regularly from local suppliers including the Japanese supply depot. The Japs had supplied canned crab, which was a pleasant addition to our regular rice.

"Are you ready to build some mines when we get back?" I asked him as I grabbed one of the rice balls.

Hoss nodded, his manner subdued.

"We'll get them put together, just as long as they bring what I asked for."

Weller's men Tirra and Anali were on their way to Balikpapan to hopefully get their hands on dynamite, blasting caps and speakers. At that point it would be up to Hoss to build a homemade mine. It seemed like a crazy way to have to fight a war, but I remembered what they preached at Quantico: adapt and get the job done. I think Major Hersch would give me a thumbs up on this one.

"I've been thinking about the timer," I said.

Right then, Weller pulled the throttles to idle. I move up to the wheel as he climbed up on the starboard gunwale.

"Listen," he said.

I heard something in the darkness, a pulsating noise, almost a low roar.

Weller jumped down to the wheel, jamming the throttles full ahead and spinning the wheel hard right. The roar was growing and off the port side I saw a huge bow wave and the bow of a warship cutting through the night. The rush of water blended with the now full-throated roar of the Jap destroyer that steamed past us no more than fifty yards abeam.

The throttles came back to idle as we all watched transfixed as the 300 feet of steel slashed past us, headed north. There was nothing to do but wait and see if we'd been spotted.

One minute, then two minutes passed, with nothing said by any man on deck. The ship continued north, no lights showing. The roar of her engines finally faded into the distance.

"Christ."

After a quiet two minutes, Weller advanced the throttles, clearly wanting to open the distance to the Jap warship. Two backfires and the engines died.

"What the hell?" he said, checking the engine gauges with a flashlight.

"Any idea?" I asked.

"I think we may be in deep shit," Weller answered and the tone in is voice told the story.

Several attempts to turn over the engine were fruitless and he switched the ignition off, leaning against the bulkhead.

No one spoke. With the sun coming up in several hours, we would be at the mercy of any Jap unit that spotted us. I found myself grasping for options and realized there weren't any. I had screwed up by not planning for something like this.

"Romeo, you've spent enough time hanging around the engine room, go take a look at the engine," I heard Pickett say.

Springer moved to the hatch.

"Can do, chief."

In less than twenty minutes, the young sailor was back out of the engine room.

"Give it a shot, Mr. Weller," he said, a dirty rag hanging from his hand.

Moving quickly to the wheel, Weller hit the ignition switch and the engine coughed once and then caught. What a beautiful sound.

"What'd ya find?" Pickett asked.

Springer grinned.

"Clogged fuel filter. No problem, but someone needs to take better care of that engine."

I think Weller just found his new chief engineer.

Clad in a pair of faded khaki shorts, a dirty t-shirt and no shoes, Finley set off in the small canoe toward the distant lights of Balikpapan. In the early morning hour, the harbor area was clearly visible, although the sea had become choppy in the hours since our encounter with the Jap destroyer. I didn't envy Finley the long pull into the harbor, but a flood tide would help him on the trip. My estimate, backed up by Weller, was that it would take about ninety minutes to paddle in, thirty minutes to check out the pier area and two hours back out to the pickup area. My Hamilton wrist watch showed 0110 as he paddled away into the darkness.

With no way on, the boat now wallowed in the waves as we all settled in for a long wait.

"What about the timer?" Hoss asked, breaking me out of my mental calculation of when we might make it back north into the inlet and safety.

For a moment, I was confused and then remembered my earlier comment.

"I've been trying to remember some things from school. What we need is a power source for the blasting cap. That should be easy using two or three flashlight batteries taped together in series. I suspect all we'd need for a current might be one amp or so and those batteries should produce two or three times that. We use the movement from a clock to control the timing and hook the leads to connect when the hands move the correct distance. We tape it all together, slip it into the gas can and seal it so it's watertight. Bingo, one mine ready to go."

"Sounds like it should work. Where do we get the clock workings?"

I laughed.

"Weller. Just like everything else."

"The pier is lit damned well if you ask me," Finley said as soon as we pulled him into the boat. After taking a swig on a bottle of Lihing, he went on, "But the hull of the ship blocks the light, so it won't be hard to get close, as long as there ain't a moon."

He took another long pull on the bottle.

"Pretty quiet, too. Didn't see much happening on the ship or the pier. Must not be a night shift."

I asked, "No Jap patrol that you could see, on water or on the pier?"

He shook his head.

A huge weight was off my shoulders with Finley back in the boat. I'd begun to have second thoughts until we saw the light. He'd started signaling twenty minutes before we expected it, but Weller had the boat in a good spot and we had him back aboard within ten minutes of spotting the flashes.

Now we had to get serious about constructing our version of Limpet mines. Wait a minute, I thought. Let the Brits have their name, we'd call our mines Lihings.

CHAPTER SEVENTEEN

Weller's Camp
Telukladang Peninsula
25 October 1942

Securing the boat just as the sun was coming up, I was ready to get some food and see if the men were back from down south. If they'd gotten their hands on the material we needed, this whole crazy plan might actually work. Once we finished putting the camouflage netting over the boat, we started single file on the hike to the camp. Stretching my legs felt good after the time in the boat and the early morning cool was a blessing. Hoss was leading the column and I brought up the rear. Watching those men walk in silence, I was struck with the dedication of them. Every one of them were going in harm's way by choice and making the best of it. The Japs would never win.

A morning shower added to our good mood. None of us were fans of the torrential downpours, but a shower went a long way to cool us down as the sun began to heat the jungle.

Voices came from ahead and brought the group to a halt. I made my way forward to find McGowan talking with Hoss. The Irishman had a Wilson in his hands and didn't look happy. The rest of the men gathered around to listen.

"The lady's gone," he said.

"What?" Weller asked.

I tried to get my hands around what he had just said, "Gone?"

People started to talk and I held my hands up.

"Shut up and let him talk."

The story quickly came out. One of Weller's younger men had been found with his throat cut. In the process of trying to sort out what had happened, it became clear that two people were missing, Lynda and a man named Alang. The only logical answer was that the man had kidnapped her and was on his way to the Japs. He would probably be able to collect a bounty and ingratiate himself with them. Several of the men had told Williams that they weren't surprised. Alang was a very recent addition to Weller's group and no one knew that much about him.

"We're searching the area from the camp, north to the river. We think he's probably trying to get to Samarinda."

The shower had stopped and water dripping from the foliage was the only sound.

"Okay, let's spread out and work our way back north," I ordered.

"He must be going for the boats," Weller said. "Batara's on guard, but Alang could surprise him."

"Larry, why don't you and Hoss head for the boats right now and make sure that doesn't happen."

"Everyone was going to meet up at the boats anyway," Mullen added, then turned to me. "Bever came down with a bad fever last night, the old witch doctor is watching him, but he's pretty much out of it."

As I worked my way back toward the river, I guessed I was a hundred yards east of the trail. I thought briefly about Dicky, he must be terrified. The best thing I could do for him would be to get his sister back. Working quickly, but as quietly as possible, I moved north, listening for anything in the jungle. I reached the river, surveying the shoreline in both directions – nothing. I heard something to my left and saw Springer emerge from the underbrush. He saw me and shook his head.

Walking down the shoreline to meet Springer I knew it was time to get to the boats and Weller. At least if the boats were safe, Lynda would still be in the area.

We started back toward the boats, still listening for anything.

"I heard the chief call you Romeo. What's that all about?" I asked the young sailor.

"Ah, kinda like a nickname I guess."

"You big with the ladies?"

"No, sir. Well, you know… Romeo is short for Romeo Foxtrot."

I recognized the phonetic pronunciation of the letters "R" and "F."

"Romeo Foxtrot?"

Springer paused as if he was considering what to say.

"Well, yes sir. Some of the guys call me Rat Fink, just a joke I guess. The chief just uses Romeo."

Probably a good story behind that one, but this was not the time to go into it.

There were twenty men gathered at the boat stash when Springer and I showed up. Williams was already there, talking to Weller. I joined them and caught the gist of what was going on. Weller's man Batara hadn't heard or seen anything. All of the boats were right where they were supposed to be.

"Are there other boats he could use?" I asked. It made sense to me that the only way he could expect to make it to Samarinda was by water.

"Hard to say," Weller said. "There are places all along the river you could stash a boat. But maybe he's still around here."

"He could be laying low until dark," Williams offered. "That's damn sure what I'd do."

He was right. If Alang could get across the river, he'd be that much closer to the Japs.

"We'd better be heading back to camp," Weller said, picking up his rifle. "It's been a damned long time since any of us slept. We can't do anything here. Batara knows what's going on and I'll send a couple of men back to stand guard with him."

"Let's go," Williams said.

"I'm gonna stay close to the river," I said. Heading back to the camp would be like abandoning Lynda. I couldn't do that.

He turned to face me.

"You've been up for twenty-four hours, lieutenant. You can't do anything more. This jungle is too goddamned big, that's just the way it is."

"I'm not going back to camp."

Williams face hardened.

"Do you want me to make that an order?"

Marines are lock-wired to follow orders. That's what we learned from day one at Quantico. But not this time.

"With all due respect, commander. I'm not going back to camp. I'll grab a quick nap right here then resume searching."

I hadn't told him to shove it, but he knew what I meant.

He nodded.

"We've been tiptoeing around who is actually running things around here. It seems that we've agreed on most things anyway, so it didn't matter. I am simply taking my authority from seniority. But that being said, you are still in charge of your men, and that's the way it has to be. I will continue to advise you on everything I can that might help you. Agreed?"

"Yes, sir, thanks."

He handed me the Wilson he was carrying.

"I'll leave McGowan here to cover your back. And Rob, watch your ass, your people need you alive."

LCDR Dave Williams smiled and strode off.

"Robby, me boy. Your time's up, let's move."

Through a fog I remembered telling McGowan to "wake me up in one hour." Checking my watch, I saw that the Irishman could tell time.

I sat up and saw that he had a battered metal cup in his hand, steam rising from it.

"Here, Batara made this. Not bad."

Rubbing my eyes, I took the cup and savored the hot steam. Despite the already sticky heat, it seemed to clear my head.

"If you were this asshole, where would you go?" I asked.

"I've been thinking on that very subject. Weller and his crew have spent most of their time east of where we sit right now. If this Alang stashed a boat it could very well be west of here."

McGowan had a point. And I didn't have any better ideas.

"I say we start up the river, sticking as close to the bank as we can. We'll be able see anyone trying to move down river. If he hid a boat, we might find it."

For a seaman, McGowan had a good grasp of the land. But then I remembered he'd been in the Irish Rebellion. I wonder how Borneo compared to Ireland?

An hour later I was thinking this was a bad idea. The tangle of vines, roots and branches made for slow going. Besides the heat and bugs, it was hard to keep the noise down. I tried as hard as I could to listen for anything happening in front of us. Would this guy still be trying to make the river or had he holed up? The whole time I kept wondering if what we were doing was a complete waste of time. Might Lynda already be miles away in a different direction? But I kept remembering what I learned at Quantico. Take all the information you know, add your best estimate of the unknowns, then press on. Until we found something that contradicted our conclusion, we would do just that.

Two more hours and we'd found, seen or heard nothing. Now I had to force myself to realize our conclusion was likely wrong. I was not going to find Lynda and she might very well be captured or dead.

"I think this is a waste of time," I told McGowan, who had just climbed over a fallen tree and slipped in the mud, falling alongside me. I helped him to his feet and he wiped mud off his face.

"You might be right. This far west makes no sense, unless this fellow wants to head farther into the jungle."

McGowan was right. Now we had a five-hour trek to get back to camp. Food and sleep were now more than just a desire, they were requirements and I needed to check on Bever.

Dave Williams, as I would have expected, had taken charge back at camp, even though it was really Weller's camp. He'd sent Moon and Hoss south to see if they could find any signs of Lynda. Weller added one of his men, who was known for his ability to track. By the time McGowan and I got back, those three had returned.

"It looks like this Alang did head south. Must be trying to make Balikpapan," Williams said.

That could only mean one thing, the son of a bitch was going to turn her into the Japs.

"We need to go after them, now," I said. "Before they make it to the city."

Weller had joined us, and said, "Damned near impossible at this point. He's too far south."

"His men got back this morning. They brought back everything we need to make the mines," Williams said. "Time to get them put together."

"The mines can wait. I'm going after her."

I suppose operating on my own had changed how I looked at things. Telling a Navy commander "no" was something I could have never imagined a year ago. Now I didn't care.

"Mr. Parker, with me, if you please."

Williams turned on his heel and headed up the trail. I followed, my Marine training kicking in.

Thirty yards down the trail, he stopped and turned.

"I gather from your remark that you feel the young woman is more important than your mission. Is that right, lieutenant?"

"That's not what I said, sir, but I can't let the Japs get her back."

"Your own men told you going after her would make no difference. Did it dawn on you that she knows what we've planned? If the Japs get that information out of her, we're done for. To say nothing of the future of this camp and Weller's men. Are you willing to put the welfare of one person ahead of your men and the mission?"

The reality hit me like a brick. I knew what the right answer was, what a Marine officer would do, but I couldn't make myself say it. Sacrificing people was not the American way.

"We can do both, sir," I said with conviction, knowing I had no idea how.

"We're short on people, supplies and time. Putting any one of those toward helping the girl…"

"Lynda. Her name is Lynda Noble," I interrupted.

He looked more exasperated than angry and said, "Splitting your forces is almost always the path to failure. Didn't they teach you that at Quantico?"

"They taught me that Marines don't abandon anyone, and by God I don't intend to start now, sir." My emphasis on "sir" was probably more exaggerated than I intended.

His eyes were drilling into me, but I was going to stand my ground, military discipline and my career be damned. He could court martial me if we ever get out of here and I didn't give a tinker's damn. I turned and walked away from him.

Amulong squatted next to Bever, who lay on his raised sleeping platform. Sweat covered the young man's flushed face. The old man turned and looked at me, his eyes sad. If Lynda was here I might be able to ask her for some advice, but I was on my own.

I asked him in Malay, "How is he?"

"A bad fever since last night."

He turned back to the young Australian and wiped his face off with a piece of tattered brown cotton cloth.

Leaning past the headman, I shook Bever gently.

"How're you doing, Jon?"

His eyes opened up, fluttered then focused on me.

"Alright…"

"Amulong will take good care of you, just take it easy for now."

What a crock of shit I told myself. This kid is deathly ill and we can't do a damn thing to help him.

I sat next to my hut, thinking about Bever and going over my other options, which were severely limited. Williams' comments about the Japs getting information out of Lynda struck home. The problem being that he was right. She knew we were going to attack the harbor with mines. While she didn't know the details, that in and of itself was enough to doom the mission to failure. And I know that anyone could be made to talk—particularly by the Japs.

Looking up, I saw Moon and Hoss coming up the path with Maksi.

"We've been talking," Moon said, sitting down on the ground next to me. Hoss and Maksi also sat down, but seemed to be looking at Moon to continue.

"Maksi said that she knows where the Japs have their military police headquarters. She used to go right by it on her way to the fish market. It makes sense that if Alang was going to turn her over, that's where the two of them would end up."

That might be the case, but what the hell good does that do us? Knowing where the Kempietai had their headquarters and getting someone out of there were two very different things.

"What are you thinking?" I asked. Increasingly I was learning to listen first before going off half-cocked.

Hoss explained, "Well, it's just possible this bloke ain't gonna walk up to the main gate with a white woman and see what they do. Wouldn't you think he'd have someone as a go between or something like that?"

That made sense. He would surely want to get some kind of assurance that he'd be rewarded, or at a minimum not be arrested himself. Setting that up might take time. Time that might allow us to catch him.

"What are you thinking?" I asked, knowing what their answer would be.

"We get the hell down there and set up a watch on the place. If we can intercept this guy, we might get Miss Noble back."

It might be our only chance. Once she was behind their walls or bars, getting her out would likely be impossible."

"Bever's sick as hell," I said, "Find the chief and ask him to come see me."

Weller and Williams both agreed that the plan to intercept Alang was worth trying. My concession was that I would stay in camp making preparations for the raid. Finley volunteered to go along with Tirra and Maksi. Weller assured me that Tirra could be counted on to do whatever was needed. I'd already seen Finley in action and had no doubts about him. As much as I wanted to go, it made no sense for me to try and disguise myself as a local. At six-foot-two, I didn't fit the profile of your average Malay. I did have dark hair, but my pale complexion certainly wouldn't blend in.

"You think this'll work?" I asked Maksi, feeling like we were grasping at straws.

She smiled. The two men were packed and ready to shove off.

"We can only try, Ajib."

And, as had been my experience growing up, she was right.

I saw Pickett walking up the trail toward me.

"Chief, Bever's not getting any better. Amulong is with him, but I think one of us should be there. I need to get busy on the explosives."

The chief understood and nodded.

Turning to Maksi I put my arms around her, hugging her with all of the love of a son.

"Thank you for doing this," I said quietly so only we could hear.

She leaned back, smiling at me and said, "You will marry Miss Lynda Noble."

Maksi kissed me on the cheek and turned to join the others. She kissed me on the cheek and smiled again.

Hoss had been able to get eighteen sticks of dynamite into the five-gallon gasoline cans and still leave room for a fuse. The screw on metal caps would make the contraption waterproof. Now we had to build a timer and detonator that would work.

Four alarm clocks, Dutch-made, had been found in Balikpapan. In short order we had the cases open and mechanisms laid bare. A spring provided the energy for the clock's motion and we fastened each movement to a small, rectangular piece of wood. It seemed to me that using the hour hand as the initiator made the most sense. That would give us more time after setting the timer to plant the mine and then get away. The question was how long to make the delay?

Hoss and I taped four flashlight batteries together as an experiment to see if they provided enough power to fire the blasting cap. The label on the cap noted that it would take ½ amp to fire. My calculation was that three batteries would do the job, but I wanted some margin for error in case any of the batteries weren't as strong.

A short walk outside camp took us to an open area. I used the extra clock mechanism to work out our design, placing wired contacts on both the hour hand and the wooden board. Setting it for about a fifteen-minute delay, we laid the detonator on the ground and retired to a safe distance.

We sat down on a log to wait.

"Is that rash getting any better?" I asked, having seen the red patches on Hoss's arms earlier.

"Bout the same. It's all right."

I glanced down and saw small gnats circling the moist inflamed skin on his forearms. Christ. All of us had been accumulating a disgusting assortment of rashes, bites and sores, but the combination of our own medicines and Amulong's ministrations had kept things bearable. Sometimes it seemed to me that westerners had no business trying to live in these jungles. We just weren't made for it.

The sharp report of the cap firing cracked through the air, flushing several birds, that squawked shrilly as they flew away from our testing area. Bingo, the design worked for timing and the power was sufficient to fire the blasting cap.

Does it make any difference if the tanker is full or empty? As I thought about the mission, it hit me that there might be a big factor on the effect of our mines if the ship was full of oil or empty. I knew that gasoline fumes could be very explosive, but I guessed that crude oil or diesel might not be the same. I needed to get more intelligence on what our target ship was actually carrying. Time to contact Coyne.

"......any information on cargos being loaded at Balikpapan. Any type more desirable for attack?"

Tirra had also returned with a dozen magnets stolen from the speakers that surrounded the perimeter of the Shell laydown area. They each were four inches in diameter and were remarkably powerful when latched on to the metal gasoline cans. As long as there wasn't too much build-up of marine growth or rust on the hull, we shouldn't have any problems securing the mines to the target.

Australia came through quickly with an answer to my question and a reason to be more positive.

".....Pandasari Refinery primary product aviation gasoline. Expect any target will be carrying very flammable cargo......."

Now it was time to set the plans in motion for the attack, but my thoughts kept returning to Lynda. If Finley and Tirra couldn't get her and we attacked the harbor, would she be the target of a Japanese reprisal? Coyne had told me about the Japs killing dozens of Dutch soldiers and civilians as a reprisal for the destruction of petroleum facilities during the invasion. The thought made me sick. I could be the cause of her torture or death. Would the damage be worth it? How does anyone measure something like that? It certainly wasn't the subject of any lectures at Quantico. According to the manual, war is very straightforward. You have an objective and allocated assets to be used for attaining it. No one ever talked about what costs were acceptable. I guess that was what they called war's gray area.

CHAPTER EIGHTEEN

Weller's Camp
Telukladang Peninsula
27 October 1942

Private Jon Bever died four days after coming down with a fever not even the locals could identify. He'd become delirious and then unconscious in quick succession, the end coming after a series of violent convulsions. We sat with him and watched helplessly. Just as the Australian doctor had told me, the jungle will take casualties.

Everyone was affected, but it seemed to hit Hoss harder than most. I remembered how the two of them had hit it off when Hoss first joined the team. Was he thinking about losing a comrade or did his thoughts move back to losing his son? The cruel reality of the jungle required that we bury him quickly. Amulong suggested a spot where it proved easy to dig a very deep grave. That would keep the jungle animals deterred from digging for the body. Weller provided a canvas tarp we used as a shroud.

All of us helped dig the grave, it was hard work in the heat. Using ropes, we lowered the private's body into the grave.

I suddenly realized that I didn't know if we should say some words now or fill in the grave first. Then I knew it really didn't matter.

Kneeling down on one knee I looked around the group and one by one they followed my example. Now I was in real trouble.

"We are here to say farewell to our comrade. He died a long way from home, but he didn't die alone. From day one, he's been a member of this team and did everything that was expected of him. None of us know how long we have. By its very nature, war makes that even more impossible. But I know we'll all remember Jon Bever as long as we live. Does anyone want to say anything?"

Hoss said quietly, "A good man."

"Aye," Moon echoed.

An hour later, we loaded the mines aboard the 46 boat. It seemed like a true naval operation with Williams supervising and Pickett barking out appropriate orders as the lethal cargo was stowed aboard. The plan was to tow three of our modified outrigger canoes behind the patrol boat. Springer stood in knee-deep water directing the men holding the small boats in place.

Williams looked like John Wayne. His khaki trousers were cut off into shorts, a crusty set of Navy wings were pinned to his worn khaki shirt and he had a ball cap pulled down tight on his head. A holstered .45 hung from a web belt that had seen better days.

"The mines are secured for sea, lieutenant," Pickett said. He lit a fragrant local cigarette and stood in the sand as the rest of our team assembled. Williams had deferred to me on who would man the canoes for the attack. He'd remain in the 46 boat with Weller and Smith, waiting to pick us up. Weller mounted the Jap machine gun on the stern and Smitty was a trained gunner. I wanted Pickett to remain behind to keep an eye on Weller's people and the camp. He wasn't happy about it, but chiefs understand how to follow orders.

I was going in the lead boat with Hoss as my second. I wanted Mullen and Abernathy as leads in the other boats. Both were solid and I could count on them to press the attack. I put McGowan behind Mullen, both were tough nuts, but they seemed to respect each other. Abernathy was going to be supported by Springer. I knew Springer was young, but he seemed unflappable. If Finley had been back I would have put him with Abernathy, but nothing had been heard from them. Those decisions, which I thought we thought out so well, proved to be something that would haunt me through the years.

A commotion pulled me from my very focused military thoughts, ones that any good commander would be reviewing as a mission was getting ready to push off. Then I heard her voice.

Turning, I saw Lynda running down the beach toward me. The sun was just beginning to dip below the mountains and the twilight made the scene almost like a dream. She was smiling, her arms outstretched. Everything around me faded into the background as I took her in my arms and lifted her off her feet.

There were no words that either of us might say. Just feeling her next to me and safe. Perhaps I had already begun to feel I had lost her forever, her fate sealed by the Japs and the cold finality of war. Now we had each other again and any pretense we had of being anything other than lovers faded away.

We kissed and then looked at each other.

"I was afraid I'd lost you," I said.

"No," she said and put her arms back around me in a fierce hug.

I looked around at the group, who stood self-consciously in the semidarkness.

"Mr. Parker, we need to shove off," I heard Commander Williams call from the boat.

He was right, darkness was coming fast and we needed to start our transit if we hoped to make the round trip by dawn.

"Lynda, I have to go."

She looked up at me, her arms still loosely around my waist.

"Rob, I… It's Maksi. I'm so sorry."

"What?"

"There was shooting. She was hit and badly wounded."

My stomach turned.

Lynda continued quietly, "We got away, Finley and Tirra carried her to where I could tend her wounds. Rob, there was nothing that I could do."

"Mr. Parker, anytime you're ready," Williams called across the water.

I stood there frozen, the horror of what had happened overwhelming me. Christ, how could this happen?

"Come on, let's get this show on the road."

"I have to go," I said, the military discipline kicking in.

"To attack the ship?" she asked, her arms tightening around me.

I nodded.

"I'll be waiting here. Come back to me."

"Dicky needs you," I said. "I'll see you in the morning."

I kissed her and said, "I love you. Don't forget that," as I pulled away.

During the trip south, everyone was quiet, spending time with their own thoughts and fears. Larry Weller stayed at the helm with Williams next to him for the entire trip. Scattered clouds hid a partial moon, allowing a horizon to stretch out in front of us. A light wind produced a chop on the water, making it a good night for what we were trying to do.

Finding a seat in the stern, I sat back against the bulkhead. My thoughts should have been on the mission, but I kept thinking about Maksi and Lynda. Until now I'd been focused on this mission, not thinking of the danger. My mindset since Quantico had been to get the job done, period. I'd thought about dying and had accepted it as a possibility, but it was something that had to be put in a box and not worried about. Losing those close to me, like Maksi, was different, though. That wasn't something that had occurred to me. Men get killed on missions, not gentle women like her. It might have been the wind, but my eyes were watering and I felt that I had failed my oldest friend. I kept telling myself that people die in wars, but it didn't help. I just had to deal with it and get this job done. But I knew that as long as I might live, Maksi's death would hurt. God damn the Japs.

An hour from Balikpapan, I got the three boat crews together and went over the procedures for the attack one more time. I would set the fuse timers for three hours just prior to loading the mines. We would stick together until we had a visual confirmation of the target and then separate. Mullen's boat would row toward the after part of the tanker and place their mine about a hundred feet forward of the stern. Hoss and I would aim for directly amidships while Abernathy would try for a spot a hundred feet back from the bow. Once our mines were attached, we would reverse track and head back out toward the patrol boat. After thirty minutes of rowing, flashlights would come on with two flashes every thirty seconds. Williams and Weller would find us, bring us aboard and abandon the canoes. Getting rid of the small boats would allow us to head north at twenty knots and expedite getting back before the sun came up. If the attack was successful, the Japs would be sending out boats and aircraft to find the attackers. Best to be long gone by then.

We'd already agreed that each man would carry his Webley and the second man would have a Wilson for more firepower. Flashlights were fastened to each man's gear for signaling. As an afterthought, I made sure Abernathy, Moon and myself each had a Mills hand grenade. One never knew when a grenade might come in handy.

The Corps had drilled into me that you had to think of contingencies. As someone once said, "no plan survives first contact with the enemy," or something like that.

"Okay, you all know the plan. But what if the shit hits the fan?" I had also learned that you can't plan for every little thing that could go wrong, but you could lay out some basic rules for everyone to follow. At least everyone would know what people were trying to do.

"And it most likely will," Moon said, but he grinned.

"Right," I agreed. "We'll stick together as long as possible, but once we split up. Everyone is on their own. Plant your mine, then head back to the rendezvous. Don't worry about anyone else."

"What happens if the boat doesn't show or if we can't find it?" McGowan asked.

"Good question. Weller could run into the Japs, or you could just get lost. The key is sunrise. The boat needs to be a long way away from here by the time the sun comes up. If you're still on a canoe, you need to act like a fisherman and work your way north along the coast. The boat, if it's still operational, will come back along the coast each night looking for stragglers. Keep heading north and go ashore if you can during the day. But stay away from people."

No one brought up being captured, but everyone accepted that it was a death sentence. The best the rest of us could do, if that happened, was to move the camp farther inland and lay low.

The glow of lights from the harbor was the first indication that we were approaching our launch point. Weller said he thought we were about two miles from the dock.

With the boat idling, we pulled the canoes up to the side. Moon went over the side and held the boat steady as we lowered the mine down to the center of the boat. The whole contraption weighed in at twenty pounds, and the square shape of the gasoline container wedged nicely in the bottom of the canoe.

"Off we go," McGowan said as he climbed down behind their mine, a Wilson over his shoulder.

Moon pulled away to allow the next canoe alongside.

As I climbed down into the boat, it seemed like a completely natural thing to do. Quickly we loaded our mine and Hoss climbed aboard.

"Let's go," I said and we moved toward where Moon was holding his boat in place against the waves.

The third outrigger was loaded and Abernathy joined us.

Our boat took the lead and I began to stroke the bow toward the lights in the distance. There was nothing to do now but paddle and watch as the lights became more distinct.

Finley had given us a good brief on what to expect and our key navigation point was a tall light post that stood at the end of the main pier, much higher than the regular pier lights. He'd said the light was high enough up, that it was clearly visible above the hull of the ship moored pier side until you got close to the hull. Fifteen minutes after leaving the patrol boat, I thought I saw the navigation light through the mist. It was difficult to make out for sure. The lights of the pier and those aboard the ship offered a confusing maze when viewed from a small boat at sea level.

The wind remained light, but I realized that a current must be setting us to the north. Rather than coming at the ship from her beam, we were being pushed to a bow on approach.

"We're coming left," I told Hoss, and began to pull hard on the right side of the canoe. Ahead, I was able to see there were some perimeter lights on the outboard lifelines of the ship's main deck. Those weren't there when Finley checked out the last tanker. The lights threw a thin illumination on the water around the ship. Now it was even more important to move our group south, abeam the ship, before we turned in for the attack.

"Look," Hoss called quietly as our little flotilla pushed out into the dark water toward the center of the shipping channel.

Ahead, I saw the lights of a boat moving toward us. I guessed the boat was making five knots and heading to our right. A small searchlight pierced the darkness and illuminated the water to our right. Nothing had ever been said by the dock workers about harbor patrols and Finley hadn't seen one. This was going bad fast.

"Left and pull hard!" I yelled back to Hoss. Our only chance was to escape into the darkness to our left and away from the tanker. Pulling with everything I had in me, I hoped each of the boats had figured out what I was doing and followed. The darkness on our bow was only broken by lights on the far shoreline. No fishing boats, patrol boats or anchored ships. This might be the way after all.

After five minutes of hard paddling, I stopped, my chest heaving and arms aching. Looking behind us I saw the other two boats not more than twenty yards away. As the canoe rocked in the waves, I felt the sweat dripping off my nose and my heart rate slowing. Mullen pulled up next to us first, followed by Abernathy a minute later.

"Everyone okay?" I asked.

I took the lack of responses as a positive, figuring they were all trying to catch their breaths too. Our panicked flight had actually set us up at a decent approach angle to the tanker, but now we must be at least two miles away. The other problem was that we'd lost thirty minutes, which cut back our margin of darkness to say nothing of the fuses ticking away on our improvised explosives I checked my watch quickly and saw the mines would detonate in an hour and forty-five minutes, give or take.

Pulling toward the ship I had a chance to get a good look at her. About five hundred feet long, she had a raised superstructure on her stern and amidships. The hull was dark, probably black, but I couldn't tell for sure in the dim light. Lights shown on the deck and from several portholes. I knew that how she rode in the water would tell the story of her cargo. It seemed that she wasn't fully loaded, as there was some free board showing. My guess was that she was three quarters full and still taking on fuel.

At what looked like a half a mile, I stopped paddling and waited for the other two boats to pull alongside.

"We split up here," I said, trying to think of something inspiring but nothing came to mind. "Everyone doing okay?"

I saw Moon, who had pulled up on our left side, nod. Abernathy gave me a thumbs up from the right.

"Right, then. Off you go. Place your mines and get the hell back to the boat." I bent to paddle, then as an afterthought said, "Good luck."

For the next fifteen minutes, my focus was on the center of the hull. We were being set left, so our paddling had to correct our track. As we closed to two hundred yards, I could hear machinery over the waves and the wind. Must've been be the pumps loading the fuel. Now the hull began to loom overhead, just as we moved from relative darkness into the area lit by the perimeter lights. The natural, weathered wood of the boats didn't stand out and we both were wearing khaki, which didn't hurt.

Two minutes of paddling carried us past the lights until we bumped up against the hull. Shoving with the paddle, I tried to fend us off as the boat rocked and banged into the steel. Hoss did the same as our left side banged into the ship. Shit, I never thought the waves would move us around like this. The boat was being pushed into the hull and then scraped against it as the waves would lift us up, then slide us away, only to begin the process again as the next wave arrived. How the hell were we going to get the mine out of the boat and attached? I could only hope that the sound of the machinery was masking the sound of our canoe knocking against the hull.

"Look," Hoss said over the sounds of the waves. "A cleat."

He was right. About three feet above our heads there was an indented circle on the hull with a vertical bar from top to bottom. It must be used to tie boats or barges to the ship's side.

The boat was moving several feet up and down as each wave passed and at the top point the cleat was at our shoulder level. Reaching forward in the boat, I grabbed the towline and cut it free with my knife. As we rose, I shoved the rope through the cleat and handed one end to Hoss.

"Hold that," I said, tying my end of the rope to the left side of the outrigger's seat. Hoss immediately realized what he should do and began to use the line to stabilize our boat.

Looking closely at the hull, there was nothing but solid steel. No weeds, barnacles, nothing. It must've been be a new ship. All I knew is that my job would be easier. The paint was in good condition, with only a few streaks of rust visible. Turning, I timed my reach to grasp the mine as the boat bottomed out. Twisting, holding the mine in a death grip, I leaned forward with the magnetic attach points toward the tanker. The boat lurched up, slamming my head into the steel hard as the mine attached to the hull. Releasing the mine, I fell backwards, lights flashing in my vision from the blow. As I landed against the side, the boat lurched and I felt myself falling into the water.

I understood the danger, but it seemed as though my body didn't care. Reaching up, I tried to grasp for the boat, but my hand felt nothing. Thrashing, I fought to get back to the surface and air. Any thoughts about the Japs or the mine were now secondary, I was in trouble. Coughing, I knew that water had gone down the wrong pipe and my chest heaved as I tried to get it up. Then I felt my shirt being grabbed and pulled backwards.

"Sweet Jesus, be quiet!" Hoss hissed at me as he steadied my back against the canoe.

Turning around, I hung onto the side, trying to catch my breath. My head hurt like hell, but my heart rate was slowing and I looked around to see we were ten feet off the side of the ship.

"The mine?" I asked.

"All set. Now let's get out of this light," Hoss said as he began to pull with his paddle. Hanging from the side with one hand, I tried to help with a bastardized side stroke to get us back out into the safety of the darkness.

Cries of alarm came from the stern as we pulled into relative darkness. Looking back, I could see a man running up the starboard side toward the mid-ship superstructure. He was yelling something, and I could see more men coming on deck.

"Here," Hoss said, reaching to help me crawl back into the boat. It took both of us and we damned near capsized the boat twice, but I got back in, tired and cold. Wiping the water out of my eyes, I saw a set of lights of a boat coming toward the tanker. There was no doubt it was a Jap patrol boat, and it was heading straight for the stern of the tanker. A searchlight snapped on, sending a beam of light across the dark water. Right where I guessed my men would be.

According to the plan, our job was now to pull seaward and get ready for Weller to pick us up. Things were rapidly going to hell and there wasn't a damn thing I could do about it.

"Pull!" I yelled back to Hoss.

As I pulled the bow of the outrigger around toward the Jap boat, I heard Hoss from behind me.

"Right."

A hundred yards separated us from the patrol boat, which was now turning away from us moving toward the stern of the tanker.

"I'll paddle......take out that light with the Wilson," I called, between gulps of air. Water slapped the bow, throwing spray over both of us.

The blast of the sub-machine gun next to my ear was deafening. Hoss fired several bursts, but the light still played across the water toward the tanker. Incredibly it appeared the Japs didn't even know we were shooting at them, their course steady toward the tanker.

Another burst from Hoss and the searchlight exploded in a shower of sparks and went dark. The patrol boat swerved hard to the right and began to accelerate, its stern whipping around in a spray of water. Without the light, they'd have trouble seeing us sitting so low in the water, but the bow was now pointed at us.

A bullet whizzed past us destroying my theory they couldn't see us. Single shots meant that the Jap must not have automatic weapons, just rifles. We might have a chance.

The range had closed to fifty yards as I realized all they had to do was run us over and the bow was now aimed directly at us.

"Fire," I yelled at Hoss, dropping my paddle and pulling the Webley out.

Holding the pistol in both hands, I aimed at the front windows of the boat, hoping to hit the driver. Behind me, Hoss continued to first short bursts, which I could see, were hitting the cabin area.

Firing the last two rounds from the Webley, I knew that we were done, the boat drove on, now only twenty yards away. I felt a sharp stab of pain above my left shoulder as more bullets whizzed by us.

Jamming the empty revolver in the holster, I yelled, "Over the side!" at Hoss and rolled left into the dark water. Pulling down with my arms, I tried to put distance and depth away from the boat as it crashed into our canoe. There was something wrong with my left shoulder, but I was still able to move my arm. Swirling water from the wake tossed me around, the sound of the crash mixing with the propeller noise and I bobbed to the surface, my lungs crying for air.

Automatic fire pierced the night as I struggled to catch my breath and stay on the surface. Never a strong swimmer, my boots were making it hard to tread water and I went down with a partial breath. Desperately, I ripped at the laces and yanked both boots off, pulling for the surface. The patrol boat was stopped about twenty yards away. Two men, standing in the rear of the boat, were firing into the darkness off their port side. They had to be shooting at Mullen and McGowan.

Looking around for Hoss, I saw him fifteen feet away, treading water, his head moving left and right.

"Over here," I called and pulled toward him.

"You all right?" I asked as I neared him and saw him nod. He was breathing hard, but showing no signs of panic. It must've been like Gallipoli all over again. Suddenly I knew what I had to do. My pistol was empty and it was impossible to reload in the water, anyways, but I still had the grenade. My shoulder throbbed, the salt water searing the wound.

"Stay here," I ordered Hoss, "I'm gonna try to put a grenade into that boat."

He nodded and said, "Right… Go!"

In less than a minute I was up to the starboard side of the patrol boat, but ominously the firing had stopped. Three feet from the side, I kicked hard to stay on the surface and pulled the grenade out of the lower pocket on my web gear. Taking it in my right hand, I pulled the pin just as I saw a face come over the side of the boat.

Like a shot putter, I heaved the Mills over the gunwale. The Jap raised a pistol, but as he raised it, the reality of what I had thrown in the boat must have dawned on him. He twisted around as I pulled myself down, the safety of the water my only thought.

I later found out that the desperate effort by the Jap to find the grenade and throw it out of the boat almost succeeded. But as the soldier rose up with the bomb in his hand, it detonated, shredding him and killing his companion.

The smell of cordite filled the air and I surfaced, not sure what to expect, but gasping. Smoke drifted over the boat. The engine was still idling, the only noise in the night. Cautiously I circled the craft, coughing several times, but keeping my eyes on the clearing smoke. It had worked. Reaching the stern, I saw two wooden steps leading up to a recessed transom. I slowly pulled myself up, my left shoulder burning like a bitch, and cautiously looked into the rear compartment. The remains of two Japs lay on the deck, damaged enough to assure me they were dead. Climbing over the transom and down into the compartment, I made a quick check of the forward area. These two Japs were it. This boat was like the 46, but smaller, so two crewmembers made sense.

Moving to the stern, I called out.

"Hoss! Hoss, where are you?"

I explored my shoulder and felt a torn flap of meat on top of my collar bone. My stomach rolled and I puked up whatever had been left in it.

"Parker, over here!" came a cry from the bow. I knew that voice. It was Moon.

A coiled line on the forward deck allowed me to throw an attached life ring toward Moon, who I could see twenty feet away.

"Grab the line!" I called. "Are you all right?"

"No," came the reply from the dark water.

Retreating to the stern compartment, I pulled Moon to the side of the boat and around to the stern transom steps. He looked up from the dark water, blood covering the right side of his head.

"Put your feet there," I said grabbing his shirt and pulling him aboard.

"McGowan?" I asked as I knelt down next to him.

Moon was on his hands and knees, catching his breath.

"Dead," he said, adding quietly, "The first Jap burst took half his head off."

I didn't have time to think about that, Hoss was still missing.

"Here, let me see your head."

Blood and matted hair was all I could see at this angle.

"Sit down over here."

Moon laid his head back against the bulkhead and I carefully examined the wound, which revealed itself as a three-inch gash. There was nothing to do for it.

"You'll be okay, I'll try to find a bandage when I can, but we need to find Hoss. Can you get this thing moving?"

He nodded and pulled himself up. Looking around, he stepped over the Jap bodies and turned on his flashlight.

"If it's like the other one."

"I think he's over there," I said, pointing to the area where I thought I'd seen him last. Looking around, I saw a rag laying on the aft ship's bench. I folded it into a square and wedged it in my shirt on top of the wound. That would have to do.

In a minute, Moon had the boat in a left turn at slow speed. I moved up the port side, hanging on to the cabin and went forward on the bow. Kneeling down, I looked left and right for anything. Several pieces of wood floated by the light sent out by my flashlight, likely pieces of our canoe. But where was Hoss? Then I saw him, he was laying with his head up, his arm around a large piece of wood debris. Turning to Moon I signaled him to stop the boat.

"I see him."

The boat was still moving too fast, heading right at Hoss.

"Reverse, turn right," I yelled back to Moon, then I jumped toward Hoss who was now moving down our port side.

By the time I pulled him around to the stern I knew he was injured, but still with us. He grunted in response to my questions and I decided that getting him out of the water was the most important thing at the moment.

"Hoss, here. Hold onto the stern," I said, putting his right hand on the raised lip of the transom. Moving around to his left side, I helped to roll him face down as Moon reached for Hoss's web gear. We managed to push and pull Hoss over and into the boat's open cockpit. I realized that Moon must have thrown the Jap bodies over the side, although the deck was still covered in blood.

Lying face down in that blood, Hoss lay still, the water dripping off his back and legs.

"Let's roll him on his back," I said to Moon.

"We don't have time for that, let's get the hell out of here," he came back, heading for the wheel.

He was right, of course.

I knelt down next to Hoss as the engine kicked into gear.

"Just lay still, we'll get you out of here," I told him, but I saw no response.

The boat accelerated, and Moon turned right toward the open sea. I had lost track of time and tried to think about the rendezvous.

A thump followed by a bright flash and explosion erupted off our port side. The first mine had worked. I could see rolling orange flames shoot up from the front of the tanker as the shock wave rolled across the water. Abernathy's mine had worked and the amount of fire was hard to believe. The forward part of the ship was now totally engulfed in flames.

"Son of a bitch!" Moon yelled.

Where were Abernathy and Springer, and where was the P46? Then it hit me, they were looking for our canoes, and would take us as a Jap boat coming after them. I remembered the machine gun that Weller had aboard the boat.

Just then a second explosion reverberated across the water, the orange flames reflecting off the bottom of the clouds.

"Moon, stop the boat! Goddammit, stop the boat!"

After explaining to Moon, we resumed at a slower speed. I saw a small compass mounted in front of the wheel and told my Australian helmsman to "just head east." Climbing forward again, I carefully made my way to the bow and began signaling with my flashlight. Two flashes every thirty seconds on different bearings, but all toward the open ocean, I hoped Weller and Williams could see the signal against the illumination from the burning tanker.

After fifteen minutes, my efforts seemed fruitless. There was nothing out in the inky darkness, the moon now completely obscured by the clouds. Turning to check on Moon, I saw a quick double flash on our port quarter.

Abernathy grinned at me as we pulled him aboard. Right behind him came Springer.

"Leave the boat," I said, turning back to Hoss who remained motionless on the cockpit deck.

"Bob, get up forward and keep signaling out to sea."

Abernathy looked around, clearly confused.

"Help me with Hoss," I said. The corporal knelt down, turning on his flashlight.

"Criminy," he said, his light illuminating a large blood stain.

His shorts were soaked with fresh blood. As I looked closer I could see the wound was from a large piece of wood, about an inch across sticking in his left butt cheek. It had to be from our canoe.

"Lieutenant, there they are," Springer called from the bow.

"Moon, you see 'em?"

"Aye," came the response, but not with Moon's normal forceful manner.

I called up forward to Springer to come down and help me with Hoss.

"Corporal, get up there with the sergeant. He's been hit and you may need to drive the boat."

Abernathy nodded and stood up.

"Lieutenant, look at this," he said without heading forward.

Standing up, I turned and looked aft to see a searchlight. In a moment it became clear there was a Jap patrol boat heading toward us, less than a mile away.

Springer jumped down into the cockpit.

"Bob, get back on the bow and keep signaling, no matter what happens."

The young sailor paused for just a second.

"Aye aye, sir."

He jumped up on the walkway and headed forward.

"I'll get the Wilson," Abernathy said. "And I still have a grenade."

The Jap would not know for sure who we were. Could we lure them into an ambush? Hoss groaned from the deck and I knelt down.

"You'll be fine, old man, just hang in there."

I stood up to see the Japs making an intercept course for us. What did they expect us to do? Heave to or reverse?

Abernathy returned, his Wilson at the ready.

"Moon, maintain course, but slow down," I called forward. The die was cast.

I saw a Japanese hat laying on the deck and pulled it on.

"Tom, get down out of sight and I'll tell you when to pop up."

Realizing I'd used the corporal's first name, I knew these were the men I was willing to die with. Strangely, I felt myself relax.

"They're 50 yards out. Plan on using the Wilson first. Keep the Mills if we get close enough."

"Right."

Suddenly I realized my Webley was in the holster, unloaded. I opened the flap on the cartridge holder, loaded six rounds, and slid the pistol back into its holster.

"Twenty yards out. I can see two men standing at the rear of the cockpit. With the driver that makes a total of three."

For a moment I thought about waving, but I didn't know what the Japs would think. Thank God, they hadn't said anything yet.

The sounds of the engine and ocean were interrupted as one of the Japs yelled something that sounded like a question. It had to happen, I thought. Now I had to bluff it out.

I cupped my hand around my ear, indicating I couldn't understand.

"Get ready. I'm not sure how long they'll buy this crap."

"Ready. Just let me know," Tom said, quietly, as if the Japs might overhear him.

Closer, I thought. Just keep coming closer, you son of a bitch.

The searchlight on the patrol boat clicked back on and swung toward us. The Japs had made the decision for us.

"Now!"

Abernathy rose up, the Wilson ready and fired two short bursts at the boat, which was now only ten yards away.

"Moon, go…go…go," I screamed.

The Japanese patrol immediately swerved left to open the distance, but they were now bow on and closing. Both boats were hitting the larger waves of the outer harbor and the motion was starting to get violent.

"Bob, get back here!" I yelled at the bow, not wanting to lose the young sailor over the side.

He came back on the port side, hand over hand, as the boat pounded into the waves, now making twenty knots into the blackness.

The spray crashed over the bow as bullets tore into us, a machine gun on the pursuing boat only fifty yards behind. Splinters exploded as bullets ripped into the wood cabin and the front windows were shattered, throwing glass shards everywhere.

Abernathy stood his ground, firing short bursts with the Wilson, but it was no match for a machine gun. Then I remembered the Type-96 we had found on the 46 boat. This must be the same, and it wasn't going to turn out well. Our only chance was to go on the offensive, otherwise they would stand off and destroy us.

Staggering forward, I grabbed Moon on the shoulder.

"We have to ram them, it's the only way," I yelled as more rounds hit the cabin.

"We'll use the Mills, but we have to get close enough."

Moon looked up at me, his hands tight on the wheel. He nodded.

"Get ready," he said.

I crouched down as another burst hit the boat and went aft.

"Stand by!" I yelled at the corporal, who was kneeling down for cover behind the transom. "Moon's gonna turn around and head right at 'em. Give me the Mills and I'll throw it while you give me cover."

He looked at me and nodded. There was nothing else to say. I felt the boat begin to turn and looked forward to make sure Moon was still operating. In the flash of the Jap searchlight I saw Springer laying on the deck, sprawled next to Hoss.

Shit.

The boat rolled wildly as we crossed the line of waves. Both of us grabbed the bulkhead to stay on our feet.

Our vulnerability was unmasked in the turn and another burst ripped at the boat. Abernathy went down, a muffled cry his only sound.

"Where are you hit?" I asked him as he tried to get back on his knees.

"Damn it, my leg. Shit, that hurts."

"Get pressure on it and gimme the Wilson," I said, knowing that his body had shielded me during the burst.

I would empty the magazine on the Wilson and hope I could throw the grenade far enough. Thank God I was right-handed, my left shoulder was still ablaze with pain.

"Get down," I told Abernathy as I moved around him to the port bulkhead. It was now or never. I fired a short burst hoping to hit their searchlight. Nothing, then the light exploded. I watched as bullets ripped into the cabin of the patrol boat, shattering their front windows.

Moon had seen the same thing and swerved to the right opening the distance to the Japs. I watched more bullets tear into the enemy patrol boat, which began slowing. Then I saw the 46 boat coming out of the darkness.

Moon circled as Weller ran in close, the machine gun continuing its destructive fire. They finished the enemy boat off with two grenades.

"Do you have everyone?" Williams called across the ten feet between the rolling boats.

"Everyone accounted for," I yelled. "We need the medical kit over here."

"Understood. Can your boat make it north?" Williams came back.

Good question.

"Moon, what do you think?" I asked.

"Yeah, I think so," he said, his voice trailing off.

Larry Weller had circled around and Dave Williams stood ready with the medical kit and several canteens. A quick handover and the other patrol boat moved ahead of us on a northerly course.

Putting the kit down, I saw Abernathy kneeling next to Bob Springer, rolling him on his back. The corporal put a life vest under his head.

"Check him out while I look at Hoss."

I began to roll Hoss on his back, my knees sliding on the bloody deck.

"Lieutenant?"

Leaving Hoss, I climbed over next to Abernathy, who had his flashlight shining on Springer's chest. A single bullet hole oozed blood from the center of his chest. I looked at the corporal, who shook his head.

"Bob... Bob," I said putting my hand on the young man's cheek.

He opened his eyes.

"Sorry," he said, his voice soft.

"Don't worry, Bob. We'll get you back to camp. You'll be fine," I said feeling like a fool. I grabbed a large compressed bandage, tearing open the package and pressing it against the wound. I tied the two cloth cords around his back and eased him back down. There was one other thing we could do for him.

"I'll give you a shot for the pain. Hang in there."

Opening the med kit, I pulled out a morphine syrette. At least we could make the pain go away for however long he had left.

"Hold the light."

Removing the syrette's cover, I twisted off the wire loop on the end of the needle. Slipping the needle at an angle into his stomach, I squeezed the tube, injecting the morphine.

"Stay with him, Tom."

Carefully as I could, I rolled Hoss over on his back. Sliding a folded life vest under his head, I went over his body, looking for any more wounds. There was so much blood from the deck on his shirt, that I slit it open to expose his chest and stomach. Thank God. No wounds, slashes or bleeding. It looked like the wood spike was our only problem.

"Christ," I heard Hoss say, his left hand coming up to wipe is face.

"Glad you're back with us. How about some water?"

"What's happening with my damn leg? What's wrong with it?"

"Drink this."

He took several long gulps and then lay back.

"We're headed north. This is the second Jap boat. The 46 is right in front of us."

"What happened?" he asked.

"I'll tell you everything later, but first I need you to lay on your stomach so I can examine that wound and get some sulfa powder on it. Then I'll fix you up with a little morphine and you can sleep the rest of the way."

I ended up giving him the morphine first. The pain when I cleaned the wound and tried to pull out the splinter put him in agony.

With Hoss on his back and starting to nod off, I went forward to check on Moon. It seemed strange that the normally loud and strident sergeant had been mum since we started north.

I sat down next to him on the bench, noting both his hands were on the wheel with a death grip.

"Are you all right?"

"My head's bleedin' coming apart. Never had such an ache."

The wound was bad enough on the outside, I wondered what it had done to his brain. A concussion at the very least, but it might have fractured the skull.

"Tom, come up here!" I called back to the corporal.

"How's Springer?" I asked when Abernathy came forward.

"Still breathing."

"How's the leg?"

"Hurts like the devil, but I can manage."

"Take the wheel from the sergeant. Keep following Weller, don't lose them. Moon, back aft with me."

Mullen stopped when he saw the two men laying on the deck, the bloody mess now visible in the early morning light.

"Christ."

"Lay down next to Hoss."

Moon complied without comment and I found another life vest for a pillow. Using a pair of scissors in the medical pack, I cut off as much of the matted hair around the wound that I could. The bleeding had stopped but it was still wet with fresh blood. I gave the wound a liberal application of sulfa powder. Thank the good Lord, the bottle of codeine tablets was full.

"Here, take two of these. We'll wait 30 minutes and if the pain isn't better, two more."

"Now lay back and try to rest."

I went forward and handed the corporal two codeine tablets and a canteen.

"Here, take these. Put your leg up on the bench. I'll get some sulfa powder on it and throw on a clean dressing."

"Your shoulder doesn't look too good, if you ask me," he said, swinging his leg up.

"It's not too bad," I lied. The bullet had gone through the fleshy part of the corporal's calf. The wound was seeping blood, but it wasn't too bad. I applied plenty of sulfa powder and as tight a dressing as I could manage.

Sitting back against the bulkhead, I found one of the canteens. I popped two codeine tablets in my mouth and washed them down. Hopefully two tablets would help the pain in my shoulder. If not, I would happily take two more. I probed my shoulder, wishing I had a mirror. Damn it hurt. For now, I'd put sulfa powder on it and that would hold me until Lynda could look at it. The sudden thought of her was pleasant. We would get everyone healthy, regroup and press on. Period.

Looking across the cockpit, I saw the terrible toll of the night. Springer was dying, Hoss and Moon were hurt bad. McGowan was dead, my shoulder was toast and Abernathy had a bullet hole in his leg. We'd have to count on the chief, Williams,

Findlay and Smitty to carry the load for a while. What a crew I thought, but I wouldn't trade them for anyone else.

I noticed Moon said something to Hoss, who was out like a light. Then I saw him pat Hoss on the leg twice. Those two had come a long way from that first day in Australia.

Thirty minutes later, Moon, the corporal and myself visited the codeine bottle again. I sat down next to Springer after passing the medication.

"Bob?"

There was no response and I felt his neck for a pulse. It was there. Erratic, but there.

With my hand on his shoulder, the young man lay quietly, his breathing shallow and jerky. Laying in the bottom of that boat with my three wounded men seemed like the most normal thing to do. I suspect I was probably in shock myself, but I managed to keep focused. After an hour, Springer's body shuddered once and his breathing stopped. There was no pulse. He was gone. I didn't say anything to anyone else right then. Moon and Hoss were quiet and I thought it was better to let that quiet continue.

As I sat there, the boat rolling slightly to the quartering waves, I thought about having another burial service. At least Bever would have some company. Then it struck me, it was a long hike up to the camp from the boats. How would we get Bob up that trail? I knew we could get it done, there would be plenty of Weller's men. But then I thought about it. He was Navy. Since time immemorial sailors have been laid to rest at sea.

Flashlight signals brought the 46 boat back alongside us in short order.

"Springer's dead," I called across the water over the idling engines. "I think we ought to bury him at sea."

Williams' face was shadowed but there was enough illumination from the moon to see his expression. He wiped his face and nodded.

"Right," he said.

In a minute, both motors were silent, the two patrol boats rolling slightly in the sea.

"Tom, give me a hand here."

I wondered how we'd do it. We had no flags, no bible, nothing formal to follow.

I looked at Moon and Hoss side by side on the deck, which was still bloody. Springer lay next to them, in his dungaree pants and shirt. That was enough. It was the uniform he wore to war, and it was enough for him to take to eternity.

I rolled him over as gently as I could manage with my shoulder and began to button his shirt. I straightened the web gear he'd been wearing and adjusted his belt. I remembered that in the days of sail, a fallen sailor would be stitched into their hammock, a cannon ball added for weight, and then sent over the side.

My senses recoiled at what I was doing, but it was for the team. For the mission. And whether Bob Springer's final resting place was in a jungle grave or at the bottom of the Makassar Strait, I didn't think it would matter much to him.

Williams threw a rope across and we pulled the boats together. Pickett scrambled across as Weller and Williams watched from the other boat. The chief knelt down next to Bob's body, putting his hand on the young man's chest. Then he stood up slowly.

"Let me get the anchor from up forward," he said.

In a few moments, we'd tied a rope around Springer's waist and attached the boat's anchor.

"Here," I said as the three of us worked to get Springer up to the gunwale. The chief had him under his torso while Tom lifted his legs. I used my good arm to support his head. We managed to get him up and ready to go over the side. We paused as if they both were waiting for me to say something, but what was there to say?

"Bob, we are committing your body to the sea. You were a good shipmate and friend. You died a long way from New York, but you did your duty. No one can ask for more."

We eased him down to the water and let him go. I watched as his arms floated upward and then he gently disappeared from sight.

I sat back against the gunwale. Suddenly exhaustion overwhelmed me. Staring forward I saw Tom Abernathy had both hands on the wheel and seemed to be in control. Hoss and Moon lay quietly on the deck. Christ, what a mess. I should go relieve Tom, but I just couldn't make myself move. My thoughts went to Maksi. I think that I had not let myself really think about her as we moved south for the attack. But now the reality hit me that I had found her then lost her. The warm and caring woman who had spent fifteen years taking care of me, teaching me and giving me the support I didn't get from my parents was gone.

CHAPTER NINETEEN

Weller's Camp
Telukladang Peninsula
28 October 1942

"So, doctor. Tell me where we stand," I asked Lynda

She'd been working steadily for the last four hours following our arrival in camp.

Brushing the hair away from her face, she sat next to me on a log.

"The corporal's doing well. The bullet went through his leg, missed any bone and I was able to clean it well. He'll be fine as long as it doesn't become infected. Sergeant Mullen is a different story. I don't think his skull is fractured, but the blow to his head must have caused internal bleeding. All we can do is watch him. There's simply nothing we can do for him out here if it starts to get worse."

I thought about Moon, realizing how much I had come to count on him.

"Hoss is another problem," she continued. "I've not been able to remove the splinter. I'm sure the combination of swelling, along with the rough pattern of the wood is serving to lock it in. The body will be working to expel the splinter, forming an abscess over time. But I have no idea how that might turn out. An infection in the area could kill him."

"Christ," I said trying to think what we could do.

"Then there's you. The bullet fractured your collarbone in addition to the torn muscle and flesh. Keeping it immobilized and watching for infection should be all that you need. But you're going to be uncomfortable for several weeks."

"Thanks. I have a lot to think about."

"Rob, two of those men need a doctor. Without more advanced medical treatment, I don't know what might happen. I'm afraid their injuries need more than a jungle medicine man," she finished. "Now sit down and let me finish dressing your shoulder."

A thought came to me as she worked on my shoulder.

"Has Amulong looked at either one of them?"

"He's not here," she replied. "A group of them left camp. I'm not sure where they were going."

She finished with the bandage and sat back against a tree trunk, closing her eyes.

"She saved my life," she said quietly.

"What's that?"

"Maksi. When they made the move for me, one of the Japanese tried to shoot me as I stumbled away. She pushed me behind a cart and the bullet intended for me hit her."

I saw her eyes were open and tears streamed down her face.

I took her in my arms and just held her.

An hour later, Dave Williams came up the trail, a bottle and two cups in his hand.

"I brought you some painkillers," he said, sitting down next to me.

He poured two glasses of Lihing and handed one to me, which I took with my free hand, the other one bound tight to my stomach with a bandage.

"How's the shoulder?"

I went over a complete update on all the wounded and told him that I was fine, just needed a little time to heal.

"We heard two explosions from the harbor, is that what you heard?"

I nodded.

"That's about the time the Jap patrol boat showed up. I only heard two explosions, no more. After that I wasn't paying any attention to the tanker."

He took a drink.

"From where we were, it looked like ship was totally ablaze. I can't imagine there was anything left after that fire. We should hear something from Weller's people soon."

The booze was going down smoothly. I suspect the codeine was helping the cause.

"Then I guess it was worth it," I said, not meaning to sound quite so sarcastic.

"Lieutenant, you put a big dent in the Japs' ability to get oil to their fleet. You're damned right it was worth it."

I thought about Marty McGowan and Bob Springer.

Williams must have been reading my thoughts.

"A lot of men died on the *Houston*, and all we accomplished was to slow the Japs down. I'm sorry we lost two men, but you got the job done. That's how you win wars, Mr. Parker, by getting the job done, regardless of the cost. It's always easy to say that in the abstract, but when it comes down to real men's lives it's never easy. You'll do yourself a favor by figuring out how to put your thoughts somewhere that you don't think about them too much."

"Yes, sir." I was still a Marine and I would do whatever it takes. I just needed to focus on the mission. The rest of it, I could deal with that later.

"Smitty can run the radio, so your broadcasts can continue. Although you might want to keep the traffic down to a minimum for a while until we find out what the Japs are gonna do."

Our intelligence chain was intact and the radio was working. He was right. We were sent here on a mission and we hadn't been relieved, but it might be time to request a submarine. Moon and Hoss needed to get back to real medicine. And how about Williams and his crewman? While John Smith may be capable of running the radio, how would I keep him here? Or the good Commander for that matter. Wasn't it time for him to get back to the war? I decided to wait two days. That would allow me to see how everyone was doing medically and if we were going to see any retaliation.

I explained my plan to Williams, then asked him, "What about you? If I ask for a sub pick up for Sergeant Mullen, that'd be a ride to Australia for you and Smitty."

He nodded.

"I've been thinking that it's time for me to get back in a cockpit. Maybe that makes sense. You could get Lynda and her brother out of this hellhole and they could swap in new team members."

There it was. Lynda deserved to leave this jungle and return to civilization. As much as I wanted to be with her, it was the only thing to do. It solved all of my problems with people, injuries and supplies. Hell, it would also let me ask Coyne for a medical corpsman, which we should've had from the very start. I wondered if Coyne would order me back to Australia. Surely, they were training more people for these types of missions, right? Suddenly things were looking pretty good to me.

"Australia?"

Lynda seemed surprised by my plan.

"You and Dicky would be able to get back the real world and to safety. You've done enough and seen more than anyone ever should. This was the plan all along, we just didn't have a good reason for a supply run. Now, with two men needing a doctor, it makes sense."

"My parents may still be alive here in one of the detention camps."

"And don't you think they would want you and your brother out of here and safe?" I said.

"Commander Williams would be there with you and you'd be able to help with the medical care for Moon and Hoss. I don't think submarines carry doctors, just corpsmen."

She stepped up next to me and took my good hand.

"And what about you?"

"I suspect I'll stay here with Abernathy and they'll send in men to fill holes in the team. I don't think they would shut down the operation."

Everything was conjecture on my part, but I think the rationale made sense. Balikpapan would still be shipping oil and the allies would want to stop it.

Lynda put her arms around me and pulled me close. I could feel her shaking and knew she was crying.

There was nothing to say, so, I kissed her.

"I love you and I want you to be safe."

I found Moon and Hoss in their hut. The last two days had been quiet as we licked our wounds. Neither man was doing better, Hoss's wound was infected and the pain showed on his face.

"I think it's time for you both to head back to Australia," I said, sitting down between the two sleeping pads.

"What do you mean?" Moon asked, his voice soft.

"I'm going to request a submarine pick up for both of you, plus Williams, Smitty, Lynda, Dicky and the chief."

Hoss struggled to turn towards me.

"And you?"

"Abernathy's leg is doing fine and my shoulder just needs time."

He closed his eyes and lay back flat on the native bed.

Moon looked at me, his focus softened with the medications.

"You'll stay here, with the radio and everything?"

I nodded.

"I'll request replacements for you two and a corpsman to boot. Shouldn't be here without some medical support. I guess we're learning."

Looking away from me and straight up, Moon said, "Not for me, you're not."

I wasn't sure I heard him right.

"What?"

"I'm staying," he said in a quiet voice, so unlike him.

"Sergeant, you're in no condition to continue with the mission. I'm compelled to get you back to Australia for proper medical treatment."

He closed his eyes, then said, "Parker, shut up and let me go back to sleep."

"I'm not leaving either," Hoss said.

Weller stuck his head into the hut.

"We've got visitors."

My first thought was that the Japs had found us.

Weller realized how I'd taken his statement and quickly added, "Some locals."

A group of men were standing near the main fire pit, all wearing nondescript western shirts and shorts. They all looked like Malays to me, none of them appearing to have any native characteristics.

Weller said, "Here is the American," to the group.

They looked at me like I was from Mars, but one man offered his hand.

"My name is Nosnah, Doctor Roger Nosnah."

His English was impeccable, which surprised me, his appearance very local. Perhaps 60, he wore his hair close cropped and looked athletic. Not what I would have expected in the middle of the Bornean jungle.

Offering my hand, I introduced myself.

The doctor continued, politely, "This is Sergeant Ilang, of our local constabulary, along with two of his men, Corporal Abu and Private Sumakil."

The two policemen looked sturdy enough, I guessed they were in their mid-twenties, the sergeant a little older.

"How did you know about us, or find us for that matter?"

"Kalimantan may seem primitive compared to what you are used to, lieutenant, but we have a very effective communication system among our people. I have been hiding north of Samarinda since the invasion. Over time, men joined our small group and we have been waiting for a chance to strike back at the Japanese."

He smiled then continued, "Finally we have a leader in our fight against the invaders. There are many more who will join us."

Thoughts flooded through my mind. This might open up a whole new ability to harass the Japs. Then it hit me. The more people who are involved, the more likely the Japs will find out about us, or even plant a spy to betray us. But for now, I'd just have to listen to what they proposed.

"You said "doctor," are you a medical doctor?"

He nodded.

"For thirty-five years."

"We have great need of medical help right now, if you would oblige us."

It turned out that Doctor Nosnah, or Rog as I came to know him, had trained in Djakarta. His real first name was Wuji, but he adopted a western first name for business reasons. For the last thirty-two years, he had taken care of the locals, including many Dutch and British. He feared for his safety because of it and took to the hills ahead of the Japanese. He apparently was well thought of and had become a magnet for those who did not want to live under Japanese rule, or were afraid they were under suspicion.

I introduced him to Lynda and she went over her treatment of the men since our return from Balikpapan. He had several packs of medical supplies with him and I showed him what we had left in our gear.

He immediately examined Hoss and Moon.

"My plan was to try and get them back to Australia. I'm just not sure how long it'll take to arrange something."

Wiping his hands on a small towel outside their hut, he looked at me like I was an idiot.

"Your Mister Hostetter will not make it to Australia, Lieutenant Parker. That splinter has to come out. Otherwise the infection will spread. There is no doubt about this. Mister Mullen is certainly concussed, but I think he would make the trip safely if kept quiet and resting. An injury such as his will take time to run its course. Head trauma is an inexact science. We simply don't have the ability to truly diagnose the damage. Most times, the body will heal itself. Unfortunately, there are also cases where the patient continues to spiral downward, and death ultimately takes them. It is simply too early to tell in his case."

An hour later he told me that Lynda had done a wonderful job on Tom's leg and my shoulder.

"We need to watch for any signs of infection, but sulfa powder is such a powerful drug, I expect no problems."

The idea of having a doctor with the team was a relief. With a corpsman from Australia and fresh medical supplies, we would be truly ready to face the challenges of this jungle.

Now, what do I tell Coyne? I decided that as soon as we got word from Weller's people in Balikpapan I would send a message.

Word came via our network that the tanker had been extensively damaged, sinking at the pier. The transshipment area on the pier had also suffered both explosions and fire, severely impacting the Japs' ability to on-load oil. We'd actually pulled it off. I should've been happy, but the loss of McGowan and Springer put a different light on it. It hurt the Japs, and my intent was to continue doing everything we could to do more of the same, but now I knew the cost.

The reaction by the Japs consisted of an increase of aircraft flying over the jungle, but nothing in the way of troop activity. The similarity to the attack on Singapore by the special boat types might have led them to believe the attackers had retired via the water, using a submarine or native lugger. But I knew not to underestimate them.

The report to Coyne was sent in five parts, each short and at random times over a sixteen-hour period. I was sure that the enemy would be actively trying to intercept radio transmissions and my intent was to move the radio deeper into the jungle. Smitty took over as the lead radio operator without a hitch. It was strange, he seemed more comfortable than any of us in the jungle, almost like it was a lark.

"Smitty, where are you from?"

He grinned.

"Iowa, sir. Central City, Iowa. It's a small town, just north of Cedar Rapids."

"You spend a lot of time outdoors growing up?"

"My folks have a dairy farm."

How different from what I'd known.

"So, you spent a lot of time milking cows?"

"I spent most of my time shoveling cow shit, actually."

I guess being in a jungle could've been worse.

That night I sat with Weller and Williams enjoying a bottle of Lihing.

"Eight more locals showed up today to join. Five men and three women."

Williams said, "You're going to have a force here if you can do some training and get some equipment."

He was right, I would ask for weapons to equip our volunteer force. That should get Coyne's attention.

Hoss had developed a fever, and the signs of infection were beginning to become very evident. The doctor was adamant the splinter had to come out as soon as possible. He sounded very sure of himself, but I had to wonder, how good was this guy?

"Lynda, the doctor's ready to operate on Hoss. According to him, the infection will only get worse. He seems like he knows what he's doing. What do you think?"

"I agree with him about the infection. The effect of a spreading infection can be fatal and it can happen quickly." Her face reflected concern along with fatigue.

"You've talked to him. Does he seem like he's the real thing?"

She asked, "Do I think he can perform the operation?" She thought for a moment. "He sounds knowledgeable. But there's no way to tell. I do know Hoss's not getting better."

"The doctor says that splinter has to come out," I told Hoss.
He lay sweating, small gnats buzzing around his head.
"Do it," he said, the pain obvious in his face.
"Lynda will assist him. We have our medical supplies and his as well."
"I think I can tell," he said as he winced with pain, "If that bloody thing doesn't come out, I'm a goner."
I nodded slowly.
"I'll talk to the doctor."

In retrospect, I should have realized the butt is mostly just flesh. There aren't critical organs or arteries to present complications. The good doctor had the splinter out of Hoss in less than twenty minutes. He cleaned the wound using plenty of sulfa powder. A very drugged Hoss was sleeping in his hut forty-five minutes after the doctor commenced the operation. Lynda told me he had been quite adept with the instruments. Now it was a waiting game, but at least he had a chance.

Moon remained quiet and resting most of the time, but he had shown no symptoms that might suggest a worsening problem. That night I asked the doctor if he saw any improvement.

"Nothing of note, lieutenant. But as I told you, this type of an injury is very unpredictable. We'll know more over the next few days."

I liked the doctor. He was pleasant and it was clear he was the leader to his group. Why else would these people have rallied to him in the jungle?

"Doctor, you mentioned a desire to fight back against the Japanese. I'm curious what that means to you and your people?"

Resistance against a vicious enemy like the Japanese Army was not something to be undertaken without understanding the danger.

"Lieutenant, you have seen what these animals have done to my people? Would you not be willing to do anything possible to resist if this was California?"

"I would. But would your men be as eager if the Japs retaliated against civilians in Samarinda?"

He stood up and walked over to the small fire, throwing a stick into it.

"They are simple people, but they are also proud. I would never expect them to journey across the water and attack others. But this is their home. They will fight for it. It is why they have followed me here. Now it is up to you."

It looked like I was going to get my platoon after all. Only they would be civilian volunteers, local natives and trained smugglers. I guess this is what Quantico would call a leadership challenge.

CHAPTER TWENTY

Weller's Camp
Telukladang Peninsula
7 November 1942

Within days, a radio message came in with a scheduled submarine rendezvous two weeks hence. Coyne had been succinct in his transmissions but acknowledged my requests. The failure by Australia to confirm anything specific was disconcerting to say the least. I requested six more Wilsons, a dozen Webley pistols and two dozen Lee Enfield rifles with appropriate ammunition. Anticipating more attacks on the Japs, I also wanted some firepower and asked for a couple of two-inch mortars. I had worked with mortars at the Basic School and knew the impact that a few well-placed rounds could have during an assault or ambush. Passing along my need for a new radio operator, I also asked for a medical corpsman. While I told them of the need to evacuate a number of people, I was vague, but on purpose. I didn't want him or anyone telling me that I couldn't put Lynda or Dicky on the boat. Understanding that he should want to return to the navy, I didn't mention Smitty, but I hoped he might want to stay with me in the jungle. He told me that he didn't have any family and seemed to like running the radio. If Coyne sent me a new radioman, that would be one more redundancy. I was learning how to play the game.

At least this operation with the submarine would not involve rubber boats. Our patrol boat would allow us to rendezvous with the sub with some control of the situation. As long as the Japs didn't show up, it should be a lot easier than the last time.

"How are you doing, old man?"

Hoss opened his eyes, then rubbed them both. He was alone in his shelter, Moon's sleeping pad empty.

"Enjoying the posh life, I'll tell you."

I knew his wound was healing well. Lynda and the doctor were both pleased.

Handing him a cup of tea, I sat down on Moon's pad.

"Ready to get on that sub and head home?"

"Not likely."

"You're a serving member of the military and duly obligated to follow all lawful orders, or have you forgot?"

"We've come too far, commander. I'm here as long as you are. Besides, this is really my home, not Australia."

Inside I felt such strong emotion for this man. He had risen to every challenge and was true to his word. But as I thought about it, my crack military team was actually more like a swashbuckling band of pirates.

"As long as your butt gets better. But if not, I'll personally throw your ancient ass on that boat." I grinned at him and he winked back at me. So much for military discipline.

But I had learned my lesson and went in search of Chief Pickett. Since Springer's death, the chief had been quiet. I'm sure he felt responsible for a junior shipmate, that's the way of NCO's.

"Chief, it's time to get you back aboard a submarine."

"Not sure what you mean."

"There'll be a submarine here in two weeks. You're going back to the Navy."

"Yes, sir," he replied, his voice neither enthusiastic or morose.

"And chief, don't ever forget that if you hadn't been with us, I doubt we would've made it."

I looked him square in the eyes.

He nodded.

"Thanks."

Over the next ten days, more people showed up looking to join Doctor Nosnah. There were now almost fifty in total, half women and children. I was surprised to see the smiles on the new arrivals. Apparently, our little camp was turning into a haven. The doctor had done a fine job of setting up his people in an expanded area of the camp. I found him there early one evening. He seemed perfectly at home, sitting in front of a small fire, a piece of meat roasting on a long stick.

"Ah, Mr. Parker, please sit down. May I offer you some roasted monkey?"

It sounded so normal, but I laughed in spite of myself.

"No, doctor, but thank you."

He tested the meat with a small knife and then sat back. I noticed his sandals. It seemed that was the foot wear of choice among his people. Shorts and simple shirts completed their uniform, very functional, while not that protective in my western mind.

"Have you been able to look at Mr. Mullen today?"

"I did," he answered. "I could detect no changes in his condition."

"But he wasn't any worse?"

The doctor laughed.

"Mr. Parker, it seems to me that you are looking for a positive response."

He was right, of course. I needed Moon and wanted him to remain with the team. But at what cost?

"I suppose I am. Medically, could you see him staying in Borneo and not returning to Australia?"

The older man smiled and tested the meat again.

"It would be wiser to send him to a hospital, but there is nothing that indicates his injury is getting worse. My experience in these cases has shown me that if he is not getting worse by now, he will then get better over time. That is the best I can do."

"Understood. Are your people getting settled?"

He nodded, pulling the stick off the fire and setting it next to him.

"They are. I would not be surprised to see more arrive over time."

That was my concern.

"Do you trust everyone? Surely the reward posted by the Japs would appeal to someone?"

"Shortly after the invasion, a reward was posted for me, by name. It was substantial by the measure of these people. Despite that, I am still here."

Trust must start somewhere.

"I'll train those who want to join us. They'll learn how to operate the weapons and the discipline of using them. Will your people accept our orders?"

"They will. Be sure of that."

I briefed the doctor on the tactical situation as I understood it. He was an attentive listener and as we talked, he brought me up to date on what his group had seen from the Japanese since the invasion. It struck me that we could make Samarinda a problem

252

for the garrison and that might divert troops from Balikpapan. Another attack on the petroleum facilities must be one of our goals.

It was time to make a decision on Moon and Hoss. The sub would be here in two days and I needed to put them aboard or not.

The two of them were sitting outside their hut, both cleaning weapons. I was happy to see Hoss actually sitting like normal, a good sign that his wound was healing.

"You two look like busy beavers," I said, sitting down next to them.

"What the hell does that mean?" Moon asked.

"American slang, sorry."

"You people do have some funny ways of talking," Hoss said, checking the slide on his Wilson.

"The pot calling the kettle black," I came back, "But I guess that's slang too."

"Stick with us, we'll get you talking fine in no time."

I came to the point.

"That's the question, are you two reprobates staying here or getting on the sub?"

"What the hell is a reprobate," Moon asked.

"A hard-headed son of a bitch," I replied.

Moon smiled.

"I like that. Fitting."

"Listen, I'll tell you straight. I'll need help with these new men, training them and getting them ready to fight the Japs. But you both have valid reasons to be sent back home to get better. I know what you said, but I want you to decide for sure. I would understand if you headed back to Australia. Think about it. I mean it."

Lynda had been quiet since I told her of the rendezvous date with the submarine. There were no arguments once she thought it through, but I know she was torn about leaving. It touched me that she would likely have remained in this miserable place with me, if it hadn't been for her brother. The idea of not having her around was hard for me, but I know I would rest easier with her safely in Australia.

We had always been able to spend time together, but the truth of the matter was that the jungle was not a romantic place, certainly not to me. For the first time in my life, I found myself knowing I would miss someone. It was strange to me, that when I'd left for school, I really didn't miss my family or even Maksi. Now I was faced with Lynda being a thousand miles away, with the very real possibility that we would never see each other again, and that was something I didn't like.

I found her washing her face in a small basin that Weller had procured for her.

"Where's Dicky?"

"He's off with our corporal. It seems the two of them have become fast friends. He'll miss Tom."

She dried her face and sat down on a log with the small towel around her shoulders.

"How are you?" she asked.

"Very much in love with you, if you must know."

Smiling, she said, "You dear man. What a tale we'll have to tell our children."

"Children?"

The thought hit me like a brick. Children, me! But she was right, if I was to have any children, I would want her as their mother.

"Yes, children, is the idea so startling? Perhaps things are done differently in America."

It was the impish smile that did me in and I knew this was the right thing to do. I knelt down in front of her.

"In America, the man gets on his knee to propose marriage."

Her eyes showed surprise, but there was no response.

"Lynda Noble, I'm asking you to marry me."

"Rob, are you serious?"

"I am."

She put her hands to her mouth and I saw tears well up in her eyes.

"Oh, yes, oh yes, I will," she said and was in my arms.

Only after the fact did I think about what my proposal meant to Lynda, and by default her brother. Not only would that give her a source of income, but she would be eligible for all of the benefits of being a U.S. citizen and the wife of an active duty Marine. In the back of my mind the thought of my government insurance also made sense. If something happened to me, my parents didn't need the money and it would be a stake for her as she made a new life.

But we were only engaged, and that would be an insurmountable problem to the bureaucrats. Perhaps Williams could marry us. He was the senior man present, surely there must be some provision for that, right? Ship's captains can conduct marriages, can't they?

"You what?"

Williams' reaction was not quite what I had expected. Congratulations were warm from everyone else on the team and Weller's folks too, but not so from the good commander.

"Sir, she's getting out of here in two days and will be safe back in Australia. And if I survive this little adventure, I want to spend the rest of my life with her."

"Goddamn it, Parker, the last thing a Marine officer needs in the middle of a war is a wife. You should know that. Don't they teach you anything at Quantico except how to crawl through the mud and polish your shoes?"

In for a penny, I told myself.

"So, you wouldn't be inclined to perform the ceremony?"

"What makes you think I can marry people?"

Suddenly I felt like a 2nd lieutenant again.

"Can't ship's captains do it?"

Williams laughed.

"Old wives' tale. They really can't. Not sure where that got started. So, it looks like you're out of luck until you get back to Australia."

Fine, if I had to wait, so be it. One more reason to make sure I got out of this in one piece.

Doctor Nosnah had his men construct a hut for use as a medical treatment location. All of the medical supplies were gathered together along with facilities for storing purified water. It made sense and when we got the new supply on the sub, we'd have a well-stocked dispensary.

Linda was in the new location working with the doctor on Abernathy's leg. The bandage needed changing, but the doctor liked to check on all injuries to make sure nothing was going bad. I was glad to have Tom staying with me, he had proved himself solid and reliable at every turn.

I sat watching until they were finished.

"Off to find Dicky," Tom said, and headed out.

"All well, doctor?" I asked.

"Fine. A superb nurse and sulfa powder makes for a powerful combination."

Lynda smiled and began to put the supplies away.

I told her, "Some bad news, I'm afraid."

"What?"

"Commander Williams can't marry us. Said that ship's captains can't either. So, I guess we'll have to wait until I get back to Australia.

The doctor looked up from one of his medical bags.

"I am permitted to conduct marriages in this province."

For a moment, I thought I'd misheard him, why would a doctor be allowed to conduct civil ceremonies?

"How's that?"

"Before the Japanese invasion, I was a civil justice for the province. A type of auxiliary official that the colonial government put in place because of the challenges of traveling to the cities from the jungle. I would conduct business while on my rounds and then file papers in Samarinda on my return. Unless you believe the Japanese are now the governing authority, I would still be able to perform weddings."

Screw them all, I'd marry Lynda before she left for Australia and let Coyne sort it out.

"Doctor, I would very much appreciate if you would marry us, and we need to expedite, if you know what I mean."

The doctor smiled, "I quite understand."

"There's one thing I need to do right away," I told Lynda.

"That is?"

"Find Dicky and ask his permission."

She looked at me, smiled and then kissed me.

That night was surreal to me. With a great deal of effort, an area was decorated with flowers, everyone cleaned themselves up as best they could. In the spirit of the moment, Weller came up with a remarkable amount of Lihing. But of all the memorable things from that night, it was Lynda who stole the show. A group of the women had taken her away once the word went out of the impending wedding. I didn't see her until she appeared, escorted by Moon and Hoss to the improvised altar.

Her willowy beauty had always taken my breath away and now I was frozen watching her approach wearing a long sarong-style dress that revealed her bare shoulders. In the firelight, the flowers that had been woven in her hair completed my vision of the perfect south seas maiden.

Standing next the doctor, I had my best man by my side. When I had asked Dicky if I could marry his sister, he had nodded, smiled a sheepish smile and touched my arm. There was nothing else to do but ask him if he knew about a best man at a wedding. Again, he nodded, and when I asked him to stand up for me he uttered the first words I had ever heard from him.

"I will."

Kneeling down I took him in my arms and told him that I couldn't wait to be his brother. And I couldn't wait to tell Lynda what had happened.

Next to the doctor, Amulong stood, a wide smile showing his several remaining teeth. He wore two crossed sashes in addition to several necklaces. Clearly this was a formal occasion for the headman.

Taking Lynda's hand, I realized I was nervous. I had intended to say something witty and light, but suddenly I felt very serious.

Doctor Nosnah looked across the group, their faces lit by two small fires that had been built for the ceremony. At least fifty people stood in around us, everyone silent as he began.

"The joining together of two people is a happy time. This is even more true today. We stand together as a group that has come together to fight the invaders, but today we have come together to see these two people become one. There can always be joy in life, despite the trials of the day."

He looked at each of us, then took my right hand and Lynda's left in both of his.

"Robyn, will you take Lynda as your wife? From today forward until the end of your days?"

It was really happening and I knew I truly meant what I said.

"I will."

"Lynda, will you take Robyn as your husband, from today forward until the end of your days?"

"Yes, I will," she said quietly.

"In keeping with the laws of the Hindia-Belanda and as authorized by the Governor General, I now declare you are man and wife."

As I stood in the middle of that jungle, a thousand miles from anywhere I took her in my arms and was happy.

CHAPTER TWENTY-ONE

Weller's Camp
Telukladang Peninsula
22 November 1943

Lynda and I were going have one day as man and wife before the submarine rendezvous in the early hours of the next morning. As nice as it would have been to spend our day together, it wasn't going to happen. There was too much to do, but we both understood.

According to our last message, the submarine was going to surface at 0100 local. Looking at the map, the area designated was about five miles northeast of where the *S-43* had surfaced to launch our rafts so long ago. The light signals to locate and identify the boat were very specific, and rightly so. The sub would be using a blue hooded light to guide us in after we signaled the recognition signal. I was sure the sub would have its deck gun manned and be ready to defend themselves if the Japs showed up.

Dave Williams assured me that he would watch over Lynda and Dicky during the passage and after they arrived in Australia. I gave him Fred Bennet's name at the support detachment. In the short time I was around Bennet, he struck me as a man that would take care of Lynda for me. Using authority, he may or may not have had, Williams authorized Smitty to remain with the team. I wasn't sure how the big brass would take that move, but I was a Marine and junior to Williams, I'd just plead ignorance. We both had approached Lester Finley and offered him a seat on the sub, assuming that was within our power to do. Surprisingly he told us he wanted to stay with Weller's group. I know that he and Larry had hit it off and I guess the seaman didn't have anyone to go home to in any case.

I also had one more run around with Hoss and Moon, after talking with the doctor and confirmed they would remain in Borneo. Despite my very Marine-like demeanor, I was damned glad they were staying with me. I had come to trust and count on them more than ever.

Lynda had been quiet, but very loving as we worked our way through the day, preparing for departure. I finally had everything covered and found her with Dicky and Abernathy.

"Your new brother-in-law has decided that he doesn't want to leave you or Tom," Lynda said. Her smile told me that Dicky's ability to speak again was a source of great joy.

I sat down next to Dicky and patted him on the leg.

"Dicky, Tom and I were talking about it and we both said that we would feel better knowing that you were with your sister to take care of her on the trip. Right, Tom?"

Abernathy smiled.

"Right you are, sir."

"Really?" Dicky asked.

"Of course. There are many situations that will need a man, and you are that man. I'm counting on you, little brother."

Dicky smiled at Tom, then me.

"Alright."

"Come on, nipper, let's go for a walk," Tom said, getting to his feet.

Once they were gone, Lynda said quietly, "He'll miss you both very much, and Mr. Hostetter is such a dear."

I decided that I wouldn't pass that on to Hoss.

"And I will miss you, my dear man."

Her arms were around me and I told her I loved her, but that love was going to have to withstand a great test. Would we part, never to see each other again? The thought weighed on me as I'm sure it did Lynda, but that's what happens in wars. At Quantico, I wasn't the most gung-ho second lieutenant, but I knew I could handle whatever the war was going to throw at me. How could I have ever imagined this? All I could do was make sure that we did see each other again, the war and Japs be damned.

"There's the light," Larry Weller said, his voice conveying the relief we all felt after an hour on station with no submarine anywhere.

A blue lamp was clearly visible on our port bow, the darkness of an overcast night making it difficult to see anything definite on the horizon. Larry turned toward the light, pushing the power up as Abernathy flashed the recognition signal.

We could hear the sub before we could make her out, the sounds of machinery and blowers were obvious across the choppy waves. A red light provided some illumination of the deck. As we closed alongside, a half of dozen sailors became visible on the deck. Smartly throwing the engine into reverse, Weller put us alongside the hull of the submarine.

More people and material began to appear on deck as we made the lines secure.

"I'll go first," Commander Williams said, "Make sure they know what they're doing, then I'll help Mrs. Parker aboard. Chief, you're with me."

I shook hands with both of them. There was nothing to say at this point, just a firm handshake and nod.

The next two minutes were something I'd never forget. A handshake with Williams, holding Lynda very tight for a moment and then handing Dicky over to them on the sub's deck. I saw her look over her shoulder one last time and then she disappeared down the rear hatch.

"Three to come aboard," I heard from a tall man using an Australian accent. The submarine was American, so this must be one of my new ones. In short order, all three men came aboard and American sailors began passing canvass musette bags of gear across to the 46. The entire operation took no more than ten minutes.

"That's it," I heard in a deep American voice, "Shove off and good luck."

"Thanks, mate," I called, realizing I had fallen into using Aussie slang.

Standing in the stern, I watched the sub disappear into the darkness.

Turning back forward I saw the tall gent and moved to his side.

"I'm Parker," I said, offering my hand.

"Andrews, Captain Harry Andrews," he said.

It hit me like a brick, if this guy was a captain, he outranked me and by default was now the mission commander.

"We've got a medic for you, Sergeant Woodley, and a radioman, Corporal Allen."

I wasn't sure how to respond, so I just said, "Glad you're here."

The noise of the engine made any real discussion a waste of time, so I gave Andrews the basic plan that we would meet Weller's gang at the beach and transport the gear back to camp. He nodded as if he had done this many times and sat back against the port bulkhead.

Standing across from the new team members, I balanced myself against the boat's movement and tried to figure out where this was going to lead. Would there be a new mission? Were more people going to be following these three? What was Coyne thinking and where did I fit in? The simple fact was that I had gotten used to being in charge.

As the gear was unloaded, it appeared that Coyne had delivered as requested, including the two mortars. The combined manpower of Weller's men and half a dozen of the villagers were able to transport all of the gear up to camp in only two hours. A quick brief to the new arrivals on the layout of the camp and everyone turned in after a long and difficult day.

Not surprisingly I woke early, just after dawn. Sleep was something that was proving more and more elusive. That must've been why I felt like an old man. But, I knew that wrestling with my thoughts made no sense, so I got up to start my first day with a new commanding officer.

"Good morning," I heard Captain Andrews call from behind me as I knelt over a tea pot on the fire.

"Good morning. How was your first night?"

He squatted down next to me and held his hands to the fire, although the temperature was already starting to warm the early morning jungle.

"Other than the odd creeper, it was quite tolerable."

'Quite tolerable,' where the hell was this guy from?

"I still don't like the little bastards, but you do get used to them. There's some coffee in that pot, unless you'd rather have tea," I said, handing him one of the tin cups sitting by the fire.

"Coffee would be splendid."

I poured and he sat down next to me on the ground.

"What can you tell me about the war?" We would get the odd report from Weller's contacts, but you never knew what was true and what was propaganda.

"It seems like the tide might be turning. The Germans are falling back in the desert and of course your chaps have landed in the west of Africa, Operation Torch they called it. Guadalcanal has given way to an invasion of New Guinea by your crew and our army working together. Of course, the biggest turn was the invasion of Russia."

"Russia?"

"Quite so. Germans attacked in late June. Changed the whole landscape."

It struck me that the world was aflame from one end to the other and I was sitting in the fucking jungle in Borneo.

"Well, you won't be seeing world changing events here, that's for sure.

"It's quite an operation you have here, Parker," he commented. "Local colonial types, native aboriginals, my God, how do you keep them all going in the same direction?"

I laughed. The son of a bitch was likable, in a British sort of way.

"So, tell me how you ended up here in our little piece of paradise."

"Of course," he said. "You're the vanguard of a new way of warfare, on two levels. Combined operations will be the key. Not that our forces will totally integrate, but instead they will communicate, coordinate and execute the war plan. Combine that with unconventional warfare behind the lines and there you go. Much like the SAS chaps in the desert, you are part of a new way of fighting. Breaking ground as it were."

Holy shit, this guy sounds like a Quantico tactics instructor. What the hell was he talking about?

"I spent the greater part of 1942 in England and North Africa," he continued, "as a liaison with the S.O.E. crew. I was being trained to come home and then facilitate future coordinated operations, such as this."

I wondered how England and North Africa could prepare him for the Bornean jungle.

"S.O.E.?" I asked.

"Special Operations Executive, the command charged with operating behind enemy lines and creating hate and discontent among the Jerries. Now my job is to help you do the same for the Japos. Although it sounds like you were doing quite alright by yourself. The attack on the harbor was quite well received as you might have expected."

"Not much of a response from Coyne, actually."

He laughed.

"Not to worry, that's just Coyne. Sometimes I think he's more British than Churchill. Trust me, your stock is quite high at headquarters."

"But you're going to replace me?"

He turned with surprise, the smiled.

"Not at all, my man. I will take over when the time is right, in perhaps three to four months. And quite frankly you look like you're due."

"Do I look that bad?" I knew I was about thirty pounds lighter than when I got here, but he didn't know that. There must be other signs.

He laughed.

"Same thing we saw in the desert, after a time, the body just gets worn out. Sometimes you can see it in the eyes. Wounds don't heal and people stop talking. You'll be fine when you get back to Australia."

Back to Australia? I had tried to put that out of my mind. Now thoughts of Lynda came flooding back to me, and nothing sounded better in the world to me than heading east.

"So, I remain in command?"

"Quite so. You're the expert in this area. Your job is to teach me and then push off home. Your shipping broadcasts are quite valuable and I need to get up to speed on that process. In the meantime, I intend on helping you misbehave. Coyne was most pleased that you initiated and pulled off the tanker attack. In fact, we brought some little toys that will help annoy the Japs to no end. Oh, and apologies, I was instructed to tell you that you've been promoted to captain. Congratulations. We shall have to toast your promotion at some point."

Captain, damn. I could remember when captains were people to be feared.

"Harry, have you ever heard of Lihing?"

Captain Harry Andrews, Royal Australian Army turned out to be everything I'd thought he wasn't when I first met him. What I thought was pretension was the driest sense of humor I had ever encountered. He capped that off with an ability to adapt to any situation with a remarkable level of aplomb. I suspect that his time in the desert had honed that ability, but I also suspect the reason he was there in the first place was because his superiors understood what a natural leader and warrior they had in Harry.

The men he brought with him were solid as the day is long. Alastair Woodley joined the army from his pre-med studies in Perth, Western Australia. He came with a full resupply of medical supplies, which pleased Doctor Nosnah to no end. Our new radioman, Alfie Allen was a no-nonsense type from Hobart, Tasmania. He was built like a prize fighter and became Abernathy's shadow in no time.

268

The new men blended in well. I don't know if Coyne evaluated personality traits, but both men seemed to hit it off well with everyone. Even Smitty, the only American besides myself, ended up wearing an Aussie bush hat and developed a bit of an accent. With two experienced radiomen available, I wanted to relocate the radio two miles further up into the hills. The Japs might look for it, but it was going to be damned hard for them to find the location or actually get to it. We continued our shipping transmissions, but had seen no evidence of the Japs' radio direction finding operations.

My biggest surprise following the arrival of the new men, was the remarkable change that took place with my two old reprobates. Moon and Hoss continued to recover from their wounds, but jumped into training our growing band of local troops with enthusiasm. It was easy to forget that Moon was a sergeant and as such, knew a thing or two about training soldiers. Hoss may have been a private, but his age, coupled with local experience, made him a superb sidekick for Moon.

Amulong went on one of his walkabouts and returned with another dozen natives from a village located north of our area, which had been brutalized by the Japanese garrison in Samarinda. By final count, we were up to fifty-five fighters who were drilled day-in and day-out by Hoss and Moon. My observation was encouraged but my interference was not tolerated. It was clear to me after seeing the new troopers in action that they were learning the right way to use their weapons and conduct effective tactics.

Amulong had told Harry and I that a number of the villages north and west of Samarinda had suffered at the hands of the Japanese Army conducting patrols from the main garrison in town. Much like Moon and I had observed at Amulong's village, the Japs would arrive, search and loot the place, often taking action against the men or headmen. It seemed to me that we had the perfect chance to fight back. If the native population was able to provide timely intelligence, we would be able to set up ambushes. Weller thought that the garrison in Samarinda numbered about one hundred soldiers, so if we could eliminate ten or twenty, that was an impact.

After discussing my idea with Harry, we briefed Weller, Amulong and our two trainers.

"Amulong's told me that the Japs run patrols about twice a month into the jungle. There doesn't seem to be any kind of a standard schedule, but the patrols last for generally two days with one night of camping. That tells me we'll have opportunity to ambush their patrols."

I saw nods around the circle as they all thought about what that might entail.

"We need to train our troops not just on using their weapons, but how to fight with discipline. I'm not going to risk their lives and yours' too with amateurs. So we'll take one month to train then make a decision on what we've got."

"Right," Harry said, "I've seen a great deal of commando training over the last two years. I'll give you some thoughts on what might be the best approach."

And so, the Samarinda Special Detachment came into being.

I would've thought that language be our biggest hurdle, but I would've been wrong. Using several of Weller's locals, who were conversant in English, we were able to keep the information flowing both ways. Amulong's son, Saba became the native leader of the troops and he worked hard to make sure his people connected with Hoss and Moon. Harry kept in the background, but his suggestions on the specific items to concentrate on during training helped focus on the most important tactical skills.

Moon slowly threw off the effects of his wound. His confrontational demeanor came back, and bit by bit we had the old son of a bitch we'd gotten used to having around. Hoss still had a bit of a limp, but the doctor assured me that he was ready for duty, the only detractor being the ongoing effect of living in the jungle for the last seven months.

In less than two weeks, five squads of ten men were operating in the jungle, attacking simulated Jap positions. Moon told me that there was a level of experience that must have come from the natural heritage of the natives, who had been involved in many local fights between tribes over the years, to say nothing of their hunting prowess. Regardless of how they came by their field sense, it was a natural step into small unit infantry tactics.

One challenge was live firing. While we'd received a good supply of small arms ammunition, there simply wasn't enough to allow our trainees to fire more than twenty rounds of target practice. Many dry firing drills served to ensure they could handle the weapons in every situation, even if they couldn't actually expend rounds. The men seemed to understand this and were enthusiastic as they went through their motions, achieving a pace and competence level that led Moon to declare them ready for the real thing.

My strongest memory of those weeks, however, was a cryptic message from Coyne:

"Your lovely package arrived safely….."

It was the best possible present as we quietly celebrated Christmas, 1942.

CHAPTER TWENTY-TWO

Weller's Camp
Telukladang Peninsula
10 January 1942

If a person didn't know better, they might think that all jungles are the same. Not true. The area northwest of Samarinda was much different than the terrain around Weller's camp. While the trees and underbrush were the same, there was a noticeable lack of vertical development. The ridges and valleys we had become used to had been replaced by wide plateaus and gentle river gullies. Maps of the area had been drawn by one of Doctor Nosnah's patients, who had been a civil engineer before the war. We were dealing with an area of fifty miles by thirty miles where the majority of people lived in a dozen or so villages. Beyond that area, the doctor told me very few people lived, except native tribes. Tributaries feeding into the large river provided the best avenues of transportation, the trusty canoes proving the best vehicle by far.

As our training program was finishing, I decided a reconnaissance was the first step we should take before starting to plan for operations. I wanted experienced men making the first run and settled on myself, Harry, and Abernathy, with Saba as our guide. A second village man, Lino, would also come along as part of our intelligence-gathering plan. After a discussion with the doctor, we decided that he would come along as well, bringing his medical kit.

Weller knew these waters well, and I was confident that even in the darkness, he'd be able to find our intended landing point.

The sticky warmth of the river seemed to be particularly oppressive that night, but the ten knots or so of progress made by the boat gave us a welcome reprieve from the flying insects that we'd come to expect after dark. The new supplies had replenished our bug repellant; my only concern was the pungent, herbal smell it gave off.

"A rather nice launch," I heard Andy comment as he joined me on the port side.

"Weller's men do a good job of keeping her running well."

"He's quite the old pirate, don't you think?"

I laughed, images of Lionel Berry in *Treasure Island* flashing across my thoughts.

"Good man in a pinch," I said, "His group is pretty savvy and tough as nails. We were lucky that Hostetter actually knew him before the war."

"Hostetter seems a little long in the tooth for active duty."

I gave him the short course on Hoss and Andy grinned.

"Just like the desert, it seems the tough times bring out the hardest old men."

"You're a long way from the desert," I commented, as Weller changed course in the darkness.

Andy laughed.

"The terrain's different, but the feeling is just the same."

The small beach that Weller found for us to disembark lay about a mile south of where we originally had planned to land. We quickly got ashore and moved inland to await sunrise.

For a time after we moved to Weller's camp from our first location, Amulong's son had been quietly in the background. His father was a strong leader and I wasn't sure how the succession of headmen worked in their culture. As it turned out, there isn't a familial right to leadership. When time came, the village would select the new headman, but from what I had seen, Saba was going to be a strong candidate. Small by American standards, he was about five feet, four inches tall, maybe a hundred and twenty pounds. But he was strong and athletic as anyone. What struck me about him from the beginning was his quiet demeanor. He wasn't shy, instead he was confident and it showed in his actions. He had made a special effort to improve his English, which only served to increase his standing among the villagers. Saba and several of the native fighters had adopted wearing shorts and light shirts instead of their traditional loincloths or wraparounds. Saba had done a good job of spanning two cultures for the good of the outfit. He would've made a great Marine.

On his recommendation, we moved north as the first light began to filter through the jungle canopy. As I expected, the going was tough, but he was good at finding the best path to avoid the thickest underbrush. Our intent was to check out several of the largest villages and the primary routes to and from. Once at a village, the doctor, Saba and Lino would enter, check out the lay of the land and see what they could find out about the Japs. Andy, Tom and I would remain out of sight, keeping the village under surveillance until our party left. By then, we should've gathered enough intel to make some decisions about what our first operation would be.

"The village of Nahallee is just there," the doctor told me as we all stopped in a clearing near a small stream.

As we all knelt around a patch of earth, the doctor drew a rough sketch of the village.

"You'll be able to see the village from this small hill right here," he said, his finger indicating a spot north of where we were.

The sun had now been up for several hours and the doctor said he was ready to move into the village.

I watched the three of them move down to the stream and head up toward the village. Seeing the two young men, carrying their rifles and moving with purpose gave me a sense of accomplishment. We were teaching the people how to fight back.

"Off we go, gents," I said, and the three of us pushed north toward the observation point.

The going wasn't bad and using my compass as a guide, we moved north, with only small deviations for the worst of the undergrowth.

"Not quite North Africa," Andy commented, dodging a thorny bush.

I was thinking of something funny to say when the sound of a rifle shot echoed off the trees.

We all stopped, looking toward the sound, not that we would be able to see anything in this deep foliage.

Another shot, then a third, came from the same direction along with shouts.

Shit.

"Let's push toward the village," I told Andy.

He nodded.

Estimating that we were a half of mile from the village, we struggled through the underbrush as fast as we could. Pushing the bush out of our way, I kept my Wilson ready, knowing that whatever was ahead could be deadly.

A crashing in the undergrowth to our right sent all of us into a crouch, weapons ready. For just an instant, I saw a flash of a shirt and knew it was Saba. What the hell was happening?

"Tom, it's Saba. Go after him. We'll screen ahead."

Several more shots rang out in front of us. The snap of bullets though the brush next to us put Andy and I on our stomachs. I aimed my Wilson at the noise coming towards us. My finger slipped around the trigger and my arms tensed like springs. Hoarse panting from a man struggling made me think he was being chased.

A face burst into view and I relaxed my finger as I recognized the doctor. More rifle rounds zipped overhead as he turned to look back, oblivious to the two of us lying prone in the grass.

"Get down, doctor!" I yelled, and watched him stop, look around then drop to the ground. Then I heard the guttural Japanese commands almost on top of us.

Two soldiers pushed into view, both carrying rifles with bayonets attached. They stopped when they saw our man, the soldier on the left lunging toward the doctor who lay face down, several steps in front of them.

My short burst caught the Jap in the chest, throwing him backwards, his rifle dropping harmlessly. Almost simultaneously, Andy hit the other Jap, the side of his face exploding in a bloody mess.

I listened, expecting to hear more pursuers, but the jungle was quiet.

In the next ten minutes, Tom returned with Saba and we had the story from the doctor. Call it bad timing, but walking into the village, they ran into a patrol of Japanese infantry. The rifles and clothes were dead giveaways and immediately the Japs started firing at them. They all fled east into the nearby jungle. Luck was with us, while they were both shook up, neither was wounded.

"What happened to Lino?" I asked.

The doctor and Saba both shook their heads.

277

"We all ran," Saba said, "He was next to me."

This was a mess, I thought and I guessed Andy felt the same way. If the Japs captured Lino, our force and plans would be compromised. We had to get him back or confirm he was dead.

What would the Japs do? Fall back to the village and make a stand or send more men to find out what happened to these two? My guess was that more would be along in short order.

Fifty yards south of us, there was a ridge that ran parallel to the direction anyone coming from the village would likely follow. If we set up an ambush, it would be possible to surprise anyone moving toward, north or south of the ridge.

I explained my plan to Andy and he agreed to set up the ambush with the doctor and Saba. Andy handed Saba his Webley, the doctor would have to fend for himself. Tom Abernathy and I would move south and west, closing with the village to see if we could discover the fate of Lino and find out more about the Japs. It wasn't a great plan, but we weren't fighting the Battle of Waterloo, either.

We moved toward the village slowly from the edge of the stream. Not surprisingly, as the first hut came into view, there was no one to be seen. Had they fled, or did the Japs kill them? Maybe they were just hiding or taking cover, which would make our job a lot harder. Then I saw three enemy soldiers standing in a common area between three huts. Kneeling, we watched the three, one of them doing all the talking. Even from a distance I knew he must be a sergeant. Two more appeared escorting a small group of natives. The villagers were carrying something and with a sick feeling I realized it was the body of a man. But was it Lino?

The sergeant barked an order and two of his men grabbed the shoulders of the man and pulled him to a sitting position, his back against a hut. It was Lino, his face was bloody, but he was alive.

The sergeant walked away, leaving the four other soldiers guarding him. Two squatted down opposite their prisoner and the other two lit cigarettes. How many other soldiers were there? The patrol we ran into at Amulong's village had eight, a Marine squad would have ten. We had killed two in the jungle, what were the odds now?

Lino's only hope of survival rested in our ability to get him back from the Japs. My instinct was to attack, but what if there were another dozen waiting on the far side of the village? But if we waited, what guarantee was there that we would get the whole picture before they did something to Lino? For a brief moment I thought that if I had a Lee Enfield with me, I could have solved the problem with one shot.

"We get as close as we can," I whispered to Tom. "Surprise those four, and get Lino out of there."

Tom wiped sweat from his face and nodded.

We moved forward twenty yards then broke cover, just as the sergeant came from behind a hut, trailed by several more soldiers.

I fired a long burst, hitting two of the soldiers next to the sergeant. Beside me, Tom fired as we both charged forward. Only a violent and vicious attack would give us any chance.

Two Japs had their rifles up as the sergeant crouched next to Lino. I fired at them, and my rounds threw them into the side of the hut. I was committed now and pressed forward, the submachine gun empty. Stumbling, I heard Tom fire once more and saw a soldier who had been on the ground fall backwards, clutching his stomach.

In a fury, I pulled my pistol and sighted along my arm, directly at the Jap sergeant's chest. My first shot missed as he ducked down next to Lino, but now I was only ten feet away and my second shot hit him in the side. The man arched his back and fell on the ground. In a rage, I fired once more into his spine.

I swung around wildly, my pistol looking for targets, but the enemy soldiers all lay on the ground, wounded or killed. It was as if all motion had stopped, the noise and screams suddenly silent. My heart pounded and my chest heaved as I caught my breath. The momentary elation of survival would be short-lived if there were more Japs in the village. Two of the wounded Japs, moaned at my feet. I aimed the Webley at the first man's head and pulled the trigger. Quickly I dispatched the second. Dead men don't talk.

"Come on!" I yelled at Tom, grabbing Lino's arm.

The two of us got him to his feet, although he seemed drugged or stunned.

"Let's go."

Lino stumbled along as we carried and dragged him into the edge of the jungle. Thirty yards in, we hear yells from behind us that could only be Japanese soldiers shouting orders. What size patrol had we run into? By my count we'd killed or wounded ten or so. How many more were there?

In the heat and humidity, Lino quickly became a burden, even with both of us helping him.

"Hold it," I said, my breath coming in gasps.

We all went down on our knees, trying to catch our breaths and see if we were being pursued.

Random jungle sounds were the only things we could hear as we continued to rest and sweat.

"Anything?" I asked Tom.

He shook his head.

"Ready?"

"Aye."

The rendezvous with Weller was delayed by almost ten hours due to carrying a concussed Lino through the dense undergrowth. The doctor had been torn by his desire to allow the injured boy to rest and our dire need to clear out of the area. In the end, the Japs were deemed to be a greater threat to the whole, even if Lino was being exposed to greater risk.

What none of us understood was the challenge of moving the injured young man through thick jungle. A litter was out of the question and we took turns on either side of him, carrying and maneuvering him through the tangle of vines and bushes. It was an exhausted crew that finally climbed aboard the 46 boat and headed south. Our foray north had not turned out as planned.

The next morning, Andy and I sat next to the morning cook fire. The meal was a treat, boiled oats with sugar. Small things made such a difference in keeping the brutality of jungle living at bay. But as much as I was enjoying breakfast, a question dominated my thoughts.

"What will the Japs do now that they know there are enemy soldiers in the area?"

Andy took a last bite of his breakfast and set it down near the fire.

"I suppose it depends on the Japanese commander and whether or not we continue to poke at the buggers."

He was right, of course. The jungle was immense and we could easily fade away. The Japs simply didn't have control of the inland areas. Our radio transmissions would likely be the only real threat they might feel compelled to deal with. Coyne would be satisfied if we simply kept up our shipping reports. But I knew that would be taking the easy way out. But if Andy was right, my time was short here. Maybe it made sense not to tempt fate. Keep the radio safe and don't stir things up. It made sense, but I knew it wasn't something I could live with.

"I say we poke 'em."

Over the next three months, that's exactly what we did. Concentrating around Samarinda, we ambushed four Jap patrols. Within eight weeks, it appeared that the enemy had ceded the countryside to us. Patrols more than ten miles from the city simply ceased. It reminded me of the Middle Ages, the evil prince retreating to the castle. That was fine with me. It allowed us to continue our radio transmissions with no interference and the doctor's people were spared the brutality they'd been suffering. But the unpredictability of war should have told me it was too good to be true.

CHAPTER TWENTY-THREE

Weller's Camp
Telukladang Peninsula
13 April 1942

A small fire burned under my coffee pot as the sun rose on another morning in the jungle. The wisps of smoke worked their way up from the flames as I waited for the water to boil. It had been almost a year since the team landed in Borneo, and at times it seemed like we'd been here forever.

"You're walking pretty good," I said as Hoss came up the trail to my hut.

He grinned at my comment. His ambling gait reflected the pain he was still in from his wound. He could get around, but slowly at best.

"It's because you took such good care of my ass," Hoss said as he sat down next to me with a grunt. "You better take care of that leg. It looks like hell."

On the last raid, I had cut my leg on a nasty thorn bush. Now my calf was sore and swollen. Over the last year our bodies had been slowly ground down. Every member on the team had suffered wounds, but the never-ending sores, diarrhea and fevers had taken the biggest toll. Hoss was in his mid-40's but looked much older. Abernathy was in his twenties and already had grey running through his dark hair. Moon had lost several teeth, and was going to need dental work back in Australia. My thoughts briefly went to Bever, who died before the wear and tear had a chance to set in, but now he lay under the stinking dirt of this jungle. Thank God Lynda was away from all of this.

"Not much longer now," I said. The rendezvous date with the submarine was now only three days away. Perhaps the reality that the end was near highlighted the ragged shape we were all in, both physically and mentally. Andy and his boys had taken over daily operations. Both the doctor and Weller reflected that subtle change by going to Andy on most issues, which was fine with me. I just wanted to be clean, healed and then sleep for a month. I felt like an old man, always tired and it hurt to just get around.

The sounds of explosions from the north put both of us on our feet. It was hard to tell the distance, but anything explosive from that direction could only mean the Japs were up to something.

Weller was coming up the trail as Hoss and I moved down it.

"Japs landed on this side," he said, bending over to catch his breath.

"How many?" I asked, knowing that our people were spread out on the peninsula and we had less than a dozen in camp.

"Several boatloads, according to Sumakil. He was going down to the river and ran into them. He thinks they must have found our boats."

Andy rushed up with Tom Abernathy. Sergeant Woodley and Corporal Allen were right behind them. All were carrying their weapons.

More explosions and automatic weapons fire told me that our lookouts were fighting back, but our plan had always been for the outposts to fight then fall back, so the Japs were likely going to be on us shortly.

Women and children began to gather in the common area and several of the men were with them, carrying their rifles and looking anxious. Saba came running from the direction of the northern outpost. He began talking before he stopped moving.

"Many Japanese coming this way….I saw at least twenty, with machine guns."

"How far?" Andy asked him.

"Two miles. Maybe less."

We had talked about the Japanese attacking the camp many times and now we'd see if Moon's plan would work.

"You all know what to do. Saba, take the women, children and the rest of your men. Go now!"

He nodded, picked up his rifle and moved down toward the women. Smitty appeared from down the trail, running at full speed.

He slid to a stop and blurted out, "The radio?"

"Get going, set the charge and catch up to us."

Smitty nodded and ran up the trail that led to the radio site.

I turned to the rest of them. "It's up to us to delay the Japs. We've got to give Saba time to get them over the bridge."

Looking around I knew we were still missing our sergeant.

"Where's Moon?"

"I'll go look," Hoss said.

"There's no time. Get going."

Hoss shook his head.

"Sorry, boss. Leg's not gonna let me. I'll slow the little bastards down for you."

Doctor Nosnah ran up to me, a bag over his shoulder.

"What can I do?" he asked.

"Help Hoss across the ravine, now!" I yelled, "Now!"

"I'm staying," Hoss said, his mind clearly made up.

"That's a goddamned order! I need you on the other side. Now get going."

He cut his eyes at me then turned for the bridge.

West of the camp, about one mile, there was a very steep ravine with a stream running at the bottom. It was almost impassable between the rocks and dense underbrush. The natural barrier was perfect for delaying a force attacking from the east. Moon's emergency plan included a rope bridge to the far bank, which we could cut once everyone had passed. There were also pre-dug fighting pits on both sides of the ravine that would allow us to set up covering fire.

As we moved toward the ravine I hoped that Smitty didn't run into any problems setting the charge on the radio. It was crucial that we destroy the radio rather than let it fall into Japanese hands. But we also knew that if the Japs didn't find the radio, we still needed to be able to transmit. Our solution was to rig a booby trap in the transmitter case. The charge utilized one of the bomb fuses that Andy had brought from Australia. If anyone moved the case, it would detonate two pounds of C-4 explosive, effectively destroying the radio and hopefully killing Japanese.

We made it to the pits in under five minutes, the sounds of gunfire dying out behind us. I was sure the Japs would move slowly once they got to the camp, assuming we would be defending it. The question was what would they do then?

"Andy, make sure everyone's in place. I'm going to backtrack and see what they're doing."

He started to object and then nodded. Turning to the men, he directed them to the two concealed pits and I headed back up the trail. I had my Wilson, pistol and three grenades. But if I had to use them, my chances of survival were going to go way down. Moving into the brush, I slowed and began to creep forward on my hands and knees. I head the occasional order barked out in Japanese, but couldn't see any troops. I jumped as a grenade exploded maybe thirty yards ahead, in the camp itself. The Japs must be using their grenades to clear out the shelters.

Kneeling in the deep grass, I asked myself what next? Could I see them soon enough to make it back to the pits, or would I lead them directly there? Maybe it made more sense to fall back and get ready to move the delaying group back over the ravine. Hearing activity in front of me, the decision was made for me.

I made it back to our defensive line and slid into the first pit next to Andy.

"They're in the camp, but I couldn't tell much else."

Andy knew what we were both thinking.

"They won't stop there, better we get across and cut the bridge."

He was right, but I kept thinking about Moon. Where was he? Or had the Japs already taken him? And had Smitty circled around north or was he stuck on this side of the ravine?

"You take the lead," I told Andy. "Get 'em across, then I'll follow."

A series of shots echoed from the direction of the camp. The distinctive sound of Arisaka rifles told me that the enemy was moving towards our position. It was time to fall back, despite missing Moon and Smitty.

Then I saw him. The young radioman was running down the trail that led from the camp. He was in full flight, no attempt at concealing himself or taking cover. Bullets cracked through the undergrowth, cutting the foliage like a knife. He stumbled once, falling face down, but was back up running in a moment, the panic of flight evident on his face.

"Smitty!" I yelled, waving one arm above my head. I fired a quick burst to Smitty's right, where I guessed some of the shots were coming from. It might keep their heads down long enough to get Smitty home.

A mortar shell exploded behind Smitty and I knew that Andy had gotten the two-inch working. Now we'd have a chance to blunt their attack and set up a withdrawal into the hills.

Another explosion rocked the jungle toward camp and I hoped the Japs would fall back to regroup, to let us get across the bridge.

"Come on, Smitty!" I yelled, hoping he could close the remaining twenty yards and take cover in the pit. He continued pumping his arms, his face contorted as he struggled up the trail. Only ten yards away, I saw the sweat pouring from his face, as he stumbled once, his arms reaching toward me. He pitched to the ground, rolling on his side, blood covering his chest. He looked up at me for a moment, then his head dropped to the ground.

In a rage, I fired again, my burst raking the jungle on either side of the trail. Dropping down, I reached Smitty and felt his neck for a pulse, but the massive blood pool under his body told me that it was pointless. God damn every fucking Jap on the earth, my mind cried. but I knew it wouldn't make any difference for Smitty. Nothing would, ever again.

The mortars were having an effect and the fire from the Japs slackened. I made for the bridge, keeping as low as I could. Seeing the ropes still in place gave me a sudden feeling of relief. Constructed from manila ropes supplied by Weller, it looked less than substantial, but was surprisingly steady as I pulled myself across using the hand supports. Abernathy was kneeling at the far end, his Wilson up and ready to provide cover.

"Cut the God damned thing down!" I spit out as I cleared the last several feet.

"Smitty?" Andy asked.

I shook my head.

We delayed at the ravine to see what the Japs were going to do. They reconnoitered the ravine, then fell back towards the village. We remained hidden until they left, then went after the villagers. We caught up with Saba two hours later.

The jungle is a terrible place to be if you don't want to be there. But now the tables had turned. It had become our refuge and the Japs seemed to want no part of it. The canopy gave us complete cover from aircraft and several of the men knew this area very well. For now, we needed to open the distance from our old camp and set up a system of lookouts to detect any Jap attempt at pushing into the jungle in pursuit.

"I believe the military requirement at this point would be to fall back and regroup as they say," Andy said, sitting now next to me.

"No arguments from me," I said. "I just wish I knew what happened to Moon."

"Let me ask around, someone must know something," Andy offered.

Two hours later, I was trying to get some rest after getting everyone settled. The people had done well in my opinion, traveling through tough terrain, with the threat of the Japs coming after them. Thank God, Moon had made sure there were stashes of provisions that would take care of the immediate need for food. We weren't in bad shape for ammunition, but that situation would get bad quickly if we engaged the Japs. Our radio was likely in a million pieces, so we'd ceased to be a functioning observation post. All things considered, we were up the creek without a paddle.

"It makes no sense for anyone to stay here without a radio," I offered to Andy as he walked up and sat down next to me."

"Have you talked with Mr. Weller?"

"For a few minutes after we got here." I laughed. "He said that they had been in this situation before and it would just take time to get squared away again."

In my mind, the big difference this time was that Weller didn't have his boats that had been crucial in staying supplied and ahead of the Japs.

"What are you thinking?" Andy asked.

"We get across the river, make our way to the inflatables and meet the sub two days from now, as scheduled."

There were a lot of assumptions in that plan, but our effectiveness as a military unit was shot without a radio or supplies.

Andy nodded.

"You're still in command, but I would heartily endorse that course of action."

"Thanks."

The next morning our exhausted, disheveled group stood around a small fire. I guess you could've called it a "council of war," but it was really a group of desperate men trying to figure out how to survive. Everyone was aware of the scheduled submarine pick up. My concern was what Weller and Saba could do in what had become a pretty shitty situation.

"We should move inland," Saba said after I asked for his ideas.

Weller nodded.

"I've heard that area is more than remote, but I also don't think the Japs will be in a big hurry to follow us. We lay low for a time, then regroup and get back at them."

It struck me that these men were on the ropes and already thinking about getting back in action against the Japs. Providing food and shelter for all of these people was going to be their first challenge, but somehow, I knew they'd be okay.

"Has anyone seen Amulong?" I asked.

Several shook their heads and I saw the look in Saba's eyes.

The young man was a strong leader, but his father had really been the spirit of the village, his loss would be felt strongly.

Weller said, "One of my men thought he might have gone off with Moon early yesterday morning, but he wasn't sure, so I don't know if it's true or not."

My thoughts went to Moon. Why would he have gone off with the headman and not told anyone? I'd talk to Weller's man before we headed out, but now it was time to lay out the plan.

"I'm going to try and make the rendezvous with the sub. If we can get word back to Australia, another team can be sent back here with a new radio. By then, I'm sure you'll be running the place," I said to Weller.

"Fair enough," he replied.

"If you send a man along with us, I'll leave all of our weapons and ammunition for you."

"I'll send Tirra."

We started for the river two hours later. Time was critical now, with the submarine scheduled to surface tomorrow night at 0200. I figured it would take a hump of just less than twenty miles to where I desperately hoped we would find our inflatables still serviceable. Looking at my beat-up Hamilton, I saw it was just past 0900. We should have had plenty of time to get there, but I wanted more time to work on the rafts if needed. I knew each one had a repair kit and hand pump in a pouch. All we could hope for was that any damage was repairable. We needed all the rafts to get everyone out to the sub, but in a pinch, as long as one raft could make it, we should be alright.

The jungle was not our friend that day. The heat and humidity were especially bad, and with our supplies left at the camp, we were out of insect repellant. Before the sun had even burned off all of the morning marine layer, we were all completely miserable from the sweat and bites. We were able to find passable areas that allowed us to miss most of the heavily thorned areas that would have slowed us down to a crawl, but that didn't help Hoss. His leg had continued to slow him down and I kept going back to urge him on. By early afternoon, we were within a mile of the river when Hoss finally collapsed.

We had time, so I thought an hour's rest might be all he needed.

"Find some shade. We'll take an hour, then tackle the river," I told group. Several nodded, but most just sat down.

I knelt by Hoss, who lay on his back, a small piece of wood serving as a makeshift pillow.

"Rest up. It's not far to the river. You can just float across."

He smiled.

"Robbie, my boy, I think this is as far as I go. The river's hard enough, but it's another five or six miles from the other bank to the rafts. I'll never make it."

"Let me worry about that, old man."

I motioned to Tom and Andy.

"Tom, there used to be two canoes stashed near here when we left the old camp. See if you can find them."

"I remember," he replied.

"Tom." I grabbed his arm. "Stay low and watch out for anyone we don't know."

My plan was to float the canoes if we could find them. We'd use logs if canoes weren't available, but we had to get across the river as soon as the sun went down. That would give us all day

292

tomorrow to get to the rafts and see if they were going to be salvageable. There were seven of us and two canoes meant we could actually paddle across the river. Otherwise, we would all be getting a good bath, which we needed anyway.

With Hoss dozing off, I headed for the river to get the lay of the land. Hopefully the current would be slack, making the distance across easy to negotiate. Andy remained behind on watch and I worked my way east. It took two tries to find a decent path all the way to the riverbank, but once there, I was able to confirm the current looked weak and the far bank was less than 100 yards away. Tom just needed to find those canoes.

My eyes caught motion to my left and I knelt down quickly. A single canoe was moving south on the river, hugging the west bank. Must be local fishermen, I thought, but better to lay low in any case.

Suddenly I found myself standing up, my hand raised high in greeting. In the canoe, paddling steadily was Amulong and Moon.

The story came out quickly. Amulong and Mullen had gone out early the morning of the Jap attack in search of a particular plant for the headman to make a tea to treat Moon's increasingly severe headaches. They had been on the Jap flank during the attack, unable to get back to the camp. Knowing the escape plan, they had worked their way around and found Weller only two hours after we'd left the makeshift camp. Amulong knew a shorter route to the river and where to get a canoe. The two made good time up the river trying to get Moon back to the team. Amulong told us he would now return to find the villagers and Weller, leaving the canoe with us to cross the river. That was just as well, Tom had found no trace of the other canoes, likely stolen by one of the many locals who used the river to travel to and from Samarinda.

I walked with the headman to the edge of the clearing. We had known each other from the second day the team came ashore and our lives had crossed in so many ways.

"Thank you for all you have done for us," I told him as we stopped at the beginning of the trail.

His wrinkled face smiled at me and he nodded.

"Be well," he said and turned, walking quietly into the jungle.

The sun was starting to set when we loaded the canoe for the first trip. Our plan was to ferry three over, have one man bring the canoe back across and repeat the process. Three trips would do it and then we could then move inland for the night toward where the rafts were hidden.

"Did you get some rest?" I asked Hoss, who was talking with Moon under a small palm tree.

"I did. But I don't know that it'll make much difference. The legs just aren't working. Not sure what's wrong."

"I'll carry you if I have to," Moon said.

"We'll go last" he told me, "don't want to hold anyone up."

That was fine with me. Once I got Hoss on the other side, it was only five miles or so to the rafts. We could rig a litter and carry him. I would get Tom busy building one when he got to the other side.

"I'll be back shortly," I told Andy as I shoved off in the canoe for the last trip. Moon and Hoss were the only ones still remaining and I wanted to get this over with. Remembering what had happened in the Balikpapan harbor, I decided to sit in the front of the canoe for the trip across. Directional control was easier sitting up front and I didn't need any problems, it was already getting dark enough to make the trip difficult.

I was halfway across when the first shots rang out. I knew the sound of a Wilson, but then came the distinctive crack of an Arisaka. They'd caught up with us.

My Wilson lay behind me on the floor of the canoe and I had a full Webley. But that wasn't much firepower if there were Japs in any strength. Several rounds whipped past me, but none were close. Straining to see in the darkness, I knew I had to get close to them if we stood any chance of getting back to the other side. There were muzzle flashes in the darkness, and coupled with the amount of fire, I guessed it was probably a Jap patrol we were dealing with.

I heard Moon call out and realized I was off course, the current had picked up and was pulling me north, away from them. The previous trip had taken it out of me and my arms were burning. As I pulled hard on the paddle, it felt like I might have opened my wound. Tracer rounds ricocheted among the trees as a light machine gun opened up on the left. With one desperate pull I drove the canoe into a large tree root bundle and jumped over the side, pushing my way to the bank

I found Hoss and Moon using a large root as cover. They'd been able to see me, calling out directions ten yards to my left.

Sprinting toward the tree, I slid in next to them as a burst of machine gun fire ripped the underbrush next to us.

Hoss lay against the tree with his Wilson on his lap. Moon knelt next to him holding his Wilson at the ready.

"How many?" I asked, catching my breath.

Two more rounds hit the tree trunk above us, spraying bark into the air.

"A dozen's my guess. One machine gun on the left," Moon said, still facing forward.

I didn't have a great plan. I thought we'd just run like hell for the canoe and start paddling.

"You ready to go?" I asked Hoss. His back was against the tree with both legs splayed out at an angle.

Shaking his head, he said, "Legs still aren't working right. Moon had to drag me this far."

"It's only ten or fifteen yards to the canoe, we'll both drag you."

"Just help me, I can move some."

Moon raised his Wilson and fired a short burst into the darkness.

"That's right," Moon said, crouching down below the tree stump. "I'll cover you, then follow."

"Hoss, gimme your arm, here."

With his right arm over my shoulder, we both lurched toward the canoe. We were like two drunks, staggering forward, stumbling over the rough ground. Covering fire from behind illuminated the two of us heading for the water. After ten yards, we both pitched forward as rifle rounds snapped past in the dark.

"Moon, let's go!" I called out, bringing my weapon to cover him.

"Right," he said.

I fired a burst at the tree line, just as the machine gun opened up, red tracers ripped over us in the darkness. Trying to make myself as flat as possible, I felt Moon stumble over my legs and crash into a bush.

"Dammit!" Moon cried in pain as he rolled to a stop.

The rifle fire continued, but thank God, the machine gun didn't join in. I crawled over to Moon to find him on his back, gasping for breath. Running my hands over his chest, I felt the stickiness of blood covering his shirt and knew his wounds were bad.

"Moon, how bad?"

His answer was a muffled groan.

Examining him closer, there were two bullet holes on the right side of his chest. Both must have hit his lung.

I could hear orders being barked out in Japanese and knew that the patrol was likely getting ready to advance and finish us off.

"We gotta get to the canoe!" I shouted at them both, "It's our only chance!"

"I'm finished," Moon gasped. "Get going."

There wasn't time to debate the issue, but how could I leave my sergeant here to die?

Moon had turned his head to look at me.

"Parker, no argument. Go, goddammit."

I knew he was right.

"Hoss, let's go."

"Do you have any Mills bombs left?"

There were two on my utility harness.

"Two, why?"

"That Jap patrol will only come after you. I'm not leaving Sergeant Mullen and I can't move anyway. Leave the grenades and when the Japs show up, I'll blow them to hell."

Hoss had crawled over to Moon and put his hand on the sergeant's blood-stained chest.

I watched that simple act of comradeship and knew that I had seen the horror of war and wonder of friendship.

"Rob, we've both reached the end. You get back across that river and get them home."

"I'd argue, but it wouldn't do any good. Here," I said handing Hoss the two grenades.

"Off you go," Hoss said. "I'll keep up firing for fifteen minutes then let them come in."

I wanted to say something but there were no words. A quick squeeze of Hoss's arm and I slid over next to Moon.

"With your permission, sergeant, I'll return to the team."

He didn't look at me, but I saw the smile.

Twenty minutes later we heard two explosions.

EPILOGUE

The rendezvous with the submarine, the *U.S.S. Cero* went off without a hitch, but I found myself going through the motions once we went below decks. My responsibility was over, after over a year in the jungle, with the burden of command on my shoulders, I was done. The commanding officer of the submarine, Commander Ed Dissette, was now responsible for getting us home. It was funny, but I really did feel that Australia was home. I guess knowing that I had someone waiting for me was part of it, but I think the bond I had developed with a small group of very brave Aussies made me feel like one of them. The events of that last night still tore me apart, though. How could we have come that far and lost Hoss and Moon like that? But as I came to know over the next three years, the tragedy of war would never change.

The *Cero* made good time on our return and eight days after we climbed aboard, the team stood on the upper deck as she pulled alongside the pier in Brisbane. I guess I was still numb from the deaths of Hoss and Moon, despite Andy's efforts to cheer me up.

That last morning at sea was beautiful. A crisp, clean breeze cut across the submarine's deck as the sea turned from deep blue to blue-green as we approached the harbor entrance. Looking up at the bridge, I saw the CO and XO talking, both had their binoculars up to their eyes. Behind them a flashing signal light was sending out a message and receiving a flashing reply from the big tender.

"Looks good, don't you think?" Andy asked me as several sailors opened hatches to retrieve lines for mooring.

"It certainly does."

He said, "There will be a very long debrief if I don't miss my mark."

Christ, I thought, that is the last thing I want to do right now is talk about the last year in the jungle.

"After a hot bath and a stiff drink, maybe," I replied.

We could see a group of cars and people on the pier, the welcoming party I was sure. I expected that Commander Coyne would be there. This really was his show, after all.

We felt the engines slow as the bow edged toward the pier, then they went into reverse and the hull vibrated slightly. I heard a loud whistle and lines unfurled as they snaked toward the pier. Then I saw her. The blonde hair had caught my attention and instantly knew it was her. Next to Lynda I recognized Commander Coyne, and then I saw Dicky running down the pier like a normal little boy. My feelings overwhelmed me. I had a family, and I was here to see them. It hit me like a rock as I thought of those who would never be able to experience this feeling. I remembered Bever, out of his mind with fever, Springer, laying in the bottom of a boat, slowing bleeding to death, and Smitty, shot down after setting the radio booby trap. How many thousands more would never return home as this miserable war dragged on? But there was nothing I could do about it and for now, I was going to put my arms around my Lynda and try to forget for a little while.

To comply with the laws of several countries, Lynda and I were married again, three days after my return. But we always recognized the date of the wedding in the jungle as our anniversary. And my fears that a romance, kindled in the jungle, would not survive the real world were totally unfounded.

As we held each other that night, the initial awkwardness long gone, I tried to tell her what had happened in the jungle with Hoss and Moon. She listened and cried. She had known them so well and the hurt was just as painful for her. We were two people who had their lives changed in the jungle of Borneo. But now it was time to get on with things.

I was surprised that my request to transfer back to the regular Marines was approved without too many objections by Captain Herrick and Commander Coyne, following a very extensive debrief. I wasn't trying to avoid the behind the lines stuff, but I had joined the Marine Corps to lead Marines in combat and that is what I truly wanted to do. In fact, I got more combat than I ever wanted, participating in three amphibious operations including the landing on Iwo Jima. I watched more good men die as we dug the Japs out of their bunkers and caves. The names have blurred over the years, but Hoss and Moon will forever be a part of who I am. With the help of Commander Coyne, I was able to submit recommendations for the Distinguished Service Cross for them. Eight months later, I found out that both had been approved and I was able to write letters to their families to express my admiration and gratitude.

It never did seem like enough.

ABOUT THE AUTHOR

John F. Schork graduated from the U.S. Naval Academy in 1972 and went on to spend 26 years in Naval Aviation, flying the iconic Grumman A-6 Intruder.

During his career, he accumulated 4,000 flight hours and over 1,000 carrier arrested landings. Operating primarily in the Pacific theater, he took part in Operations Frequent Wind, Praying Mantis and Southern Watch among others.

As the last Executive Officer of the USS Midway (CV-41), he took part in Desert Storm and the evacuation of U.S. personnel from the Philippines following the eruption of Mt. Pinatubo. He commanded an A-6 Intruder Squadron, VA-95 and Naval Air

Station Whidbey Island. His final tour was as the Chief of Staff of the Kitty Hawk Battle Group.

John is the author of adventure novels based upon historical events. He resides with his wife, Carole, in Sammamish, Washington.

John Schork Titles

A Light in the Jungle
An Echo of War
Destiny In the Pacific
Journey of Honor
The Deadly Sky
The Falkenberg Riddle
The Flames of Deliverance
The King's Commander
The Right War
Winds of Battle

www.ingramcontent.com/pod-product-compliance
Lightning Source LLC
Chambersburg PA
CBHW030933260626
47169CB00002B/459